Through My Father's Eyes

A Son's Awakening

Linda Meyerholz

Eloquent Books
Durham, Connecticut

Eloquent Books
An imprint of Strategic Book Group
P.O. Box 333
Durham CT 06422
www.strategicbookgroup.com

ISBN: 978-1-60911-036-9

Book Design: Bruce Salender

Printed in the United States of America.

DEDICATION

This book is dedicated to ... millions of souls who have gone before or are now involved in recovery from addictions and the myriad obsessive-compulsive behaviors that plague mankind in the Twenty-First Century... the movement that Dr. Carl Jung said was the closest thing to First Century Christianity ... a tidal wave of souls, moving together to heal from unbridled worship of the material to balanced living in an unbalanced society.

ACKNOWLEDGMENTS

Acknowledging everyone who played into the writing of this book would take another book. Needless to say, I thank my parents for many things, but especially for an education that taught me how to write. Thanks to my husband for his support and love in my recovery and my work. Special thanks to my editor, Erica Wisner, who patiently corrected not only grammar and syntax, but converted the manuscript from one word processing program to the one required by our publisher. I assure you this is no small feat. Bless you, Erica. To all the folks at AEG Eloquent Books who patiently worked with me as I managed a full-time therapy practice and pulled together the many bits and pieces of a novel. I'm grateful for my years of experience as a broadcast journalist in Denver, Colorado and San Francisco, California. It was through those experiences that I began to understand the massive pain that tears so many families apart. Lastly, thanks to my hundreds of recovery friends and to my clients, many of whom suffer the pain of parental alienation in its many forms.

PROLOGUE

It was as cold and miserably grey outside as I felt on the inside the day I was told I had to meet Elizabeth Grayson. I felt intense dislike for the woman although I had never met her. What I knew of her came through a videotape of a talk show. I was told to meet her or be fired. I had to keep my job, which meant I had to be civil to this person, no matter what. Everything I hated about life was thrown in my face that day.

The nightmare that centered on Elizabeth Grayson and her work began when my boss, Ed Wainwright, called me into his office and ordered me to sit down and pay very close attention to what he was going to say.

"Here's a videotape I want you to watch with me, and then I'll tell you what I need for you to do."

We watched the tape. Elizabeth Grayson's three children had appeared on the Leslie Wilder Show. They were obviously hurt and embittered by their mother's material success and lack of interest in their lives. I didn't miss the irony of it all. Elizabeth Grayson was being hailed as an innovator who had developed a psychological theory that seemed to be changing the way many counselors and clinicians were working with their patients. Grayson had written a self-help book that was on all the major best seller lists. People were coming out of the woodwork to give testimony to the wonders of Mrs. Grayson's new idea. People were acting as if their lives had been saved by this new view of human psychology.

As I watched the tape, I felt loathing for Elizabeth Grayson. The children, all well into their forties, recalled with tears and sadness the cruelties of their childhoods with Elizabeth Grayson. So many of the things they complained about were very close to the terrors my own mother had inflicted on me. I had tried to forget I ever had a mother, but there she was, being talked about by three complete strangers. They weren't really talking about Angela Howard but they could have been. I felt they were.

I fought a desire to rip the tape out of the recorder. Ed sat there watching me. He was a seasoned, hardened editor. I remember wondering how he could watch the tape without revulsion. Ed may have sensed my thoughts because he threw a smoldering look of anger at me. It was at this point I decided to watch the rest of the tape more closely. I figured he would probably test me on it when it finished. I tried to observe what the people were wearing, the words they said, everything he might ask me about. As I did this, my discomfort rose. Ed fast-forwarded through the commercials. To me, the tape seemed endless. By the time the credits rolled I was almost beside myself. I felt I would explode.

Ed got up from his chair, stopped the machine, rewound the tape and then ejected it. He handed it to me.

"I got this tape special delivery from Martha Bullock yesterday afternoon. She thinks we should do an article and a book on Elizabeth Grayson. She's the boss and it's not an idea I can afford to ignore."

"Screw Martha Bullock," I protested. "Why give any more ink to a bitch who did what this woman did to her children?"

"In my wildest dreams I wouldn't screw Martha Bullock. She's probably nice enough," Ed chuckled, "but at my age, sexual energy needs to be carefully depleted with someone more suited to my tastes than the good Mrs. Bullock."

The tape was still warm from the VCR. I felt repulsed by the heat, by Martha Bullock, and by Ed. Ed's attempt at humor sickened me. We had many laughs together over the years. This was definitely not one of them. I looked at my old friend and tried to figure out why he had shown me the tape and was telling me about Martha Bullock's request. My head ached. My stomach was turning. I think my gut knew before I did that something I wouldn't like was on its way to me.

"Evan, I have to be honest with you. You're on very thin ice with me and with this magazine. We've been friends most of our lives, but you're becoming someone I don't know. I don't know what the problem is. What I do know is I can't depend on you. You're not the same Evan Howard I thought I knew. The last thing I want to do is fire you, but I have a responsibility to my publisher, to everyone else who works here, to myself, to our readers, and to you. You call in sick, don't meet deadlines. I've asked you to get a medical checkup and you've refused. I've asked you to see our company counselor and you've refused."

"Ed, there's nothing wrong with me."

"Evan, your clothes look like hell, your office looks like hell, you look like hell."

I didn't like what he was saying, but I became vaguely aware of the pain on my oldest friend's face. I had a glimmer of understanding about the seriousness of his words. It would take me weeks to realize that I had destroyed years and years of trust that we had between us. Fortunately, I was able to play this conversation back in my mind later that day. As I thought about Ed's words later, I had enough smarts remaining to realize that I had been given an ultimatum. I know that what mattered to me more on that day was the paycheck, not the friendship. But I'm getting ahead of myself.

Ed told me I was to go out to Elizabeth Grayson's home. She already knew I was coming. Martha Bullock had talked to her personally and requested a long interview. Ed decided to give me one last chance to keep my job.

"If you don't put together a fair, honest piece on this woman, Evan, you will have your walking papers. The deadline is two weeks from today. That means you'll have it to me in ten days so that you can reconnect with people you've interviewed for the article for any revisions. If it isn't on my desk, fully edited and ready to go two weeks from tomorrow, clean out your desk. Don't come to me with any excuses. There are a lot of people here carrying resentments because they've seen you get away with stuff they aren't permitted to do. Your friend Ed is gone, Evan. I'm your boss now and that won't last long if you don't get your act together."

"We just sat here and heard what a bitch this woman is. I don't want to write a single word about Elizabeth Grayson. I know all about these selfish, self-centered career women. She probably never cooked a meal for her kids."

"There was a time when you were one of the best journalists in this country, Evan. If you prejudged people or situations, you never let on and it never came across in your stories. Over the past couple of years I've seen your high-and-mighty self-righteousness pour out into this office and into your work. Get a hold of yourself, do this story right, or pick up your last check today."

"That's how it is?" I asked.

"That's how it is, Evan. And I mean it. I'm not going to cover for you again. I've done it too many times, and frankly, our friendship is leaving me drained. I've read Elizabeth Grayson's latest book. You better read it before you go out and interview her." Ed picked a book out of his bookcase and handed it to me.

I snapped the book out of his hand and charged out the door, slamming it behind me. I looked back through the blinds of Ed's office and saw him holding his head in his hands. I whispered something about an ungrateful bastard under my breath and walked to the hole I called my office. I looked at the book he gave me. The book was titled <u>Spiritual Disconnection: The Root of Addiction and Domestic Violence</u>.

"Oh, my God. What has become of Ed's good sense? That son-of-a-bitch has gone insane even thinking of doing such a kiss-ass story," I thought. My opinion of Ed hadn't been very high for several years, but at that moment, I felt nothing but disgust and contempt for him. I knew I couldn't read in my office. I needed to get home and get a good bottle of whiskey. That would be the only way I could bear reading anything written by a woman the likes of Elizabeth Grayson. So home I went.

PART I

THE ARTICLE

CHAPTER 1

The fog was rolling in over the city early that afternoon. I left the office on Market Street and rode the cable car up California to Van Ness. I walked from the end of the line to home. If there was any light in the world, I couldn't see it. I felt I was in a black hole so deep I could hardly put one foot in front of the other to get to my front door. My feet felt like they were buried in mud. All I could think of was getting a drink and going to sleep. There was nothing but blackness to greet me as I opened my door. I threw my coat in a heap on the chair beside the door. My coat hadn't been hung up in years. It fell on the chair in the same lines it always did. I threw Elizabeth Grayson's book and the tape on the small table next to the chair. Something was pushed off to make room and it thudded to the floor. I didn't care.

I turned on the living room light and saw the mess of the last week strewn everywhere—pizza boxes, Chinese takeout boxes, plastic spoons and forks, newspapers, junk mail. I lifted the lid of the newest pizza box and jumped when several large cockroaches scurried out of it and over the table and my arm. I slumped down to the floor and felt loathing for everything in my life. I loathed myself. It was bad enough to have cockroaches in my living room, but even worse to cringe in terror because they ran across my arm. "God, why am I here? What's the purpose of all this shit?" No one answered. I slumped onto the sofa and stared at the mess.

"What kind of a miserable coward have you become?" I wondered out loud. "You're a miserable failure in everything. You came from a family of losers and you're the biggest loser of them all, Howard. You sorry son-of-a-bitch." I detested where I was. I detested being alive.

There had been many moments of self-loathing, but for some reason that was a turning moment in my life. I decided against the drink and decided to begin cleaning. My old lady had been a perfectionist house cleaner. Before I hit my teens I vowed to never be enslaved to cleaning of any kind. It was a marvelous decision in my youth because it drove my mother crazy. About every fourth week I would come home and my room would have mysteriously cleaned itself. Everything was dusted. The sheets were fresh and smelled of the outdoors. Being a slob worked well in my youth. As an adult, 45-year-old male living in San Francisco, my rebellion hurt only me. The depth of my own stupidity was beginning to dawn on me in the midst of the garbage and roaches in my living room.

Until that bleak afternoon, I can honestly say that I did a thorough cleaning about every fourth year, or when I met someone I wanted to impress, or when I had to move. In my twenties I lived with a couple of women who seemed like very nice women in the beginning. I broke up with both of them because they constantly fought with me about my living habits. I figured they either accepted me as I was or they could leave. They left— and I was alone right up to the day Ed Wainwright threatened to fire me.

I cleaned out piles of papers and garbage that afternoon. I made twelve trips to the dumpster, dragging at least one or two large bags of garbage behind me while carrying another one or two. I found shirts and socks that I had thought were long lost and never to be seen again. I went to the laundry on the third floor of my building and put in five loads of wash. Someone had left a box of detergent. I helped myself to a cup for each load. I didn't stay to see the wash and rinse cycle through, as was suggested in several bulletins plastered on the laundry walls. I figured this was all new-found wealth, and if someone stole the stuff, fine. I hadn't used some of the clothes in years, so what the hell.

When I returned to the apartment, I searched for my kitchen timer. It was actually in the drawer where I thought I had put it. That felt like a victory of sorts. At least I hadn't lost all my mental faculties. I set it for forty minutes and carried it with me. I planned to go back to the laundry when the timer went off and put the newly washed clothing into dryers—if, that is, someone hadn't stolen it by then. It was now five o'clock. Ordinarily I would be coming in from the office, throwing my coat on the chair, and pouring myself a good stiff drink. Good old bourbon on the rocks. I had finished yesterday's supply, so there was nothing to drink in my apartment. I had this feeling of blackness that kept moving me to sit down and do some serious thinking. So I sat down on the newly cleared recliner. I picked up a yellow legal pad and a pen—two of the few items I had left on my coffee table. I wrote down my assignment.

> *Do article on Elizabeth Grayson in next two weeks. Article should be the basis for a book which Martha Bullock would like to publish. If article isn't acceptable to Ed Wainwright you will be fired. Deadline: 10 days for first editing. Two weeks for publication in next month's issue.*

I looked at what I had written. My job was the only thing in the world that I had. Something told me that losing my job would be a death sentence. If I lost the job and didn't get a recommendation from Ed, I'd probably end up on skid row.

"No," I thought out loud. "No probably about it. I will end up on skid row. I'll lose this lousy apartment, my stuff will be thrown on the street, and I will end up on skid row."

Some choice. Do an article and maybe even a book on some bitchy psychologist or lose your livelihood. My stomach turned upside down.

I went to the bathroom and vomited. There was blood clearly visible in the mucus that poured out of my throat. This wasn't a new experience for me. I had spent countless hours hanging my head in toilets, but for some reason, the seriousness of what was happening was finally registering with me.

When the vomiting stopped, I stood up and felt my body begin screaming for a drink. My hands began to shake. Bourbon always calmed the shakes. Instead of rushing for the kitchen in the hope of finding a forgotten bottle, I opened the medicine cabinet and searched the prescription bottles for a tranquilizer. Every bottle was empty. When I slammed the cabinet door I saw my face in the mirror. Even through the filth on the mirror, the sight of me was awful. I was visibly exhausted, needed a shave and a haircut. I was considered handsome by many in my younger years. Now, there was no trace of handsomeness—only darkness, dirt, and depression.

"What have you come to?" I asked myself. The sorriest face stared back at me. I wanted desperately for someone to comfort me, but I knew comfort was nowhere to be found.

What I was becoming was dawning on me, whether I wanted it to or not.

I returned to the living room and sat once again in the recliner and looked at the yellow pad. It was clear I had to make a decision. Would I accept the challenge of doing an article on a person who offended every sensibility I had, and do it fairly, or would I just tell Ed Wainwright to take his assignment and shove it?

The shaking of my body got worse. I sat in the shadows, thinking, until the timer went off. By then, my physical being relaxed somewhat. I was able to move. I went to my bedroom, gathered up more quarters from the change box on my dresser, then headed to the laundry. The clothes were still there and they were clean. I put all the loads into two dryers, deposited the quarters, and started the machines. I returned to my apartment and hugged the cool wall as soon as I closed the door behind me. When I finally felt able to walk again, I found the timer and reset it for an hour.

I took it with me into the bedroom and lied down on the bed. The only light came from the lamp in the living room. I couldn't see the dirty sheets. I hoped my body would stop shaking. I put the timer near my head and pulled the covers up over me. Blessed sleep came over me for an hour.

The timer went off and my body woke up in a panic. The noise jangled every cell of my being. I realized I was sweating profusely. Through sheer force of will, I pulled myself up to my full six feet and staggered out to find some clean garbage bags for the dried clothes. The dryers were still warm. The clothes hadn't packed down. I threw the clothes into a large basket on wheels. I actually separated things and put the underwear in one bag, socks in another, and shirts in yet another. When I returned to the apartment I dragged the bags into the bedroom. I crammed as much clean underwear as possible into its proper drawer and stashed the remaining underwear in the bottom of the closet, still in its garbage bag. I did the same thing with the socks. I surprised myself by remembering that the shirts should be put on hangers. There were plenty of empty hangers, and I did a half-assed job of getting the shirts in wearable order.

That done, I returned to the living room and felt a sense of accomplishment that hadn't visited me in a long, long time. Once again, I sat down with my yellow pad. The hour of sleep had helped. I hadn't had anything to drink at lunch because Ed Wainwright pre-empted my lunch plans. I came right home after my meeting with Ed and didn't drink. Only God knows why. Having a drink when I walked into my apartment was a sacred rite. I'll probably never know exactly why I didn't drink that night.

I went to the kitchen to see if I could find something to eat. Cockroaches scattered the second I turned on the lights. The kitchen looked as bad as the living room. Usually, if I ate anything at all in the evening, I would grab a sandwich at one of the delicatessens on Polk Street. On payday I usually stopped for a nice meal in one of the restaurants on Van Ness. I hadn't cooked in my kitchen in years. There were some cans of soup in the cupboard. They had been there for years and the dust on top of them proved it. The soup was probably seven years old. I wondered if anyone ever died of old soup, but I opened the can anyway. As best I knew, it smelled okay.

There weren't any clean dishes, so I cleared the sink and ran hot water into it. I found detergent and washed a pan for heating the soup. While the soup was heating I soaked a full sink of dirty dishes. I cleaned a bowl and spoon and took my nourishment to the living room to watch the news. It felt strange to be eating a bowl of soup instead of having a drink. I was shaky, but the hot soup felt comforting. I turned on the news in the hope that I could distract myself from the rising feeling of anxiety.

No luck. The news was as depressing as ever, and there was no distraction from the butterflies in my stomach. I was shaking, but I refused to give in to the urge to get a drink. Ordinarily, I would have stopped at the nearby liquor store and gotten the evening's supply. I never got more than a pint because I didn't want to be an alcoholic. A pint was a lot less than I was capable of drinking, but a pint usually got me to the passing out stage.

I decided to clean the kitchen and get the grime off my bathroom mirror before I turned in. Because I hadn't cooked in the kitchen, there weren't layers of grease and rotted food to be cleaned off. It was a small space and cleaned up pretty easily. I looked in the refrigerator and decided that would have to wait for another day. The dishes soaked clean, and I piled them in the dishwasher. I was feeling a real sense of accomplishment.

"Weird," I thought.

I looked under the sink for window cleaner. I remembered seeing some somewhere in the apartment. It wasn't in the kitchen and it wasn't under the sink in the bathroom. I decided I'd borrow some from the only neighbor I knew. I walked to Apartment 5B and knocked on the door.

Madge Underwood answered the door.

"Well for heaven's sake. What are you doing out of your apartment at this hour? And by the way, you look like hell."

"Thanks. You look wonderful too. I'm doing some cleaning and I can't find my window cleaner. I was wondering if I could borrow some from you."

"You're doing what?"

"Please, Madge. I just need some window cleaner."

Madge Underwood was a big woman. She was part Black-foot Indian and the rest was African-American. She once told me that she had been dropped off at an orphanage when she was six with a note explaining her ancestry. She was beautiful and sensual and way too smart to get involved with me. God knows I had tried to get her to go to bed with me, but for some reason she was never interested. She had also tried to get me to look at my drinking, which ended any romantic notions I might have had about her. I never wanted to listen to what she had to say. I figured she was Native American, and those people haven't a clue about how to drink, so there was nothing she could tell me concerning alcohol.

Madge left me at the door, and when she returned she handed me a bottle of cleaner and a roll of paper towels.

"Are you having a party?"

"No. I just figured I need to clean the place up a little. I hadn't realized it had gotten so dirty."

"Evan, the neighbors have been complaining about your place for years. Don't tell me you didn't know how dirty it was."

"Yeah. Well thanks for the cleaner. I'll bring it back as soon as I'm through."

"Yeah, yeah. I'll believe it when I see it, Evan."

Madge closed her door as I walked back to my place. I think she mentally said goodbye to her window cleaner. She'd loaned me many things over the years and almost never saw their return. I would remember this conversation and come to a new understanding of my life during the next couple of weeks. It was another measure of how I had drained the good will of those around me.

I cleaned the bathroom mirror. I looked up and saw cobwebs and dust covering the light fixture. I cleaned it, my hands shaking all the while. The entire bathroom lit up to a level that

21

probably had happened only during my first week of occupancy. The brightness hurt my eyes. It also made the filth of the rest of the room all too apparent.

"Oh, what the hell," I muttered. I got the detergent from the kitchen and cleaned the sink, the back of the toilet and the bowl. I decided the shower and the floor would have to wait. After that, I only remember walking into the darkness of my bedroom and dropping like a rock onto the bed. I heard nothing until five o'clock the next morning.

CHAPTER 2

A little ray of sunshine broke through the tattered shade on the window of my bedroom and it startled me. My heart began to race. It felt as though it were trying to explode out of my chest. I lay as quietly as I could. After a few minutes, the mass in my chest began to beat normally. I pushed myself over to the nightstand and studied the face of the clock. It said five o'clock. My body hadn't gotten up at five o'clock in at least twenty years. I felt like hell had worked me over and spit me through a hole in a cement doughnut. As I look back on that morning, I realize I had a vague awareness that something wasn't hurting quite as much as usual. I pulled myself upright and sat on the edge of my bed and looked around me. The rumpled shirt and slacks of yesterday looked like I felt. Ed Wainwright's assignment flashed across my mind. I knew I had to look halfway presentable when I went to the office that day. I'm not sure how I knew that. My mind was fogged up, but I knew it and didn't argue with it.

I stripped and did something I hadn't done in years. I actually tried to throw my dirty clothes into the dilapidated wicker hamper that someone had given me years before. The second I opened the lid, roaches tumbled out. I looked in to find piles of paper and garbage. Since no one had been in my apartment for at least a year, I admitted I was probably responsible for the mess in the hamper. Another round of self loathing surged through me. I'm sure today that the vermin-filled mess was made during some of those long winter evenings when I drank myself into blackouts.

I slammed the lid shut and went to the kitchen to look for a spray can of pesticide I had brought with me from my last apartment. It was under the sink.

"Viola," I exclaimed out loud. I marched back to the bedroom and sprayed the entire can into the hamper. A cloud of noxious gas filled the room. I covered my face and walked a few feet away, listening until the scurrying stopped. When all was quiet, I poured the mess into a garbage bag. I knotted the top to be sure nothing could escape.

The prior evening was coming back to me. I remembered putting the clean clothes away. I also remembered throwing the extras in the bottom of the closet. I turned on the closet light and helped myself to clean underwear and socks. I pulled out a clean shirt and found the cleanest pair of pants available. There was a pair on a hanger that looked fairly respectable.

I showered, shaved, brushed my teeth, and even flossed.

I looked at myself in the mirror when I was through, and saw that I was no longer the hunk of my earlier days.

"Actually, Evan Howard, you're just an average looking, middle-aged man." I told myself.

"No. Not so," I argued. "You can never be average."

"Oh yes you can. And you can be a jerk, too," the face in the mirror said to me.

"Words right out of my mother's mouth," I thought. And with that thought came the realization of the decision I was facing. Panic began to take hold of me. I walked to the living room and checked the clock. It was just a few minutes after six. My body began to shake again, and my heart raced. I sat for several moments. My body shook, my heart raced faster. Finally it settled back to normal.

"I need some coffee." I moved to the kitchen to see if I could find some way to put together a hot cup of coffee.

Chapter 2

There was no coffee in the kitchen, so I decided to go to the convenience store on Van Ness for coffee and something to eat. It occurred to me that some of my shaking might be due to hunger. I realized I hadn't died of old soup, but had consumed very few calories during the past twenty-four hours.

When I walked out the front door of my building, I felt as though I had stepped into a movie set. The sun was just breaking through the night's fog. The shadows of the buildings were long. The air was brisk. I could hear a trolley on Van Ness. I wasn't sure I had ever been out in my neighborhood at that hour. Everything was so quiet, so calm.

It took only a few minutes to get to the convenience store. The clerk was an Asian woman who seemed to recognize me.

"Good morning, Mister," she said sweetly.

I nodded and walked over to the coffee pots. I poured a large cup and loaded it with cream and sugar. The donut trays were just being filled by the driver of a bakery truck. I waited until he finished his work and then helped myself to a half-dozen donuts, using a tissue to place each one in a paper bag. Ordinarily, that would have been my breakfast for the day, but something made me think about getting some fruit. I picked out two apples and two bananas. Most of what I did that morning was totally out of character for me.

Picking up that day's edition of the *San Francisco Examiner* wasn't out of character, though. I had to get an in-depth look at world and local events. I'd never get over being a news junky. I had a feeling that things would really spin out of control if I didn't keep up with current events. Yes—I was indeed a news junky.

I placed my purchases on the counter. The Asian lady rang them up. I paid her and she put the entire order in a large bag. As I walked back to my apartment, I breathed in the smell of ocean air that is always present in San Francisco. It had been years since I had thought about the freshness of the air that flowed constantly through the city, thanks to the bodies of water that surround it. My body began to shake again. I hurried back to my apartment, fearing I was going to die on the way.

I made it to my kitchen. I put the groceries on the table and held onto the back of the closest chair. Finally I was able to sit. I took the lid off my coffee and sipped it slowly. It was very hot. It was delicious. I was grateful for the taste and for the nourishment. I ate a donut and a banana and finished the coffee while trying to read the paper. For some reason it was impossible to concentrate on anything in the paper.

I looked at the clock on the stove. It was now a few minutes before seven. I decided to knock on Madge Underwood's door. I even remembered to take the remaining window cleaner back to her, and I thought to bring the tape of the talk show and Elizabeth Grayson's book. As I stood at Madge's door, I could hear someone rustling around. I knocked and waited quietly for the door to open.

Who is it?"

"It's me, Madge. Evan."

The door opened slowly. Madge was in a battered terrycloth robe. You know, the kind you never want to throw away because it's warm and soft and comfortable. She waved me in and padded slowly to the kitchen.

I sat down at her kitchen table. She put together the makings of a pot of coffee.

"Give me a minute, Evan. I'll be back in a few minutes. Pour yourself a cup as soon as it's done."

With that she disappeared into her bedroom. I heard the toilet flush and water run in the sink. I looked at her kitchen. It was very welcoming, actually. Spotlessly clean. The curtains were bright. Very Native American in design. A tower of coffee mugs stood beside the coffee maker. I took one and filled it. I found the half-and-half in the refrigerator, which was also spotless. I looked for sugar and a spoon, and found both in the usual places. The front of our apartments faced west. Light radiated off the building across the street and brightened Madge's kitchen. I realized the brightness was hurting my eyes. I turned the louver blind covering the kitchen window to deflect the light. I wondered if light broke into my apartment that same way and told myself I'd be sure to check that out if I ever got up this early again.

Madge returned to the kitchen looking as though she had been up for hours.

"I'm sorry to wake you. I brought back the window cleaner."

"You didn't wake me. I was doing my meditations. My God, Evan. What's happening with you?" Madge looked at me curiously. I looked just as curiously at her. I didn't understand how ludicrous and rigidly out of touch with life I had been. What seemed to me to be curiosity was actually genuine concern for my sanity on Madge's part.

"Ed Wainwright threw down the gauntlet yesterday. I have to make a decision today and I don't know if I can do what he's ordered me to do. I thought maybe you could give me some perspective."

Madge stared at me. She had the most piercing grey-black eyes, and they were burning a hole through me.

"First of all," she said, "what are you doing knocking on my door at this hour? As far as I know, you've never gotten up before eleven a.m. This has to be a damn serious assignment he's thrown at you."

He's ordered me to do a major article on Elizabeth Grayson, Ph.D. He told me to start with this tape of Grayson's kids on Leslie Wilder's talk show. The article has to be done in less than two weeks, and if I do that well, I'll be kept on and will be expected to do a book on the bitch."

"You know this woman, I take it."

"Naw. I mean, I've heard of her. You can't work for *World of Psychology Magazine* and not have heard of Elizabeth Grayson. Supposedly, she's done some work concerning emotional disability. There are a lot of respected people in the field who think her work is groundbreaking. I didn't have feelings about her one way or the other until I saw a tape of her kids."

"You mean this tape?" Madge picked up the cassette.

"Are you in a hurry, Madge? I really need some guidance," I pleaded.

"I don't have to be anywhere until ten. What do you want me to do?"

"Watch the tape with me. Scan the book and see what your feelings are about Grayson."

Madge gave me another of those curious looks.

"You're looking for advice from me, Evan?"

"Well, I don't know if I'd go so far as to call it advice."

"Is this going to be another one of those 'I'll ask for input but ignore it completely when I make my decision' things? Because if it is, you can go back to your apartment right now." Madge was clearly confrontational. I didn't understand why she was so sharp in her reaction.

"We've been through this kind of thing often, Evan. I'm sick of you asking me what I think and then doing the exact opposite. I don't know why I let you in. I guess I'm surprised to see you up so early and I'm flabbergasted that you're returning my window cleaner."

"I don't know what you're talking about. I don't remember ever asking your advice on anything. But I'm dead serious about asking your advice now. I'm hoping you can help me understand why my boss is yanking my chain like this."

"I've met Ed Wainwright, Evan. You took me to the magazine's Christmas party two years ago, remember? He seemed to be a good man, a caring man. But he's not stupid. I'm sure he's a very good editor. I think he knows you're a good reporter—otherwise he wouldn't have given you this story to do."

I explained that the person behind the story was actually Martha Bullock, the publisher of the magazine and owner of the Bullock Publishing Company. I also explained how it angered me to see Ed allowing a woman to manipulate him as Martha Bullock was.

"I don't understand why you believe Martha Bullock is 'manipulating' anyone. She owns the company, she went to her editor, and she asked him to do a story on someone she admires. I believe manipulation is underhanded and devious, not open and direct as she was in this case." Madge sat down across the table from me and looked me square in the eye. I took a deep breath and tried to change the subject.

"Will you watch this tape with me or not?"

"I'll watch. And I'll give you my honest opinion."

Madge picked up the tape and walked into her living room. I followed. She inserted the tape into her VCR.

"Why isn't this on a DVD?" Madge looked at me for an answer.

"I told Ed I don't have a DVD player. I guess he assumed I had whatever it takes to play the tape. I don't have any electronics except for my TV. I promised myself a long time ago I wasn't going to be trapped by technology, and I haven't been.

Madge said nothing. She turned her television on and started the tape. Watching it was as painful as it had been when Ed made me watch it with him. Madge fast-forwarded through the commercials just as Ed had. Each segment reinforced the pain of my own childhood. When the daughter cried, I found myself experiencing another of those shaking episodes. I hoped Madge wouldn't notice. Fortunately, she was quite taken with the tape of Elizabeth Grayson's children.

My body settled down again. As soon as my physical crisis passed, my anger began to rise. I heard Grayson's children fight to be heard, to be understood, to be apologized to, and to be loved by their mother as they, nor I, had been loved in our growing up years. Again, I wanted to smash Elizabeth Grayson in the face. When the program finished, Madge rewound the tape. She said nothing.

"Well?" I asked.

"Well, what?" she responded.

"Do you see why I don't think I can do an article, much less an entire book?"

"Frankly, I don't. These people are in their forties and they sound like they're five or six years old. 'Mommy didn't do this for me, Mommy didn't do that for me.' I'd be fascinated to know how someone ever gets one kid like that, much less three."

I became infuriated and slammed my empty coffee cup on the coffee table.

"That's it, Evan. Go back to your apartment." Madge was on her feet, ready for a fight.

"Wait a minute, Madge. Please. I'm sorry I slammed the cup down. It's just that these people suffered through the same shit I did. I know how they feel. Their mother only cared about herself and her precious career, her precious house, her precious feelings. Don't you see? Ed Wainwright is asking me to do an article on a woman who is almost identical to the person who destroyed me?"

"I'm seeing a lot, Evan. I'm understanding a lot. If you want my advice, I think you'd better do this article and you'd better listen to all sides of this story. My gut tells me there's something very fishy about the stories these people are telling. I'd very much like to learn more about their father and to actually hear Elizabeth Grayson's side of the story."

"Are you saying they're lying? That I'm lying?"

"No, I'm not saying anyone is lying. I can only tell you from my own personal experience that things I remember from childhood look quite different now that I see the whole picture. I don't think those three people are telling anywhere near the whole story. Maybe you're not seeing the whole picture about your mother either. So do the story. Maybe you'll help them out of their pain and maybe you'll be able to let go of some of your pain, too."

I stood staring at my neighbor and one of the few friends I had in the world.

"I'll never be able to let go of my pain. My mother is dead. She'll never be able to apologize to me and make amends for all the harm she did me."

"You know, Evan, I used to believe that way. I was a 'nigger,' an 'injun,' and I spent years nursing my hatred for everyone and anyone who had more than me, or was white. I almost killed myself with my own negativity. You're doing the same thing. There's a different way. Maybe Ed Wainwright's assignment is the best thing that could happen to you. Do the article. Learn from it."

Chapter 2

I don't know if it was anger or my body shaking apart again. All I could do was sit down and hold my head in my hands. I felt tears in my eyes. I would rather die than cry in front of anyone. I hadn't cried since I was four years old, and I was damned if I would cry in Madge's living room. Despite my best efforts to stop them, the tears came.

Madge walked over and stood behind me. She rubbed my shoulders.

"Evan, I think I know what's happening to you. You're in your forties and this is mid-life crisis time. We all come to a crossroad in our lives and this may be yours. When I came to mine, I had to look at what really happened in my childhood, not at what I thought happened."

"I know what happened in my childhood, godammit." I looked at her and the rage in my eyes caused her to step back from me. The tears burned my cheek. Madge took a step forward and brushed my cheek with her hand. I felt the moisture she lifted from my face. Even in that emotionally charged moment, I could still worry that Madge might think I was gay. I felt nauseous. My body seemed to be in complete revulsion. All the aching in my head, heart, and joints couldn't shut out the sound or the meaning of what Madge said to me next.

"You don't know what happened, Evan. You know what you think happened, just as Elizabeth Grayson's children think they know what happened. Healthy people come to terms with the disappointments and hurts of childhood. Unhealthy people let those hurts fester into hatred and revenge. Those are not healthy people on that tape. If you'll find their truth, you may very well find your own truth. Do the story, Evan. And get all sides of the story."

"And if I don't?"

"Then don't ever ask me for advice again. And I mean it."

CHAPTER 3

I wandered back to my apartment in a stupor. Now it was Madge giving me an ultimatum. Everyone I cared about seemed to be turning against me. I sat in my living room and stared at the legal pad on which I had listed the choices I was facing. Next to it laid Elizabeth Grayson's latest book and the tape of her children on the talk show. My job was my lifeline. I could not lose it. Every job I had lost had led me to accept something inferior in order to keep body and soul together.

Feeling like a whipped child, I washed my face, combed my hair, and got myself looking as professional as possible under the circumstances. Most of my clothes were clean. My shirt looked better than usual. I found a clean tie and put on my best Pendleton jacket—a camelhair that looked fairly good no matter what you did to it. The reflection in the mirror looked weary, bone weary. Tears came. I fought them with fear and anger but still they came. I slumped onto the toilet and let the pain roll through me. My world was falling apart. I wanted a drink but something in me said I could not drink that day. I hated, truly hated, my alcoholic mother for having done all of this to me. I vowed again to never forgive her, and then wondered how in God's name I could ever do a story on someone just like her.

Chapter 3

I must have used half a roll of toilet paper blowing my nose and wiping my face. Finally, I pulled myself together and made the decision that Ed Wainwright and my friend Madge hoped I would make.

"Okay," I said to myself. "I'll do this story on Elizabeth Grayson and I'll show the world what a hypocrite she is. I'll interview everyone I can find and I'll prove to everyone what a bitch this woman is. I'll show 'em, by God—I'll show 'em."

On this note, I headed to the office on Market Street and my meeting with Ed Wainwright.

***

I stepped into my office and was astounded at the clutter. I wondered if cockroaches were making homes in the piles of paper that had accumulated everywhere. Ed told me later that he had my office "bombed" with roach bombs at least twice when coworkers complained about bugs invading their offices from my office. Ed was in a meeting with some sales people which gave me time to do some straightening and cleaning. I headed to the office kitchen for garbage bags and cleaning supplies. I washed my coffee cup, which held about two ounces of green, moldy liquid. My stomach turned as the slimy stuff slid out of the cup and down the drain. Hot water and detergent sanitized the cup. I dried it carefully and then poured myself a cup of fresh brew. I gathered spray cleaner, furniture polish and garbage bags.

At least one coworker commented on my "ambition." I was, of course, insulted by her comment. Fortunately, my turmoil over Ed's assignment prevented me from giving her the usual verbal assault that such insults warranted.

It didn't take long for me to fill two of the garbage bags. It astounded me that I had done so much eating while at work. I wondered if perhaps some office slobs had piled their garbage in my office so they would look good and I would look bad. Again, I would later learn that the entire mess was mine.

When I looked at how full the garbage bags were, I wondered how I could get them out of the office without being seen.

"Good morning, Evan."

Ed stuck his head in the door of my office. I tried to hide the bags by kicking the first one behind my desk.

"Are you cleaning out your office to leave?"

"No."

"Do you want to talk here or in my office?"

"Let's go to your office."

"Okay. Bring that tape and book with you."

I picked up the tape and book and followed Ed into his office. He seated himself behind his desk. My mother used to talk about positions of authority/inferiority. Here I was, understanding what she meant by that, probably for the first time in my life.

But Ed didn't stay there. He took something out of a drawer, then came around and sat in a chair right next to me.

"Equal/equal, win/win," mother would say. I had a vague feeling of comfort as my best friend took the chair beside me.

"So," Ed said, "what have you decided?"

"I feel I have no choice, Ed. I have to do this assignment, and it galls me because I'm being forced to do something that renews a lot of my childhood pain. I don't understand why you would be so insistent on me doing this story. You know what my home was like when I was growing up. I've always thought we were best friends, Ed."

"I'm a better friend than you can see right now, Evan. I'm sorry you feel badly about the assignment. Frankly, you're the only person in this office who sees this as a negative thing. I've told T.J. he'll get this assignment if you decide not to take it. He's hoping you'll turn it down. Elizabeth Grayson is an exceptional person. I've met her and I've read every book she's written. She lives with deep hurt and disappointment that comes from the loss of her children."

"She brought it on herself." I interjected. I was so busy hating Elizabeth Grayson that I didn't connect with Ed's comment about giving the assignment to someone else. I would later be enormously insulted that Ed even thought of giving something assigned to me to the youngest reporter on the staff. It was my opinion that T.J. Froeling was a snot-nosed little brown-noser who was always asking questions and always overdoing the eager-beaver role.

"Oh really." Ed gave me one of his statements of disbelief that always stopped me mid-sentence. Ed was a born questioner. If I, or anyone, said something was thus-and-such, he'd say, "Oh really. Prove it."

"Have you read the book yet?"

"No."

"I strongly suggest you read the book before you meet Mrs. Grayson. She won't mess with you, Evan. She's expecting a professional reporter and you'd better not show up at her home as anything else."

"Anything else? I am a professional, Ed. I'm insulted that you would infer I would ever be anything else."

"Ten years ago I would have had no qualms about sending you on this story, Evan. You were the best reporter in San Francisco. Maybe even California. But something's happened to you. You've been fired from three jobs. When you applied to work here you promised you'd work like hell for me. Martha Bullock allowed me to hire you only because I vouched for you. I haven't told her how much rewriting I've done of your work or how often I've covered for you in front of the rest of the staff."

"What rewriting have you done for me?" I couldn't believe my ears.

"I'm not getting into an argument with you, Evan. I'm tired of that game. I'm tired of your crap. We both know your time is limited and you have a lot of work to do in the next two weeks. I suggest you call and arrange to meet with Mrs. Grayson before you leave this office."

I nodded and shrugged my shoulders in my usual way. I rose to leave the room.

"Evan."

"Yes?"

"Don't forget the tape and the book. And shine your shoes before you meet with her."

Ed handed me a fifty-dollar bill.

"And buy a new belt. Your paunch has stretched the one you're wearing to its limit. I'd hate to have you meet her and have your pants fall down."

I took the money but felt contempt for the giver. I wondered where Ed Wainwright got off patronizing me. Still, I didn't have but a few dollars left in my wallet and almost nothing in my checking account. I shoved the bill into my pocket and promised I'd pay him back if it killed me. I couldn't foresee how close to right I was with that thought. I headed for the bathroom. Once inside I realized how poor the lighting and the mirror in my bathroom at home were. I saw myself as I hadn't seen myself in years. My eyes were puffy and red, and my nose looked swollen, almost bulbous. My hair was turning gray—and it wasn't the suave and debonair graying at the temples men are supposed to get as they age. It was a clump here and a clump there. And I was getting paunchy. I looked closely at the belt Ed asked me to replace. It did look stressed.

When I finished in the bathroom, I called Elizabeth Grayson. She answered the phone herself. That surprised me. I figured she had servants and a large mansion. I asked if she would be able to meet with me in the morning. She said she would, and asked if I needed directions to her home. I told her I would take BART to Walnut Creek. She asked me to call her from the BART station and she would send a car for me.

I hung up the phone and felt nothing. I thought it strange that she aroused no feelings in me. Her voice was pleasant. She seemed sincere about doing all she could to help me get a good story. She was more than accommodating about the fact that I didn't have a car and would be taking the Bay Area Rapid Transit to the East Bay. I gave up driving years before. Actually a judge had urged me to do so after my third DUI. Those were the days before Mothers Against Drunk Driving, when you could still get multiple DUIs and almost nothing happened to you. One of the best things about San Francisco is its transit system. Cars are an unnecessary bother and expense in the city, especially if you have a tendency to get into trouble while driving. It would take a while for me to understand that Elizabeth Grayson knew a great deal about me when I called her the first time.

I spent another half an hour cleaning out papers, straightening and dusting in my office. I made three trips to the dumpster behind the building, and returned the extra garbage bags and cleaning supplies to the kitchen. I looked at "my office" and felt proud. My mother would have called it a disgrace but, by my standards, my office was in amazingly good shape.

Next, I gathered "the" tape, "the" book, a couple of notebooks, my tape recorder, pens and pencils, and realized my load would be handled better if I had something to carry everything in. I remembered having an old briefcase somewhere, and found it behind a box of old wire copy. I stuffed everything in the case and headed for the street. Ed waved to me through the window of his office as I passed. I nodded, but mentally gave him the finger. When I got to the street, I headed for a menswear store just a few blocks away. I bought a new belt and then walked to the Embarcadero and got a shine from Big John's Shoe Shine Stand.

I headed back home, fully intending to read "the" book. I stopped at my favorite sandwich shop on Polk Street and had the Gold Miner's Special—beef and Cheddar piled high on sourdough bread with a dill sauce. It came on a huge platter, next to a large, crisp slab of dill pickle and a pile of French fries. For some reason, everything tasted better than it had ever tasted in all the years I'd been eating there. Instead of my usual beer, I ordered a soda. My body seemed to be settling down, and food was remaining in my stomach. This was unusual and welcome. The waiter was friendlier than usual, too. I cleaned the plate and didn't throw up a single bite. Something strange was happening to me.

The fog was rolling in over the city as I walked from Van Ness to my apartment. I knocked on Madge's door and wondered why. Fortunately, there was no answer, so I went home feeling totally wiped out. As I started to throw my coat on its chair, I stopped myself and hung it on the coat rack next to the door. All my body wanted was rest. I put the briefcase in the living room and took out "the" book. I lied down on the couch and turned on the lamp above my head. I began to read Elizabeth Grayson's latest work. I got through the first paragraph of the Introduction and was off to a very deep sleep. I look back on that sleep now and understand that it was the first sleep of true healing. I'll never forget how deep and pure and refreshing that sleep was.

CHAPTER 4

I slept for more than three hours. I probably would have slept through the night except someone knocked loudly on my door a little before eight. I struggled to my feet and made my way to the door in a stupor—more coherent and aware than I usually was when I was in a stupor.

I opened the door to Madge Underwood.

"Hi. Did I wake you, Evan?"

"Yes, you did."

"Sorry about that, but I'm going to a meeting tonight and I think you should come with me."

"What kind of meeting?"

"It's an Open 12-Step Recovery meeting."

"A what?"

"A 12-Step Recovery meeting. You know, for alcoholics, drug addicts, gamblers, sex and love addicts, anyone with an addiction problem."

"What?" I couldn't believe what I was hearing. "Are you trying to drag me to an AA meeting, Madge? Don't you ever give up? I've told you I'm not an alcoholic."

"Well actually, the meeting I'm trying to drag you to permits people with any kind of an addiction to attend. There aren't many pure alcoholics anymore, at least not in California."

"What do you mean by that?"

"Most people use drugs and alcohol together, or they smoke and drink, or they gamble and drink and drug, or they destroy themselves through obsessive sexual behaviors. The day of the alcoholic who uses only booze is long gone. So now we have Open 12-Step Recovery meetings. The 12 Steps have always worked with any addiction, but those of us who use more than one substance to medicate ourselves needed a different kind of meeting."

"I don't understand a word you're saying, Madge."

"That figures. Have you had dinner?"

"Yes."

"Have you been drinking today?"

"No. I haven't had a drink since yesterday. I feel lousy and I'm having problems with sweats and panic attacks."

"Terrific. It's dangerous to stop drinking or drugging cold turkey. Do you want me to take you to a doctor or to an emergency room?"

"No. I don't want you to take me anywhere."

"You owe me money and you owe me time, Evan. You're going to my meeting with me tonight. And since you haven't had a drink since yesterday, you can pick up a white chip this evening for having 24 hours clean and sober."

"Oh no you don't, Madge. No! No! No!" My voice was strained. I thought my brain was going to burst. "I promised myself a long time ago I wasn't ever going to get into anything like AA. My mother went to AA and it never made her a better person."

"And how do you know that, Evan Howard? You told me you never had anything to do with your mother once she divorced your father."

"Don't give me any of your psycho-babble bullshit," I said. "You don't know anything about me or my family other than what I've told you—therefore you know nothing."

"Don't give me bullshit, Evan. I've known you most of your adult life and I'm finished watching you rewrite your mother's life to suit your agenda. It's time you start learning that you don't know everything. I want you to come to this meeting with me. You've imposed on my friendship for years and it's payback time. Go wash your face and comb your hair. I promise to have you home in less than two hours." Madge pushed me toward the bathroom. She was a powerful woman in more ways than one.

"But Madge, you don't understand. I have to be in Walnut Creek tomorrow morning and I have to read Elizabeth Grayson's book by then."

"Yeah, yeah. If I hadn't come over you would have slept all night and probably missed getting out to Walnut Creek in the morning, and then you'd be fired for sure. When we get back we'll set your alarm and get clean clothes laid out. I'll even come over in the morning and make sure you get off on time."

I sat on the toilet and stared into the sink.

"Come on, Evan." Madge rooted around in my medicine chest and found my almost empty tube of toothpaste. She turned the water on, dampened my toothbrush, put some paste on it and ordered me to get going. I brushed, rinsed, swizzled, and spit.

"Good boy. Now comb your hair and wipe your face if you need to. We've got just fifteen minutes to get to the meeting."

I didn't argue. I did as I was told.

When I walked out of the bathroom, Madge was waiting with my camelhair jacket. She helped me into it and pushed me out the door. She checked to see if it locked behind us. It did. She then took me by the arm and walked me down to the parking garage. I hadn't been down there since I sold my car years before.

Madge pushed me into the front seat of what appeared to be a new sedan.

"Nice car. Is it new?"

"Yes. This is the kind of stuff that happens when you get sober and stay sober."

"What happens if you don't get sober and stay sober?" I felt like an impish little brother trying to taunt an older, domineering sister.

"What happens if you don't get sober and stay sober is what's been happening to you, dummy. You run out of family and friends, jobs, cars, homes. You end up on the street and eventually you die and get put in a pauper's grave."

"Fuck you!"

"I don't get fucked anymore, Mr. Howard. I have healthy re-lationships with people who talk and behave respectfully toward me. No one's been messing with you except you. So don't give me attitude. For some reason you haven't had a drink for an en-tire day. There's a reason for that. I'm sick of watching you kill yourself with booze and self pity so I'm taking you where the answers are. Now will you go into this meeting with me and try to listen to what other people say? Just listen to the feelings ex-pressed. Don't compare yourself with what they've done or ha-ven't done. Compare yourself with the feelings these people had while they were drinking."

"I'll go, but I don't have to like being there."

"Just try to open your mind for once in your life."

Once again I felt whipped. I prided myself on being open minded. At any other time Madge would have had a real fight on her hands, but I just didn't have the strength to fight with her. I slumped deeper into the seat and shut my mouth. Madge turned the car into a church parking lot somewhere north of Van Ness but I wasn't sure exactly where.

"Look, Evan, I care. I honestly want to help you. Your life is far enough into the dumpster that I sense you're open to chang-ing some things about yourself. Leave your pictures of AA and your mother's recovery out here. Please. You've never attended a meeting. Go in there with your reporter's objectivity."

"I'll try," I said. "But I don't know which hurt me more, my mother's alcoholism or her so-called recovery. I'm sorry I can't be positive about something you clearly treasure, but you ha-ven't had my experiences with it."

"Your experiences are what you've made of them, Evan. It's possible that at least one or two things you've told me weren't what really happened. Until now, there was no sense trying to get you to see things differently. We learn in recovery not to deal with people until they show signs of real change. One day isn't a lot to hang my hopes on, but by God, I'm going to try to help you see the light. I'm glad your job is on the line. The chance of losing it may be the only thing that would get your attention."

We arrived at the door of the church. Madge stepped behind me and opened the door for me, shoving me into the vestibule. The hall was dimly lit. She directed me down a stairway. When we reached the bottom of the steps, a brightly lit room full of people came into view. Immediately, people rushed to give Madge hugs and to shake my hand. Women were welcoming me, men were patting me on the back. Faces were blurs, voices blended together. I began to panic.

Suddenly there was the sound of a gavel.

"It's time to bring this meeting to order, ladies and gentlemen." The man with a gavel looked like a judge. I was to learn later that he was, indeed, a judge. He was a man whose name was in the news frequently.

"Good evening, everybody. I'm Jim and I'm an alcoholic/addict, and I'm pleased to have been asked to lead the Wednesday Evening Recoverers Anonymous Group. Is there anyone here for their first meeting?"

I thought I would die until at least six people stood up. Madge gave me her "are you going to be honest and stand up" look—so I stood up.

"We want to welcome you to Recoverers Anonymous. Because there are new people here, we will focus on the first of the twelve steps of recovery. As many people as possible will tell you how it was for them when they first came into the program. We'd like to have you tell us your first name, if you will, so that we can talk with you after the meeting to see if there's anything in particular we can help you with as you begin learning about 12-Step Recovery."

Madge had seated us in the first row, much against my wishes. Most of that meeting is still a blur in my mind, but I remember the wave of nausea that swept over me when the judge pointed the gavel at me.

"All you have to say, sir, is 'my name is so-and-so' and then be seated."

"Uh, hi," I said. "My name is Evan and my friend Madge dragged me here." I sat down immediately.

People chuckled. Everyone in the room said, "Welcome, Evan." My eyes automatically rolled to the back of my head. I slouched in my chair wishing an earthquake would split the floor wide open and suck the entire room into it and crush us all to death as it closed. I hated attention from others. I hated this experience. I looked at Madge, who was nodding her approval of me, and I hated her. The only thing that kept me in my seat was the realization that getting up and walking out would put a hundred or more pairs of eyes directly on me.

The judge allowed the other six to introduce themselves, and each of them got welcomed in that stomach-turning chorus of voices. The judge had different people read things. I tried to bring my reporter's mind to the meeting. One person read the Preamble, another the 12 Steps, another the 12 Traditions. I had a notebook on me, and it helped me stay in my chair to try to write down what was going on. I didn't hear much of what was said in the readings, but I did hear a lot of what people in the room said about the last days of their drinking and drugging. Many of them had circumstances similar to mine with Ed Wainwright. Some of their problem people weren't bosses. Some of them were spouses, children, parents, lovers, girlfriends or boyfriends. Some of them had their entire family ordering them to shape up or ship out.

Most talked with a sense of amazement that they had made it through their crises and come out the other side feeling okay about themselves. It was discouraging to hear that some of them had lost their jobs; others ended up divorced even though they got sober and stayed sober. In every case, they talked about how good their lives had gotten no matter what they lost. I was gagging on the syrupy sweetness and concern they were directing at us "newcomers."

At the end of the meeting there was a ceremony. It confused me, but I ended up holding an aluminum coin because I had gone 24 hours straight without a drink. People came up after the meeting and pressed their phone numbers and business cards into my hands. A few asked if they could give me a hug. I let a couple of women hug me, but drew the line when men came up and looked in the least bit like they wanted to hug me. I was in the heart of San Francisco, after all. We had coffee and cake to celebrate sobriety anniversaries in the group. One man had thirty-three years. He blew out the candles on the cake. I couldn't imagine going without a drink or a drug for thirty-three years.

Madge and I drove home in silence. She walked me to my apartment and helped me get ready for the next morning as she promised. The alarm was set for six-thirty. She took my suit home to spot and press and told me to come to her place early to pick it up. She said if I wasn't there by seven she would come to get me. I thanked her and mumbled a half-hearted apology for my angry outburst earlier in the evening.

"It's okay, Evan. There'll be more of those outbursts. Thanks for going to the meeting with me. See you in the morning."

I sincerely thanked God when she walked out the door. I was sick of people. I took everything out of my pockets and placed it on my dresser. I looked at the 24-hour coin. It felt warm in my hand. I didn't feel angry at it, at Madge, or at the people in the meeting. I was disconcerted by the absence of anger. Anger was my friend. It was my truest connection to life. The weight of my anger held me in place. Without it, I usually experienced free-floating anxiety. So how come I wasn't experiencing anxiety right now? I felt the absence but was too tired to think any more about it.

I crawled into bed and thought about the day. It dawned on me that I hadn't read "the" book. I went to the living room, retrieved the book, crawled back into bed, and began reading again. I didn't make it past the second paragraph of the Introduction. I was gone and heard nothing until 6:30 the next morning.

CHAPTER 5

The alarm went off and I rose straight out of bed. My sleep had been so deep that I had difficulty figuring out where I was. Some of my confusion may have been due to the fact that my room was relatively clean and therefore unfamiliar. I shook myself awake. A feeling of doom and gloom hung over me. My head hurt but not quite as bad as usual. I threw myself back on my bed and pulled the covers over my head. I was dozing off when the phone rang.

"Yes, Madge. Whaddaya want?"

"I want you out of bed. Did the alarm go off?"

"Yes, it went off."

"Are you up?"

"Can't I sleep just a little more, please?"

Click.

Before I knew it Madge was storming through the door.

"Damn," I thought. "Why did I ever give her a key?"

Instinctively, I stood up and dashed into the bathroom, dragging my underwear with me. I heard the apartment door shut. I took care of my morning "necessaries," as my mother used to call them, and walked into my bedroom in my tee shirt and BVDs. Madge was standing in the doorway of the bedroom holding a large mug of coffee and my suit. Her black eyes pierced my being. I remembered the many withering looks my mother had given me under similar circumstances.

"For God's sake, can't a man have some privacy?" I protested.

"Oh sure. ...Like you've got so much to hide."

"Yeah, well how would you know?"

"Do you have any idea how many times I've had to put you to bed when you were passed out? Do you know how many times I've had to clean you up when you've thrown up on yourself or gotten beaten up?"

"You looked?" My first instinct was to feel ashamed of being seen by Madge, but just as quickly I felt a rush of excitement.

"You'll never know, Hot Shot. Here's some good hot coffee. Now get dressed. You can probably read a little of the book before you have to leave for BART. And don't forget, you can read all the way out to Walnut Creek. Just don't fall asleep on the train and miss your stop."

"Yes, Mommy."

"Don't smart mouth me, Evan. You owe me."

"I thought we were even when I went to that damn meeting with you last night."

"That was just the beginning. But we'll talk about that later. Now get busy."

Madge left. I stood there feeling totally foolish. I looked at myself in the mirror on the back of my closet door. The thought of Madge taking a peek was an interesting concept. It became much less interesting when I looked at my paunch and my fading youth.

I pulled on my clothes and then carried my mug of coffee to the kitchen. I turned my radio on and listened to the news. Nothing of any note was happening. Traffic reports indicated several messes around the Bay Area. I was grateful again that I was carless. Mass transit was moving just fine, and besides, I was going to the East Bay. Most of the crowds would be coming west into the city while I would be going east and away from rush hour.

As I sat in the shadows of my dreary little kitchen drinking Madge's coffee, I renewed my acquaintance with the feeling of doom that hung over me when I first greeted that day. Memories of the previous two days rolled over me. Again I felt nauseated, but the feeling soon left me. What remained was a sense of being weighted down with a blackness I didn't understand and couldn't define. I was frightened and I didn't know why. I was able to tell myself that I hadn't felt the type of fear I was facing since I was little.

"That's what I feel like! I feel like I'm five years old." I put my head down on the table. I was aware that the joints in my body ached, my head ached, and my stomach ached. I'm pretty sure my hair ached.

"I hate life!" I said out loud. "I hate all you bitches and sons-of-bitches. I hate your freaking technology!"

I proceeded to enumerate all the people who had worked to make me a failure, and number one on that list was my dear, departed mother. It was then that another huge wave of nausea washed over me. I rushed to the bathroom and knelt over the toilet. I surrendered Madge's coffee to the bowl. I wretched everything from my stomach.

"Oh God, how much longer do I have to go through this kind of crap?" Long ago I had given up on the idea of a good God. When I used the word it was with as much derision as I could muster.

I lied down on my bed and picked up "the" book. I tried to read, but nothing of what I read made any sense. I began to dose off. A loud rap on my door ended my flirtation with sleep.

Madge had let herself in again.

"Evan?"

"Yeah. I'm coming." I jumped up, dashed into the bathroom, combed my hair into place and splashed a little cold water on my face.

"I'll take you to the BART station."

"Thanks."

I grabbed my briefcase and stuffed the book and the tape into it while pulling on my suit jacket. I took a last look in the

48

full-length mirror. The suit looked good. Madge was a master of making old stuff look new. I had to admit I looked better than I had in years. Still the wear and tear of my hard living was obvious. I shook my head and turned to face the world. Right then the world was a very tall, very powerful Native-American/African-American woman named Madge.

"You look pretty good for a white man, Mr. Howard."

"Thanks."

"No smart-ass back talk this morning?"

"No."

"My, my," Madge chuckled. "Miracles really do happen."

With that we headed for her car. Neither of us said anything on the way to the BART station. She stopped the car to let me out.

"Good luck, Evan. Keep an open mind."

I tried to say thank you but it stuck in my throat. I hoped the fear I was feeling didn't show. I felt like a lost child. I was as vulnerable as a human being can be.

I closed the car door and began the trek to the trains. It occurred to me that I could turn and run. As I rode the escalator down, I toyed with the idea of chucking it all and just going to work in a convenience store or fast-food chain. And then I remembered Madge's statement about what happens to people who don't get sober. If I went to a less challenging and poorer paying job, I would be following the spiral she told me about the night before. No way was I going to let Madge be right about something. I was not a drunk on the way down and I would prove that or die in the doing.

My stubbornness and need to be right about everything wasn't always a bad thing. At times bullheadedness saved my ego or my ass and this was one of those times. I got on the train to Walnut Creek and tried to read the blankety-blankety book all the way out. It wasn't easy.

There were plenty of seats on the train. I picked one as far away from other people as possible and hoped no one would come near me on any part of this trip. At the next stop several people got on. A 40-ish guy—one of those pictures of success—

eyed what I was reading, walked over to where I was sitting and sat down.

"Great book! I finished it a couple of months ago. I can't tell you what great changes I've made in my life since reading it."

I nodded.

"I can see you're not very far into it. That's okay. I think I learned something on every page."

I thought about telling him that I was on my way to interview the author but realized I'd never get rid of him if I did. I listened to him prattle on about the improvements he gained in his life and felt nauseated. Mercifully, he got off at the next stop. I tried to go back to my reading as the train slid into the darkness of the tube under San Francisco Bay. On those rare occasions when I rode BART to the East Bay, I always wished the tube would flood and everyone on board would be wiped out, including me. That thought occurred to me this time, but for some reason I took no pleasure in it. In fact, I found myself trying to reverse the thought. I didn't feel like dying that day. I dreaded going to interview Elizabeth Grayson but I didn't want to die. Conflicting feelings always caused me distress, and I was truly distressed that day.

When we came out from under the Bay and into the light of day, the brightness hurt my eyes. I was surprised to see several people coming toward me. A young woman sat next to me and an older woman sat in the seat directly behind me. They, too, were interested in what I was reading.

"Isn't that a great book?" the younger woman asked.

"Oh, I've read it too. I've changed so many things for the better since I read it," said the older woman.

I slammed the book shut, but that did nothing to stop either woman.

"It's so good to know why men are so attached to the television remote control and why women aren't," the younger woman went on.

"Well, my husband read it, and believe me, he's not a reader, but even he's making some positive changes because of that book," said the older woman. "It's a miracle, I tell you."

"Wow! That's awesome," said the younger woman. "Is it helping you understand why American men and women go at life so differently?"

I realized she was talking to me. I was aware that the young woman was attractive, and decided I needed to respond positively. This might lead to a date maybe.

"Well, I've just begun reading it, but it seems Mrs. Grayson's theories may hold some promise of answers to the male/female struggle."

The older woman laughed loudly and slapped me on the back.

"You got that right, mister. If I had known why men are forced to disconnect from their emotions and why women are ashamed of theirs, I guarantee you my whole life would have been different."

The young woman nodded her head in agreement.

"I'll never go through the stuff my mother, aunts, and grandmothers went through," said the pretty young thing.

"What?" I asked "If you read this book do you automatically trash men?"

"Not at all," the young woman answered. "You just don't play the games that come out of their emotional disconnectedness. By not playing the games, you force them to connect to their own emotions rather than live off yours. But you haven't read enough of the book to get to that part. Keep reading. You'll be glad you did."

Both women got off at the next stop. I realized I needed to look at the BART map to make sure the train hadn't already stopped at Walnut Creek. The women had taken up more time than I had realized. My first feeling was resentment. My second feeling was gratitude. I would use their descriptions of their discoveries and perhaps Elizabeth Grayson would believe I'd read more of the book than I'd had time for.

"Yeah," I thought, "that'll help a lot. I can tell her I was discussing it with people on the train who had read the book and approved highly of it." And then I wondered just how much tap dancing I'd get away with in the ordeal I knew was waiting for me in Walnut Creek.

The train stopped. People got off. People got on. The train moved again. Panic began to rise in my middle. The next stop was Walnut Creek. The train pulled into the station. The doors opened and I stepped onto the platform. I rode the escalator down and began to perspire profusely. Panic was setting in as I looked for the Grayson's telephone number. I wondered if I had left it on my desk at the office. I searched every pocket and then remembered that I stuck it in the last page of "the" book so I wouldn't forget where I put it. The relief of finding the number almost compensated for the anxiety I felt about calling Elizabeth Grayson again. But call I did, and once again she was gracious and accommodating. She told me which part of the station to go to and that someone would arrive shortly to pick me up.

I went to the designated waiting area, sat on one of the benches and tried again to read "the" book. I actually read one or two pages and was getting interested in the message when someone walked up to me.

"Mr. Howard?"

"Yes." I looked up and saw what seemed to be a beautiful woman surrounded by a brilliant light. The sun was behind her and shining in my face, and I had to put my hand above my eyes in order to see her face. She was pretty, not beautiful. Blondish. Forty-ish. Well built.

"I'm Denise Kinzler, Mrs. Grayson's secretary."

She stuck her hand out and I shook it.

"The car is over here. I found a parking space close by. Sometimes people confuse the east side of the station with the west side and I'm waiting on one side while they're waiting on the other. I've found it's easier to park and walk around to find them."

I followed her to her car, a zippy convertible with the top down. I thought about slinging my briefcase in the back and jumping over the door into the passenger seat. It occurred to me this could go badly at my age, and in my condition, so I opened the door, set my briefcase carefully on the floor, slid into the

Chapter 5

passenger seat and pulled the door closed. Denise Kinzler backed out of the parking space and moved out into open traffic. She drove with confidence through the winding streets of Walnut Creek, California. I liked her. Not sexually at this moment. I just liked her.

"Do you get out of San Francisco much, Mr. Howard?"

"Please call me Evan, Ms. Kinzler."

"Please call me Denise, Evan."

"Done." With that I reached the end of my conversational abilities with a good looking, intriguing woman. This was not like me. I could bullshit women with the best of them. Suddenly I found myself lost for words. The knot in my stomach got bigger. I was already intimidated by Elizabeth Grayson, and now I was stymied with what to say to one of her employees.

"So, Evan, do you get out of San Francisco much?"

"No. Actually, there's little reason for anyone to go out of the city. Anything a human being could wish for is there."

"Don't get me wrong, I love the city. I lived and worked in the heart of it for years. But the time came when I had to change, so I looked for a job that would give me a change of scenery. You know, a geographic cure. Luckily, I answered an ad for an administrative assistant in Walnut Creek and I've been with Mrs. Grayson ever since."

"So you live out here now?"

"Yep."

I had no idea where I was being driven. We wandered down curvy boulevards and eventually turned into a driveway that sat between two very nice homes. Quickly the narrow driveway became a circle that was the centerpiece of a beautifully landscaped yard. In the center of the circled driveway was a lovely garden with a fountain. Denise drove into a vacant spot in the three-car garage. There was plenty of room for me to open the car door and pull my briefcase out behind me. I looked at the garage and observed the neatest, cleanest garage I had ever seen. There were built-in cupboards, tool racks, peg boards. Everything appeared to be in an exact place. Instantly I felt anger. Elizabeth Grayson was indeed my mother. I wanted to run.

"Elizabeth is looking forward to meeting you, Evan. We went out and did some shopping this morning. She's a great cook and is making a lovely lunch for all of us."

"Oh, I really wish she hadn't gone to any trouble."

"No trouble. Honest. We'll go through the garage into the house if that's okay with you."

"Fine," I snapped. I wondered why my opinion about where we went mattered, and it irked me that anything was said. Years of rage at female considerations were ready to explode out of me at that moment. Good sense came over me.

"Is there a restroom I can use before I meet Mrs. Grayson?"

We stepped into the coolness of a long hall.

"Second door on the right," said Denise. "When you're ready, just come into the day room and have a seat. She may be in the middle of something in the kitchen."

I nodded and ducked into the bathroom and relieved myself. I flushed, closed the lid, sat down and held my head in my hands. I became aware of a pain in my chest that hurt in a way I had never felt before. I began to sweat profusely and once again experienced the rapid heart beat.

Eventually my heart settled down. I washed my face, combed my hair and straightened my tie. I picked up my briefcase, took a very deep breath, and opened the door. In a few short steps I walked into my worst nightmare.

CHAPTER 6

I walked into the hall and turned right per Denise Kinzler's instructions. I came into a cheerful room that opened onto a wide porch. A wall of windows looked out on the porch. A gentle breeze blew curtains inward wrinkling the sunlight as it hit the floor or flew across a table or chair. My first impression was of warmth and cheerfulness. The room was out of character with the woman described on the talk show tape. The charm of the room disconcerted me. I looked around and saw no one. I was aware that a kitchen lay beyond the door at the far side of the room. The sounds that came from the kitchen were a clear indication that someone was cooking or cleaning up pots and pans.

"Have a seat, Mr. Howard. Elizabeth will be with you shortly." Denise Kinzler poked her head through a doorway to my left. I took a few steps and watched her walk down another long hallway toward more doors and open spaces. I realized I was in a large, expensive home. I had not been aware of the size of the house when we drove up the circular driveway. The garden and fountain in the center of the driveway had captured my attention. Inside, I could only guess at the size of the house. The size of the room I was in told me the house was very large.

I began to study the decorative pieces that were everywhere in the room. Everything complemented everything else. I picked up a colorful piece of hand blown glass and held it up to the sunlight. Color danced into my eyes from within the glass—so much color that my eyes hurt. My mother had a similar piece in our home when I was young. The weight of the glass and the range of color within these kinds of glass pieces had always fascinated me. I felt a stab of pain in my chest. I carefully put the piece of glass back on its table and slumped into the chair next to it. I wondered if my heart was going to race out of my chest again. But that didn't happen. I looked at the glass again and felt the pain in my chest again.

I rubbed my chest but the pain continued. My mind wandered back to the home I grew up in. The piece of glass seemed so familiar. I'd almost swear my mother had a piece just like it. My father called that piece of glass a waste of money, but my mother had loved it and bought it despite his objections. I remember sitting and staring at the piece when I was young. I remembered the morning sun breaking through our living room window and hitting it. The explosion of light and color that followed kept me rapt for hours. There were little bubbles inside the glass. Swirls of soft yellow, blue, red, turquoise, and green seemed to move through it, just as the colors in this piece were doing. My father said we could use a brick for a paper weight rather than spend good money on an expensive piece of glass. He became visibly upset whenever he found one of us paying attention to the paper weight. I learned to leave it alone rather than be ridiculed for having an attachment to it. As a child, I knew that liking things my mother liked would earn me the wrath of the person whose love I most craved.

"Hello, Mr. Howard. How are you?"

I jumped and stood up.

"Forgive me for startling you. I'm Elizabeth Grayson."

The bitch didn't look like a bitch at all. She was small, about five feet tall, neither plump nor skinny. She had salt-and-pepper gray hair, what appeared to be her own teeth, and she had blue eyes that looked straight into mine.

"Good morning."

"Do you like it?"

Chapter 6

"I beg your pardon."

"The paper weight … do you like it?"

"It's beautiful. For some reason I have a fascination with glass pieces like this."

"That's a special piece. It was a gift from a very dear friend of mine."

I began to sweat. My heart started to race out of my chest. I couldn't think of what to say next.

"Please, have a seat. Let me get you something to drink. It's a long ride from the city out to Walnut Creek. You must be thirsty."

"Water will be fine, thank you."

"With ice and lemon?"

"That would be fine."

Elizabeth Grayson returned to the kitchen. I sat down. My head began to spin, so I placed my hands firmly on my temples, hoping to squeeze the pain out of my reality.

"Are you all right, Mr. Howard? You don't look well."

"I'm getting over something, Mrs. Grayson. Just had a touch of the flu I think."

"Ah," she said. "I used to have the flu all the time when I was drinking. In the twenty years since I quit drinking I've had it only twice. But twice was enough to make me understand how sick we can be when we really have the flu. Perhaps we should cancel this interview. If you're just getting over the flu, you might be better off to go home and spend another couple of days in bed."

"No, no, we need to do it now. I hope you know I'm past being contagious. I'll get home early tonight and I should be good as new in three or four days. But we really need to get this initial interview done. My magazine wants a thorough article completed, which means I only have about nine more days before submitting the first draft."

"Can't it be postponed? I mean, when a person has had the flu, your body needs rest."

I gritted my teeth and stifled myself. I wanted to scream at her.

"Please don't fuss over this, Mrs. Grayson. I'm just fine. The issue of the magazine that hit the news stands last week promoted an in-depth article on you. That means I have several other interviews and a good deal of writing and rewriting to do in less than two weeks if the article we promised is to be published."

"Very well. What do you wish for me to do?"

I took a deep breath and tried to think of what I really needed her to do. "My editor has told me that Mrs. Bullock wants this article to be the basis of a book. That means I'll have to question you a bit more than I would for a simple magazine article."

"Really? And you're going to do the article and the book, Mr. Howard?"

"If the article goes well, it's probable I'll be assigned to do the book."

"Martha Bullock is a good friend. She can seem pushy sometimes. Are you sure you want to do this work?"

"I'm a journalist, Mrs. Grayson. I can write any article or write any book." I was becoming irritated and it showed in my voice. What's worse, I could see she sensed my irritation. She said nothing. The silence was deafening. Finally I connected my thoughts enough to find a starting point. I took the tape of Leslie Wilder's talk show out of my briefcase and began at what I believed was the most obvious point of the article I was to do.

"I'm told you saw your children on the Leslie Wilder Show."

"I did."

If she had any emotions about the program I couldn't see them.

"Because you're highly regarded in the field of psychology, my editor feels your side of the story should be presented somewhere." My tactfulness surprised me. "It's my understanding that you were invited to be on the program with your children but that you declined."

"I did. I trust you've seen the tape. Wouldn't you turn down such an invitation?"

"I'm not here to judge you, Mrs. Grayson, but your children say all they want is for you to apologize because you and your alcoholism destroyed their childhood home."

"I have apologized for my part in the dysfunctions that developed in their childhood home, Mr. Howard. But that isn't really what they want. Perhaps we need to just talk. I'm sure you have plenty of questions after seeing that tape. I agreed to this interview because I trust Martha Bullock completely. She is an honest and generous person. I think she feels an article or book will bring some fairness and balance to the story of my first marriage family."

Elizabeth Grayson pulled a chair over to a space just opposite mine. She didn't invade my space, I'll give her that, but I've never been one for that face-to-face brand of interviewing. I took out a notebook and my tape recorder. She pointed to a plug. I obeyed. I also felt a sense of *déjà vu*. She pointed in the same way my mother gave directions. I resisted the temptation to slap her arm away.

"She's so like my mother. Run, you fool, run," I thought. But something held me in that room. My flight button failed me for the first time in years. Before sitting again, I tried to move my chair just enough so that I wouldn't have to look at those piercing blue eyes straight on. I hoped she didn't notice the move.

"I'll be recording our conversation, Mrs. Grayson, and I'll take some notes as well."

"Fine."

"Your children seem to believe that your career was the only thing you really cared about in their growing-up years. They're very bitter about that."

"Let me say that I understand they are sincere in their perceptions of me. I also understand that they reinforce each other's negativism toward me with every get-together they have. There are still people in their circles who have contact with me who hear the same complaints and criticisms repeatedly. I despise gossip, but grapevines sometimes help one understand what's going on with people they're no longer safe with."

"Did you drink all through their growing-up years?"

"No. Socially once in a while. Fortunately, we were very middle class and there simply wasn't any money for alcohol or drugs in the early years of that marriage. I didn't begin drinking on a daily basis until after our twelfth anniversary."

"Really? One of your sons states on the tape that you were a drunk from the minute he can remember."

"That was Jeff. He's the most distant and the most angry of my children. He was always very closed to any kind of a relationship with me. Friends of ours used to say that Jeff had to be his father's clone. He's not a clone, but he's the one most like Matthew Monahan, and he's also the one who adopted all of Matt's strategies for living."

"Although Jeff is mistaken about my drinking, I understand why he felt I was drunk during all of his growing-up years. May I give you a little history of that family from my perspective?"

"Certainly." I placed the microphone of the tape recorder in her hand and sat back to listen.

"I need to begin with the earliest days of my marriage to Matt. We were to be married in Matt's church, and before we could be married we had to go through a great deal of counseling. The religion Matt belonged to would be considered a fundamentalist religion today. To be a member, one can't use tobacco, can only use alcohol for religious rites, and can use no birth control whatsoever. We were asked point blank if we were prepared not to use birth control and to welcome any child who came at any time. Both of us replied firmly that we were indeed ready for any eventuality as far as children were concerned.

"That meant a lot to me since I came from a less fundamentalist Christian background, but my church also did not permit birth control. This was a vitally important issue to me, and I truly believed Matt was equally dedicated to allowing God to decide when our children should be conceived."

I was fascinated but wondered what the hell any of this had to do with the abuse she inflicted upon her children. She continued.

Chapter 6

"We got married, and I must confess that the night before our wedding was filled with worry on my part. I cried almost all night and I couldn't understand why. I knew my husband-to-be had come up in chaos. His father was a loving, funny man, but he also drank from morning to night. His mother abandoned the family when Matt was very young, and his father left his young children to fend for themselves most of the time. Matt ended up being raised by different families in the Church he eventually joined.

"One of the most destructive beliefs I had at that time was that if you love someone deeply enough you can fix anything. I believed that my love for Matt would fix any problem he or I had. Today I know that my love can't fix, mend, or heal the holes in the souls of others, but that knowledge was a long time coming. I love my children, but no matter how much I love them, I can't fix them or change them. Only they can do that.

"But to get back to the early days of my marriage to their father. We were married and connected sexually in very clumsy, unsatisfactory ways. I lied to everyone about how wonderful our new life together was. Matt was going to school to become a medical researcher. I worked as a secretary to pay the bills. One of the courses he took fascinated me. It concerned the psychology of human illnesses. I read his text book and devoured the information like a sponge. I think I knew I wanted to become a psychologist at that time.

"Within three months of our marriage I was pregnant. I went to the doctor and got confirmation of the fact. I have never been so excited about anything as I was about the child within me. I rushed into the door of our little apartment. Matt was asleep on the couch. He slept most of the time during our first year of marriage.

"I shook him gently and gave him a few minutes to wake up. I knelt on the floor before him and told him I had the most wonderful news. We were going to have a baby.

"With that he pushed me back and screamed at me. 'That's the last thing I need right now,' he said. He pushed me away, got up and went to the bathroom, leaving me in a heap on the floor in front of our sofa."

I nodded as I always did during interviews. People always went away from my interviews thinking I agreed with everything they said. Elizabeth Grayson continued.

"After he yelled at me, I lay on the floor and agonized about what my baby and I were going to do. I was devastated. He was so angry I worried he was going to leave me. Although my baby was legitimate, I was just a secretary and didn't know if I would be able to support both of us and still give the baby proper care. I held my stomach and told the baby it was loved by me. I don't know how long I lay there. It was dark when I got up and went back to bed. Matt was already there, sleeping as though nothing had happened. I hadn't had dinner. We couldn't afford much food because Matt insisted on every bill being paid exactly on time and whatever was left we could use for food. There was never much left, so the most I probably could have had this close to payday was a few crackers and maybe a little milk. I know today that both my baby and I suffered emotional trauma that day. Research is just beginning to show fetuses can and do suffer trauma when their mothers suffer trauma.

"When we got up the next morning, he said nothing. I had hardly slept. He went out to his morning classes. I dressed, packed an apple and some crackers, and got myself to work. He didn't speak to me for weeks after that except to ask me to pass the salt or something like that. I felt worthless and lost, feelings I would have many, many times in that marriage. Both my religion and Matt's religion forbade divorce, so there was no real out for either of us, not in our minds and, therefore, not in reality.

"I came home that day and found a package of soup mix in a cupboard. Matt was sleeping again. I fixed the soup and poured myself a bowl. It was hot. With crackers and the last glass of milk it filled me. I went into the living room and sat staring out the window into the darkness of night. It was late fall and night came early. I was lonely and frightened.

"I realize now, Mr. Howard, that I was always alone in that marriage. I never got any closer to my husband than I was that night. More than forty years later, I truly know nothing more about my first husband than I knew three days before I met him. Strangely, he had been quite romantic when he was courting me. The day we were married, he shut down emotionally. I spent more than twenty years trying to find the man I had dated, but he never came back."

"Do you hate your ex-husband, Mrs. Grayson?"

"I've certainly had my moments, Mr. Howard. I loved Matt with all my heart for the first seven or eight years. I longed to reach him. And then I began to go into anger at his emotional unavailability. I didn't know that this was what I was angry about at the time, but I know today that was the real point of my anger. Even after we divorced, my heart longed to have some sort of resolution with him, but I think I'm past that finally. Therapy and group work have helped me give up that hope."

Both of us sat quietly. I was thinking about what was just said. I heard Elizabeth Grayson tell her side of the story. It would be years before I would be able to wonder why I was able to listen to this woman who represented so much of what I hated in my own childhood.

"Mrs. Grayson, do your children know about your husband's treatment of you when you told him you were pregnant?"

"I don't know if they really comprehend what happened in the first years of their parents' marriage, but I did try to tell them my side. I've realized that their perceptions of anything I've ever said are always colored by the early discipline they received from me. They've always feared me, which makes it hard to listen fairly to anything I've ever said to them. Trying to get them to understand what happened to me in those early years was one of the greatest mistakes of my life. But that comes later in this story. There's so much more to the destruction of that family that happened before the children were even born."

I leaned toward Elizabeth Grayson and checked the meter on my tape recorder to make sure it was running. The thought occurred to me that she was a wonderful storyteller. I wondered if I was getting sucked in. The thought of being sucked in by another manipulating career woman helped me feel some of the deep anger I had carried since childhood. I actually felt better because I was back in familiar emotional territory.

"I'd like to freshen up my water. Would you like yours freshened up, Mr. Howard?"

"That would be fine."

In a minute she returned and placed the fresh water in front of us. She seated herself, picked up the microphone and began to talk again.

"Only a few weeks later my husband's father died. I barely made it through the funeral because I had morning sickness morning, noon, and night. It was all I could do to sit through the funeral without tossing my cookies. The gathering afterward is still a blur in my memory. I would visit with one or two people, eat a little, throw up, and lay down. I did this several times. It was not a good day for me."

"Did this affect your health and your baby?" I asked.

"I weighed less than ninety pounds, and I'm sure it didn't help the baby. My son, Bud, was born hungry. He's had difficulties with food and weight ever since. But that wasn't the worst thing that came out of Matt's father's death. What happened is something that took me years to forgive. Hurting me was one thing, but when Matt neglected his own child, that was almost more than I could stand."

She had me hooked.

"Matt had five brothers. One night they all got together to divide up their father's estate. The oldest brother had two children. Keep in mind that at the time they were dividing the estate, I was six months pregnant with Bud. Another brother was married and he and his wife were trying very hard to get pregnant. Eventually they had three children."

I nodded to show her I would keep that factor in mind.

"The oldest brother said he thought his two children should be included in the settlement. And so they were. The estate wasn't much, but it was divided into eight portions. Three of the portions were given to the oldest son, who proceeded to drink up every cent within three months. In the meantime, I was still hungry and Matt's child got nothing. When Matt came home and told me what had been done, I was furious. I asked him if he had any caring for the child I would soon give birth to. He told me I was the most selfish, self-centered, greedy person he had ever known. Again, he didn't talk to me for weeks. Unfortunately, I brought this up often and Matt would again tell me how viciously selfish and un-Christian I was because I always noted that his brother had been able to be drunk for weeks after the settlement."

"That does seem unfair considering the fact that you felt hungry so much of the time."

Elizabeth Grayson nodded and took a drink of water. She looked sad, but there were no tears.

"It's probably important that you know I grew up in a home where my parents fought every day. When I was very young, I vowed I wouldn't have a marriage like that. Interestingly, I married someone who would never argue with me. I would scream at him and he would give me the silent treatment. In the last several years I became the embodiment of both of my parents. I couldn't stand his coldness and unreachableness just as my father couldn't stand those things in my mother. I couldn't stand my own doggedness in trying to change Matt into something I could live with, just as my father had tried to do with my mother and my mother had tried to do with my father."

I made notes of the numbers on the tape recorder's counter so that I could easily go back to certain places in the interview.

"When Bud was born, Matt became a different person. He quit school and got a job managing the business end of a building supply company here in the East Bay. Bud was three days old when we brought him home from the hospital. Matt's depression lifted and we began to look like a healthy, wholesome family. I was thrilled. We had normalcy. There was still no connection between me and my husband—I gave all the hugs and he took them. I greeted him with open arms and he greeted me with indifference. But to the outside world we looked just fine, thank you, and I did everything I could to keep up the illusion. And that is what that marriage was, Mr. Howard. Actually, it was a delusion, and I was the most deluded of all."

"I believe your son Jeff stated on the talk show that you used his father to get your schooling, and that if you were so unhappy, you should have left the marriage."

"I already told you, in both Matt's mind and my mind that wasn't an option. Our religious values didn't permit divorce. That was a critical part of both our value systems. Jeff refuses to blame his father for continuing our marriage, but he condemns me for not ending it. I lived with that double standard for more than twenty years. It's always been my hope that my children will someday see how unfair they are in this regard ... and so many others."

"This makes you angry?"

"Unfairness always makes me angry. But that's just me." Elizabeth Grayson looked at her watch. "I need to get back to the points I was trying to make. I do realize you're working under a deadline. Let's see, where was I?"

I rewound the tape and stopped at the last number I had recorded.

"Ah yes. After Bud was born ... Matt went to work and I cleaned and cooked and mothered. Bud blossomed. He was bright and wonderful and when he was about five months old, I did the most destructive thing I could do as a mother. I became a member of Matt's church and we went there every Sunday. It was made clear that children were to be there and they were to be well behaved. Bud had begun to assert his personality and became wild during the service. I tried to hand him to his father, but Matt just shrugged and waved me off. When the baby began screaming and banging his head against mine, I did what I had seen many other parents do. I took him out of the church. Once in our car, I pulled down his little diaper, whacked him and screamed at him to settle down and behave. I had watched my own mother do the same thing to younger siblings. It was very effective. Very."

Elizabeth Grayson began to weep. She reached for a tissue on the table in front of her. She blew her nose and composed herself.

Chapter 6

"I did that to every one of my children, Mr. Howard. I became their worst enemy. They feared me. They were the love of my life, my whole reason for being, and they feared me from very early on. To this day I'm not able to forgive myself for becoming the strict disciplinarian of those children. From their earliest days they saw me as an oppressive jailer. They saw their father as a quiet, non-threatening victim, a comrade in the war against me—their mother, his wife.

"When we went out to restaurants to eat, servers would compliment us on how well behaved our children were and how rare it was for children to be so well behaved. I thought that was high praise at the time. Today I would be defined as a child abuser and rightly so. But that's how I was raised, and it seemed perfectly natural and normal to me."

"Are you admitting that you really were the sole source of your children's problems, Mrs. Grayson?"

"On the contrary, I'm admitting my part in their problems. My children want me to accept total responsibility for what they see as abuses in their childhood. I'm only willing to accept fifty percent of the responsibility, and that is what drives their rage at me."

"I don't understand. You admit that you abused them."

"I admit that I did very hurtful things to them, but their father was quite happy to go along with everything I did. Although he said very little, he obviously reveled in the compliments our children received. They were very bright. Most dinners at our house revolved around the retelling of the children's happy, accomplishment-filled days. As they got older, we talked about what they had learned each day. When Bud first tied his shoes, I made a cake and wrote Bud's name on it with a brand new, red shoelace. It had three candles because he tied his shoes three times that day. One of the best things I did for my children happened when each turned five. We always made a trip to the library and they got their own library card that birthday. They got to take out a bunch of books, and the whole family celebrated this great moment. As far as I know, all three children still love to read—so my efforts weren't all negative despite what the children say.

"But I need to tell you how Matt and I set our children up for the rage and hatred they feel toward me now."

"Really," I said. I was totally engrossed at this point. I wondered how she would ever be able to shift blame back to a guy who may have been emotionally detached but, by her own admission, had taken no action to inflict pain on his children.

"Please note that I said we both destroyed any hope for a good relationship between me and my children."

"I don't understand, Mrs. Grayson."

"Matt used to tell the children, 'If you have problems when you get older, it's your mother's fault. She's the active one, she's the doer.' I remember thinking how wonderful it was that my husband was so truthful about his lack of emotional involvement in the children's lives. I felt sure the children would see the truth when they got older. Today, I know that my silence confirmed to my children that I was and would always be the culprit. By saying nothing, by allowing his statement to go unchallenged, I accepted all the blame for all their problems into eternity."

"Yes, but they're in their forties now. Surely they can look at things differently."

"Obviously they don't, Mr. Howard. You've seen the tape. It's their hope, I think, to destroy me as they feel I destroyed them. The world is full of people who blame others for their problems. Hitler blamed the Jews and brought about a global war and the annihilation of millions of people. Our family war is no different. The problem comes because I refuse to accept total blame for their problems, sadness, and losses in childhood."

"What would it cost to just say 'I accept the blame for all your problems. I'm sorry, and can we now just get on with life and be friends'?"

"It would cost me my truth, my personhood. I lost it for more than twenty years in that family, Mr. Howard. I would do great harm to myself and to my children if I allowed myself to lose it again. The truth is, their father was as responsible for the development of the home they grew up in as I was. If those children were subjected to so much abuse, why didn't he rescue them? He had a good position, he has an extraordinary IQ. He could have gotten us help as a family. Remember, he had more than a year of advanced education, some of it in the field of psychology. If I was so sick, why didn't he seek help—at least for the children if not for me?"

"That's a good question." I had to admit that I hadn't thought of the situation from that angle. I did need to try to get an answer either from Matthew Monahan or from the children. I was becoming fascinated with this family and how its members had come to be so public with their pain and suffering. I went deeper into thought.

"Mr. Howard?"

"Yes?"

"Would this be a good time to take a break? I've fixed some lunch for us and I'm getting hungry. May I set it out?"

"That would be very nice. Thank you."

Elizabeth Grayson left the room. I sat with some troubling thoughts. I wanted to fight the fact that this woman might have some points in her favor that her children needed to address. The journalist in me accepted the challenge, but the rest of me felt lost. I wished I had a drink. A good, stiff drink always made me feel better.

"It's ready, Mr. Howard."

I sighed and pulled myself out of the chair with great difficulty. I walked into the kitchen and lunch with Elizabeth Grayson, her husband, and Denise Kinzler.

CHAPTER 7

The smells in Elizabeth Grayson's kitchen were among the most welcoming I've ever experienced. She had baked fresh bread in one of those bread machines, and the smell as she opened the lid of the machine made me totally aware of my stomach and how empty it felt. The table was set for four, which surprised me for some reason.

The kitchen looked like something out of a magazine. To me, it smelled like something out of heaven. My mother always said that the Howard men could only be reached through their stomachs, and at this moment I couldn't argue the point. Mrs. Grayson directed me to a chair at the table that allowed me to look out on a garden area and the swimming pool. Another picture from a magazine. A large, stern looking man was walking through the garden. He looked into the window, saw me, smiled and waved. He disappeared from view and then entered the kitchen through a set of French doors at the other end of the room.

"I see you found your way here, Mr. Howard."

"This is my husband, Marshall, Mr. Howard."

He thrust his hand toward me and I shook it. "How do you do, Mr. Grayson."

"Please," he said. "Call me Marshall."

"Ah, if you don't mind, sir, I'd feel better if I called you Mr. Grayson." The words came out with much more power than I had intended.

He nodded his head and said, "As you wish, Mr. Howard. I hope you brought an appetite with you. Elizabeth is a wonderful cook." He seated himself next to me and didn't seem bothered by my request.

"The smell of fresh bread gets me every time, Mr. Grayson."

And that was the truth. One of the few good memories I had of my mother was the wonderful smells that used to come from the kitchen of my childhood home. We always had good food and plenty of it. Suddenly I felt a choking feeling. My heart was racing again.

"Would you mind if I take a minute to freshen up before lunch, Mrs. Grayson?"

"Of course not. I'll wait a few minutes before I put everything on. Do you need anything? A wash cloth?"

"No. No. Just give me a couple of minutes." I returned to the bathroom I had used earlier in the day. I turned the light on, closed the door, and stood with my head braced against the door. My forehead dripped with sweat and my heart beat like a teenager on a new set of drums. In a minute the worst of my panic passed. I relieved myself, made sure I was zipped properly, threw some water on my face, washed my hands and dried them. I took a deep breath and returned to the kitchen.

"Are you all right?" Elizabeth Grayson asked.

"I'm fine, thank you. As I said earlier, I'm just getting over a bug of some sort." I looked toward Marshall Grayson, hoping I was convincing him that what I was saying was true.

I returned to my designated seat next to Marshall Grayson. Silently, Denise Kinzler entered the room and seated herself across from me. I acknowledged her with a nod of my head. She nodded back.

While I was away, a delicious looking spread had been set out. Elizabeth Grayson placed a large bowl in the center of the table. She removed a lid and placed it on the counter.

"Lobster salad. I hope you like it." She set the uncovered dish in front of me.

"I don't think I've ever had it." I had long ago stopped eating lobster. The last time I had it was at my last newspaper's Christmas party. I vaguely remember standing on a table holding a hot, red-clawed creature above my head and telling my editor we shouldn't have to work so hard for our food on Christmas. I have been told that later in the evening I criticized the editor because there wasn't enough drawn butter on the tables. That was a few days before Christmas about six years ago. A few days after Christmas I was fired. I couldn't believe the guy had such a shaky sense of humor. Since that experience I had never eaten lobster.

"You'll love this stuff, Mr. Howard. I make sandwiches of it. There's nothing like it," said Marshall Grayson, proudly.

"He's very prejudiced about my cooking, Mr. Howard."

"I am too," chimed in Denise Kinzler. "One of the biggest benefits of this job is lunch in this kitchen five days a week. Healthiest eating I've ever done."

"Well, I guess I'll have to try this dish," I said, feeling a little pressured by them and very pressured by my empty stomach. I placed a healthy scoop of the lobster salad on my plate and passed the dish to Denise Kinzler. Next came the bread. I took a large slab. The butter came next. I slathered some of the yellow stuff on the warm bread. The smells were almost more than I could stand. I put a fork full of the salad on a corner of the bread. I took a huge bite and chewed slowly. The flavors were perfectly blended. The lobster was tender and chilled with finely chopped celery, a delicious mayonnaise, and several other things I couldn't identify. I ate without saying a word. I didn't hear much of what was said by the others. I was so hungry and the food was so good. My hunger didn't permit me my usual anger at lobster for getting me fired from my last newspaper job. This was indeed, a very strange day.

Everyone quieted as each plate was filled and then emptied. We were united in the enjoyment of this moment. I will never forget that meal. I was in the midst of people I believed were my enemies, and yet there was a sense of peace at this table that was wonderfully strange and addicting.

When we finished, Denise cleared the table and filled the dishwasher. Marshall Grayson excused himself and said he had things to do in his office. Elizabeth Grayson ushered me back into the family room, asking if I wished to continue the interview.

"If you don't mind, Mrs. Grayson, I'd like to review the tape briefly. There were some questions that came out of this morning's session, but I'm too full to remember them right now."

"Tell you what. Lie down on the couch here. We're great believers in siestas. I'm going to take a half hour nap and I suggest you do the same. I'll wake you in a half hour or so and we can get back to work again. How's that sound to you?"

"Actually, that sounds wonderful. Thank you." I watched her leave the room. I made a restroom stop and then stretched out on the sofa. I looked at the ceiling for perhaps a minute and then was gone into some very deep part of the Universe. I heard nothing until the next morning.

CHAPTER 8

I became faintly aware of daylight coming through the windows and pouring over the back of the couch and into my face.

"My God, what time is it?" I sat upright and panicked. It was eight a.m. according to the digital clock on the table. There was a blanket over me. I tried to remember where I was. I soon realized I was in Elizabeth Grayson's family room, not my bedroom. I knew I was too refreshed to have had a thirty minute nap. The doors to other parts of the house were closed. I went to the bathroom down the hall. Someone had put a toothbrush, toothpaste, a razor, shaving gel, towels and soap out for me. I used everything and regretted I had no clean clothes available. Still, I felt better this morning than I had in a very long time. I found my comb in my pants pocket and got my wet hair in order. I wondered if sleeping through the last eighteen hours would mean the end of this job. I wondered if there had been a drug in the lobster salad that knocked me for a loop. Would lobster mark another step backward in my checkered career as a journalist?

I walked back into the day room and the doors to the other wings of the house were now open. I smelled coffee. Elizabeth Grayson heard me and stuck her head into the room.

"Have a good sleep, Mr. Howard?"

"I did. I am deeply embarrassed, Mrs. Grayson. I thought you were going to call me in a half hour."

"I would have, but you were sleeping so deeply that we all got together and decided to let you sleep as long as possible."

"Who's we?"

"We, is Marshall, Denise, and myself." I sat in my designated chair at the kitchen table. She poured a cup of coffee for me. "Cream, milk, sugar...?"

"Cream and sugar, thank you."

Elizabeth Grayson pushed the cream and sugar toward me. I filled my cup to the brim with cream and added as much sugar as I could. I stirred, watching the excess pour into my saucer. I drank some out of the cup and gingerly poured the overflow back into my cup.

"Cereal, eggs, bacon, toast, donuts?"

"Donuts are fine, thank you."

Out came a plate full of several kinds of pastries including glazed donuts. I ate three different kinds and then helped myself to an apple. My coffee was freshened, and again I felt very much at home in this kitchen.

"Good morning, everyone. How are you feeling, Mr. Howard?"

Denise Kinzler came through the hallway from the garage. She laid her briefcase and jacket next to her chair and sat down to a cup of coffee that was apparently prepared just as she liked it.

"I'm feeling refreshed and terribly embarrassed, thank you."

"Your body needed rest. Those flu bugs really take a lot out of you. No need to feel embarrassed around here, I can assure you."

Elizabeth Grayson sat quietly, sipping her coffee and finishing a bowl of cereal. She got up from the table and put her dishes in the dishwasher.

"Shall we get back to work, Mr. Howard?"

"Please allow me to apologize, Mrs. Grayson. I don't know what happened."

"As Denise said, there's no need for apology or embarrassment, Mr. Howard. I understand perfectly."

Now those were fighting words. My mother always said she understood perfectly and she never understood at all. I snapped back that I didn't believe others understand us at all much less perfectly.

"It was just a figure of speech, Mr. Howard. I'm sorry if it upset you. Please forgive me."

I realized I was pushing an envelope I had no right to push. I could hear Ed Wainwright reaming me for insolence and stupidity. I realized she could tell Ed that I slept eighteen hours on her couch, which would do nothing for my shaky status with Ed.

"I guess I was sicker than I realized. Would you mind if I go over the tape from yesterday and get the questions I need to ask clearly in my mind?"

"That will be fine. I'll be in the garden when you're ready."

I listened to the parts of the tape I'd made notes on during the interview the day before and wrote down some questions. Then I went to find her in the garden. I stood at the French doors. She put her gardening gloves in a tub by the door, brushed her clothing, and moved past me. As she did, I caught a wisp of a familiar scent. It wasn't an unpleasant fragrance, and yet it stirred something in my mid-section. I shook my head. I was tiring of trying to figure out why smells and words were causing me to feel so many emotions.

I followed her into the family room. She took the microphone to my tape recorder back in her hands and sat quietly, waiting for my questions.

"As I listened to the tape from yesterday, two questions occurred to me. The first is, if you do this article and it's published, might this not mean the absolute end of any chance of a relationship with your children?"

"They've already told me there is no chance for a relationship with them. I'm not stupid. I know I must make something worthwhile come out of this life I've been given. My life work is helping families like my first marriage family understand the part each plays in the destruction or the salvation of their family.

76

Since the people I gave birth to have gone so public in their hatred of me, I'm going use what I've learned from them and from my own harmful attitudes and behaviors to help other families avoid total destruction. I firmly believe in an eternal life, Mr. Howard. My children and I will be healed someday. Maybe not in this world, but we will be healed. In the meantime, I'm going to use my own pain and sadness as best I can to help others. You are the one doing this article, and I'm told an article will be done whether I consent to an interview or not. I think it best I talk to you. I expect fairness and truth in this setting. It won't stop the tabloids from doing their thing, but a more accurate picture of my point of view will exist somewhere in hard copy."

"My second question is, can you give me a list of people to talk to about your theory on emotional disability, and are there people I might interview who can verify what you've told me about your early marriage?"

"I've had the same friends for many, many years. Even though I've been in recovery for more than twenty years, I've been blessed to still have contact with my original addiction counselor, and people I was in treatment with. Here are their addresses and phone numbers. I knew you'd probably want to interview them. I've drawn up and signed release forms so that my addictions counselor can tell you what she is legitimately permitted to tell about my treatment and recovery. She's still my counselor and she's got my records from the treatment center. I also have listed Matthew's address and the children's addresses and phone numbers. Also, a former sister-in-law is alive. We were good friends in those days. I don't know if she'll meet with you, but she does know about the settlement of the estate. She understood what I felt and said so at the time. There are a couple of psychologists and psychiatrists listed who know of my work and use it in their practices."

I took the list. "I appreciate your time and hospitality, Mrs. Grayson."

"One last thing, Mr. Howard."

"Yes, Mrs. Grayson?"

"My children are not crazy. Their father was always totally controlled in his responses to life. They saw their mother deteriorate into alcoholism and insanity. Matt was the same from the first day of our marriage to the last. Today I believe I was relatively healthy when I entered that marriage. Twenty years later I was spiritually and emotionally bankrupt. My children aren't crazy in their reverence for their father and their hatred of me. What they didn't see and haven't looked at is their father's cooperative role in all that occurred in that marriage. Please don't be hard on them."

"I'll do my best to be fair to everyone, Mrs. Grayson."

"I've enjoyed meeting you, Mr. Howard. I hope we meet again."

With that I packed up all my equipment. Denise Kinzler was called. She took me back to the BART Station. She also said it was nice to have met me. I thanked her for all her help. I was sick of hearing myself say thank you and I'm sorry. I found my ticket, pushed it through the turnstile and headed up to the trains. A train came almost immediately. I took a seat as far away from people as possible. This time I held the book high up in front of my face and began reading it in earnest. I did not want to hear about the wonders of Elizabeth Grayson's book. I just wanted to read it and understand it.

CHAPTER 9

As the train took me back to the city, I began to learn about Elizabeth Grayson's theory on emotional disability. She argued convincingly that the worst elements of human emotional dysfunction are socially induced and taught. For the first time I could see how rearing male children to not feel emotions that might cause tears stopped males from bonding with others. I also understood that programming girl children to feel all their softer emotions but to never get angry, crippled females when it came to setting boundaries with others, particularly the men in their lives. Elizabeth Grayson, the author, asked me, the reader, to keep an open mind and look at emotional disconnectedness as a natural byproduct of the American socialization process. She also wrote that emotional disconnectedness is measurable and treatable in most people. Her style of writing was quite pleasant. The journalist in me approved of this work, but part of me felt the type of fear I used to experience when watching a good horror movie. And that's what hooked me and enabled me to continue reading a book by a woman who was, according to her children, disturbingly like my mother.

No one bothered me during this trip. Before I knew it I was on Market Street. I debated whether to stop in the office. Should I tell Ed I slept all afternoon, evening, and night on EG's couch?

"Nah," I thought. "If she tells him, I'll deal with it then. If she doesn't tell him, I'll just act like I stayed in the East Bay and went to her house this morning." Sounded good to me. I decided to go to the office but to say nothing.

I picked up a couple of pens and a new typewriter ribbon. I was a relic of the 1950s according to my coworkers. I knew nothing about computers. I could hunt and peck with the best of them and was damned if I was ever going to get trapped in the computer world. Just as Ed was about to force me to take a computer class, the magazine got a scanner. Now I could hunt and peck out an article on paper and the scanner would put it into the computer. I was supposed to learn how I could use a computer keyboard to clean up an article, print it, and put it on a floppy disk that I could hand to Ed. I kissed the scanner the day it came to work at *World Of Psychology Magazine,* and I never did take the class. I was happy and Ed was free of any need to make me computer literate. And then I wondered if Ed had cleaned up the scanned copy and if that was what he meant when he said he'd done a lot of rewriting for me. I quickly dropped that thought as irrelevant.

I went to the supply cabinet and picked up some cassette tapes for my recorder. I had plenty of interviewing to do for this article. I would mark each cassette carefully with the name of the person interviewed and the date and times. You can't be too careful when writing an article concerning such volatile people.

I walked past Ed's office. The lights were off. He was already gone for the weekend. I was relieved to not have to say anything to him. I left the office and sat on a bench on Market Street and read for a couple of hours. Then I headed up California Street to Van Ness via cable car. The weather was cool, as usual. The car was full of tourists jumping on and off. I was able to read a few more pages of "the" book. The end of the line came too soon. The clarity and simplicity of Elizabeth Grayson's theory fascinated me. As I walked toward my apartment, my thoughts went to her words.

"Males explode from unfelt, unexpressed soft emotions. Females implode from unexpressed harder emotions. That's why we see boys and men acting out violently and why we see women suffer high levels of depression that kill their chances at happiness in life. And the level of violence generated in succeeding generations increases incrementally..."

I thought about the rising tide of mass murders in American schools and businesses. I'd done several stories on domestic violence. I had interviewed ten men who had murdered their wives or lovers. I remember being told by a psychologist that the most dangerous time is when the victim partner has decided to leave. According to Elizabeth Grayson, the victim partner usually is the partner who is connected to the softer, bonding emotions. This person is the only connection the battering partner has to his own softer feelings. He's disowned them in himself, so he artificially connects to them in his partner. It occurred to me that I might have to do that story over if Grayson's theory was correct.

And then I thought how sympathetic I had been to the men in their prison cells. I really believed that the women had gotten what they deserved, but again, I did my best to keep that bias out of my writing. I knew if I didn't, Ed Wainwright would fire my ass faster than I could say vodka and tonic. And then I thought about a vodka and tonic. The bars I could have stopped at were behind me. I was just yards from my apartment. I may never know why I did it, but I went to Madge's door and knocked. There was no answer.

I went to the mail room and picked up a pitiful pile of junk mail and then walked to my apartment. There was a note stuck on the door.

Where have you been? Are you all right? Don't plan anything for this evening. I'll pick you up at six o'clock. Madge

It was just four o'clock. I still had time to pick up a bottle before Madge would swoop down. But I was hungry to read more of the Grayson book. Could emotional disconnection be the basis for all human dysfunction? Grayson argued that we've known for generations that sociopaths don't bond with others and this is why they are unable to develop a conscience. Grayson postulated that people who learn their feelings don't matter or who are shamed for feeling feelings, try to repress or kill their feelings. She wrote: "It is only through full utilization of all our emotions that we are able to bond healthfully with other human beings. Our softer emotions allow us to bond with others. Our harder emotions allow us to set healthy boundaries with ourselves and others. We can then adopt values society holds as good and worthwhile or we can establish an even stronger set of values that comes from our full connectedness to the creative force of the Universe."

I sat in my living room and read with an interest I had not had in years.

On each page I questioned how connected I was emotionally. Looking back on that experience, it amazes me how non-threatening EG's written challenges were. I would learn over the next two weeks that many people were entranced by the challenges contained in Elizabeth Grayson's writing. The book suggested that I begin writing about my childhood home and how emotions were perceived in that home.

"Later," I thought. And then I was off to sleep again.

***

An hour later Madge was shaking me awake. My living room was darkening, and once again I struggled to remember where I was.

"Evan..."

"Huh?"

"Wake up. It's almost six o'clock. I'm taking you out to dinner and to a meeting." Madge didn't leave room for argument.

"Uh, I don't think so, Madge. I'm whipped."

"How long have you been napping?"

She sounded like my mother, and my anger responded immediately. "It's none of your damn business how long I've been napping."

Chapter 9

"Yes it is. I'm the only damn friend you have left and I want to know what happened to you last night and how long you've been napping right now."

"I fell asleep yesterday after lunch on Elizabeth Grayson's couch and didn't wake up until this morning."

"No." She said it with that female tone of exasperation that infuriated me.

"Yes," I shot back, with that male tone of exasperation that I hoped would infuriate her.

"Good for you. Did you tell Mrs. Grayson that you're detoxing from years of alcohol abuse and that your body is struggling to recover and needs tons of sleep?"

"Of course I didn't. Do you think I'm totally stupid? I told her I've had the flu and I'm just getting over a bout with the bug."

"She works with alcoholics and addicts all the time, Evan. She probably spotted your problem the minute you walked in the door."

"If she did, she was polite enough not to say anything, which is more than I can say for you."

Madge decided to change the subject, which was disconcerting. I was in the mood for a good fight and she was the most likely opponent.

"Get cleaned up. We're leaving in ten minutes for dinner and a meeting. Have you had anything to drink today?"

I had to think about Madge's question. It took several seconds to remember whether I'd had a drink or not.

"I haven't had a drop. It's really strange. Yesterday I had lunch with the Graysons and her assistant, Denise Kinzler. The food was very good. EG takes siestas and suggested I do the same. I fell into a sound sleep and didn't wake up until this morning. We had a nice breakfast. Pleasant. We did some more work on the interview for the article and then I came back to the city. I stopped at the office and did a few things and then I sat on a bench on Market Street and read her book for quite a while. I read the book on the cable car home. I thought about going out to pick up some booze but I fell asleep reading here in the chair."

"Did you have lunch?"

"No."

"Not good. You have to begin eating healthy meals regularly three times a day. Your body has a lot of repair work to do."

"Yes, Mother."

I dutifully went to the bathroom, washed my face, brushed my teeth and did a quick shave. I decided to change into clean clothes. I could feel Madge pacing in the living room. I sat on the bed and thought.

"You know what?" I shouted to the living room.

"What?" Madge shouted back.

"I don't feel like going anywhere. And did you say you were taking me to a meeting afterward?"

"I did."

"I already went to one and I wasn't very impressed. I don't like all that huggy-huggy crap."

When I looked up, Madge—big, black Madge—was in my face.

"You will go to meetings for the rest of your life if you want to get healthy."

"Why would you go to meetings for the rest of your life for Christ's sake? Isn't that just another addiction?"

"You asshole." Madge was still in my face. "If people didn't come back year after year even after alcohol and drugs are no longer a threat, there would be no one around to help jerks like you when they try to get sober."

"Damn. I really don't feel like going out, Madge."

"Most of us don't at first. But there are two times you must go to meetings in the beginning. You go when you want to and you go when you don't want to. And to be honest, you're not going to want to go more often than you're going to want to go in the beginning."

I didn't understand a word the woman had said. I just realized I wasn't going to get out of this evening with her. I finished dressing and followed her into the living room.

Chapter 9

"We're late. Let's go," she said.

Before I knew it, we were in her car and on our way down California Street. We ended up at Washington Square and went into one of the restaurants just off the square. Italian. God, it smelled like heaven again. My stomach rumbled. The room was dimly lit but Madge seemed to know exactly where to go. I tagged along and smelled a basket of bread that passed under my nose on its way to a table. My stomach growled loudly. I hoped the noise of the crowd covered it up. People at every table seemed to greet Madge. She seemed to know everyone in the restaurant.

"Here's our table, Evan."

Madge hugged and kissed several people at a large round table. Two seats were still vacant.

"Evan, this is Hardaway Hawthorne. He's going to be a very important person in your life." Madge acted as though she was giving me a great gift. She waved her hand toward a man seated on the far side of the two empty chairs.

A giant of a man rose slightly to shake my hand. He had a white handlebar mustache, a bolo tie, a western jacket. When he shook my hand he held my elbow like it was a ton of steel. My hand hurt. I figured he was probably wearing blue jeans and boots. After dinner I watched him swagger out of the restaurant. I was right about what he wore beneath the table cloth. I could not have imagined anyone further from my sphere of reference.

"Just call me, Hardy, son. Hardy Haw-Haw according to some people around this table." He didn't take a breath or wait for a word from me. "Evan Howard, huh? I used to read you every day in the Chronicle. Why'd you ever leave there?"

"It's a long story. Maybe someday…"

Hardy slapped me on the back and pushed me into the seat next to his. Madge slid into the chair beside me. I looked around the table and noticed that all the wine glasses had been cleared. Instinctively I realized the table was full of reformed alcoholics. I decided I wouldn't insult or tempt them by ordering a glass of wine for myself. Ordinarily, I wouldn't have been so thoughtful, but these were really impaired people. I felt a rush of good will as I looked at the odd gathering of people around the table. There was a beautiful young woman—couldn't have been more than twenty-five. After her, everyone was downhill. There was a guy who looked like he left his job as a construction worker to come for dinner. He was missing a couple of teeth in front. He had a mustache and a paunch and a sleeveless denim shirt. There were two guys who looked like they came from court to the restaurant. White shirts, three piece suits, cuff links—the works. There was a woman of about fifty, rather plain, who looked like she might be a teacher. A very strange combination of people to be sure.

All were chattering away. I grabbed my menu and studied the offerings. I settled on the special of the evening, a seafood marinara with linguini. I could almost afford to pay the asking price if I shaved a little off the tip.

"Order anything you want, Evan. I'd like to treat you this evening," said Hardy.

"Ah, thanks, but that won't be necessary," I said.

"It is necessary, son. Order whatever you want and I'll pay for it. Part of becoming a healthy human being is letting others do nice things for us."

I had really wanted to order one of the veal dishes, but had decided against it because of the price. My stomach, more than my mind, opted to go along with Hardy Haw-Haw Hawthorne. Much as I hated to be owing to anyone, I was hungry for a truly Italian veal parmesan.

Madge passed me the bread. She introduced to me to the others at the table and told me a little about each of them. The young woman was a child of drug addicts who saw herself falling into the trap of addiction and came to recovery through the Adult Children of Alcoholics Program. The man I thought worked in construction actually owned his own roofing company. He was in the middle of dental work to repair teeth that were knocked out years before in a barroom brawl. The two men I thought were lawyers were actually financial consultants. The school teacher was actually an assistant to the mayor. I was right

86

Chapter 9

about one thing—they all claimed to be recovering from alcoholism or addiction.

I asked the young woman if she felt out of place in this group. She said, "Not at all. When you're raised in alcoholism or addiction, you get all the crazy thinking and behaviors without ever having to take a drink or drug."

"Hmmm," I said.

"It's not the drinkin'," said Hardy, "It's the thinkin'."

"Hmmm," I said again. I bit into my third hunk of Italian bread dipped into olive oil and spices. My stomach was in heaven and I wasn't terribly concerned about where the conversation was going. It soon became clear I should have been.

"Were you raised around alcoholism or drug addiction?" The question came from the mayor's assistant.

"My mother was alcoholic. She went into AA about twenty years ago. Maybe you knew her. Angela Howard."

"I've heard the name," the woman answered.

"She's been dead about three years now."

"Oh. I'm sorry," said the lady.

"Don't be. It's good riddance. She was nothing but a drunk."

"Excuse me. Didn't you say she was in AA? Did she stay in the program?" One of the financial consultants was asking.

"Yeah. Supposedly she did. She claimed she didn't have a drink for more than seventeen years when she died."

"Then how can you say she was nothing but a drunk?"

"Once a drunk always a drunk. I didn't have anything to do with my mother for all those years." I reached for another piece of bread. A waiter placed a salad in front of me. Everyone else was served a salad. The dressing was excellent.

"We're all sorry to hear that," said the young woman. "One of the greatest gifts I've ever been given is the ability to understand addiction and to understand and forgive my parents. I'm sorry you didn't experience the joy of knowing your mother in sobriety."

"Lady, if you had my mother you would understand why I feel I was given a gift by not having to ever see her face again after she left my father." I glared at the young woman across the

87

table. I saw tears well up in her eyes and wondered what the hell was wrong with her. I went back to my salad.

Madge broke in. "It's clear you've been very hurt by your mother's addiction, Evan. We'll hope you'll stick with the program long enough to understand and forgive as the rest of us have. We were all injured in childhood—some of us in the most brutal ways possible. But we've all been able to get past the hurt and into forgiveness and we'll hope the same for you."

I glared at Madge. Hardy Haw-Haw broke the tension.

"How's that salad going down, Evan?"

"Great. You know, the food I've been eating the past several days has been outstanding. There's always been an abundance of good food available in the Bay Area, but for some reason it's unusually good this week."

We ate the rest of the meal in relative quiet. I would soon learn that people in recovery make healthy eating a spiritual experience. People passed things to others, all the while consuming the food on their plates with silent gusto. I told Hardy that money was a little tight this week and I was going to settle for the special of the day until he offered to buy—that I was glad he offered because the veal was just about the best I'd ever had. He laughed and patted me on the back and said, "Keep coming back. There's lots more good things in store for you."

When we finished, the bills were quickly paid. As we left, the majority of the people in the restaurant also departed. Everyone walked across the Square to the white church across the way. We walked to the back of the church and entered the parish hall. Tables were set out in rows. Three large candles sat on brass plates at the front table. A single large candle sat in the middle of the other tables. Madge and Hardy guided me into a chair between the two of them. I was so full I didn't care what they did with me. The mayor's assistant lit the candles on the front table. Others lit the rest of the candles. One of the financial consultants began leading the meeting. He asked someone to read the preamble—a statement of what the group was gathered to do. I heard something about becoming free of addictions, our own and others. There was a reading of the twelve steps and twelve traditions. Again, people attending their first, second, or third meetings were asked to stand and give a first name. Madge elbowed me again. I stood and said my name was "Evan, and I don't know what I am." Everyone laughed. Then someone read the Promises of 12-Step Recovery. Elizabeth Grayson had said something to me about the Promises.

Madge pushed a copy of the Promises in front of me.

The Promises

- *We are going to know a new freedom.*
- *We are going to know a new happiness.*
- *We will not regret the past nor wish to shut the door on it.*
- *We will comprehend the word serenity.*
- *We will know peace.*
- *We will see how our experience can benefit others.*
- *That feeling of uselessness and self-pity will disappear.*
- *We will lose interest in selfish things and gain interest in our fellows.*
- *Self-seeking will slip away.*
- *Our whole attitude and outlook upon life will change.*
- *Fear of people will leave us.*
- *Fear of economic insecurity will leave us.*
- *We will intuitively know how to handle situations that used to baffle us.*
- *We will suddenly realize that God is doing for us what we could not do for ourselves.*

I read the sheet and remembered what EG had said. In her first week of sobriety, she had gone to a Promises meeting and had been taken with the eleventh promise and its prediction of intuitive powers. She said that had been the beginning of her understanding of emotional/spiritual disconnectedness. It occurred to me that the gaining of intuitive powers from working a 12-Step program was a curious result. My intellect was getting teased into further study of this thing called the 12-Step process. Nothing but an intellectual pursuit would have tempted me to go further into investigation of what I believe was my mother's sick resolution for her life. I began to pay attention to what people were saying.

Everyone talked about wondrous powers that had been opened to them as they worked the 12 Steps. I pretty much tuned out remarks about becoming less selfish and more giving as pure bullshit. I very much tuned into comments about losing the fear of financial insecurity. One man said he was still financially insecure, but he didn't have any fear of it. The whole room broke into laughter. I could only think how sick these people were. Still, I wanted to be financially secure, something I'd never known as an adult on my own. Many of the people in the meeting appeared to be financially secure and I wanted to find out why. There were plenty of expensive clothes, diamonds and Rolex watches in that room. True, there were people who appeared to be homeless and without resources, but they were a distinct minority. Oddly, no one appeared to be repulsed by the down-and-outers. The "haves" interacted genuinely with the "have nots." What I didn't understand that night was the fact that, to all intents and purposes, I looked the part of a "have not." Indeed, I was a "have not."

The meeting closed with everyone holding hands and saying the Our Father. I nearly gagged. When we finished, everyone, still holding hands in a circle, shook their arms and said, "Keep coming back. It works if you work it." A dozen people rushed at me, gave me business cards and told me to call if I needed to talk to someone. I took the cards and shoved them in my pocket. I think I mumbled some thanks.

Hardy walked over and towered over me. I felt like a child looking up at him.

"Son, I'd like to be your temporary sponsor if you'd let me."

"Ah, well…"

"Take him up on the offer," said Madge. "You need a man who's been where you are and who will help you during the first months of sobriety."

"Sobriety?" I was dumbfounded. "I don't need sobriety. I don't want sobriety. My mother got sober and it did nothing for her."

"How do you know it did nothing for her, Evan?" Madge was right in my face, and I could feel the heat of her anger and saw rage in her eyes. "You never spoke to her after she got sober. You never took the time to meet the person she really was. You chose to keep her frozen in alcohol in your mind."

"How do you know what I knew or didn't know? What makes you an authority on me and my mother?"

"You've told me you never talked to her after she got sober. You've said you were glad she was dead. You've come over to my apartment crying in your beer about how she destroyed you and how much you hated her. You get a couple of shots of booze in your craw and you swell with hatred for someone you never really knew."

Hardy stepped in between us. He directed me to a chair as far away from Madge as he could without being completely rude. He sat beside me. I looked at him and wondered what I was doing in this room with this strange man and a very angry woman who used to be my friend.

"Look, Evan, I don't know if you want this thing called sobriety, but Madge has told me that you better stay clean for at least a couple of weeks if you want to finish an article for your magazine and keep your job. If you'll work with me and come to meetings with me, you'll be able to get the article done and keep your job. What say?"

The old man had piercing hazel eyes. I put my head in my hands so that I could look at the floor rather than at him. I didn't want him to see how afraid I was of the chaos that seemed to be filling every part of my being. He patted my back and said he could help. I mumbled that I didn't think he could.

"Well, why don't we try it for a week or two, and we can make a decision on whether to continue after you get your article finished." And then he was silent.

I stared at the floor for a while longer. Still he was silent. Finally I realized he was waiting for me to answer.

"Madge has a big mouth," I said. "But I do need to get myself together enough to get this article written. What does it mean to have a temporary sponsor?"

"Well, we talk every day and we go to a meeting or two every day. I help you get good food and rest and you talk to me when you feel like having a drink or you feel like your feelings are going to kill you."

"We have to go to meetings every day?"

"Yes sir, we do."

The man was so genuinely sincere it seemed impossible to say no. I especially liked the part where he said his job would be to help me get good food and rest. I thought about the veal dish and decided I had nothing to lose by giving this sponsorship thing a try.

"I'll try this until I get the article done, Hardy. After that I make no promises."

"Good enough," said Hardy. "Now let's go have coffee with the gang."

We went to a great coffee shop on Broadway. There were tables full of people from the meeting. They were laughing and welcomed me to the inner circle. Several people were great story tellers, and soon I found myself laughing as I hadn't laughed in years. They bought me cheesecake and gourmet coffee. I had to admit that my first three days without booze held some positive things. But I definitely didn't think I wanted to live forever without a drink or uppers and downers. I didn't really believe that all these people actually lived without pills or booze to

change their moods. But it was interesting to watch them socialize with only food and non-alcoholic drinks to make them
happy.

CHAPTER 10

Madge drove us home. She asked me to promise to let Hardy pick me up in the morning for a men's AA meeting. I didn't have the energy to fight her so I made the promise. We walked from the garage to her apartment door in silence.

"I'm sorry for losing my temper with you, Evan."

"Yeah. I keep forgetting I've told you a lot of things about my family. I don't remember telling you, but I guess I must have. I guess I talked more about my mother the bitch than I thought I had."

"Would you like a cup of coffee? I can put a fresh pot on."

"No thanks. I'm about coffeed out. I need to do some more reading and start making a list of interviews for next week."

"Set your alarm for eight. The men's meeting is at nine."

I shook my hand toward her as I walked to my door. Once inside, I undressed, set the alarm and crawled into bed with EG's book. I read several chapters and finally dosed off. The next thing I heard was the alarm. For some reason, I was able to hear it, turn it off, and stand up without grogginess. I did my bathroom routine and put on fresh clothes. I actually threw the dirty clothes from the day before into the hamper.

At 8:40 there was a knock on my door. Hardy blocked most of the daylight that tried to break through the door.

Chapter 10

"Mornin' Evan. Ready to go?"

"Yeah. Give me just a minute, will you?" I returned to the bedroom and threw the bed together. I realized I was relieved there were no roaches scurrying about or piles of fast food boxes to apologize for. I grabbed my jacket and followed Hardy out the door. In a matter of minutes we were in the level below a printing office on Van Ness Street. It had been made into a club-room. It was filled with comfortable, masculine furniture. At the far end of the room was a pool table and a table filled with cof-fee pots, baked goods, soft drinks, juices and a large bowl of fruit. Hardy helped himself to a plastic plate and utensils and filled his plate with goodies. I followed his lead and seated my-self gingerly, trying not to dump my plate or coffee. We ate in silence as at least twenty-five more men poured into the room.

Again we went through the routine readings, this time the preamble, 12 Steps, 12 Traditions, and a thing called "How It Works," which I was told is the first part of Chapter Five of the Big Book of Alcoholics Anonymous. Again the leader asked if there were newcomers. I didn't put my hand up because he didn't say anything about first, second, or third meetings. Hardy read my mind and raised his hand. "I'd like to introduce a new friend of mine. This is Evan. He's been to a couple of meetings and is going to give the program a try for a couple of weeks."

Everyone said, "Hi, Evan. Welcome."

"Damn, I hate this stuff," I thought.

The meeting went on. The leader said he picked the subject of hope as the topic for the meeting. And then he talked about his need for hope when he first came into the program. He said his father was an alcoholic and that he hated the man who sired him with all his might.

"Now this I can identify with," I thought.

"But since getting sober," the leader said, "I've come to un-derstand and forgive my father. I only hope my children will someday be able to forgive me. In some ways I wish I had never gotten married, because I did things just as painful to my chil-dren as my father did to me. But for now, my struggle is to forgive myself. Until I'm able to forgive myself, no one else will be able to forgive me."

"More bullshit," I thought.

The meeting droned on. Suddenly someone in the back of the room asked to talk. The leader nodded.

"Hi, everyone. My name is Paranoid Robinson."

I turned around to look at the remains of one of the greatest linebackers in NFL history. He looked like hell. His clothes were dirty and ragged. His eyes were red. His gut was huge. This wasn't the man who was the most valuable player in two All Star games and one Super Bowl game. He got his name because he seemed to have a sixth sense about people coming at him from behind. He was a brilliant player for several NFL teams. He was one of those players who was so good at what he did that he could have spent all of his career in one town with one team. He was like an eel, and watched his back better than anyone else in the game. That was when he was in his prime. Rumor had it that Paranoid lost most of his abilities as an athlete because he induced real paranoia through too much of the good life, too much money, and too many drugs.

"I'm Paranoid and I hate alcohol and drugs. I'm back again and I know you guys have every right to throw me out, but I really want to get sober. I've been on a binge for more than three weeks. I hocked my Super Bowl ring and I've been doing coke and booze and pot. Someone wanted to get me on crack last night, and I knew I'd better get here or be gone permanently. I've lost everything. I've been on the streets now for three or four months. I've lost my wife, my kids, my house, every cent I ever had. Please help me. I don't know what to do."

"Thanks, Paranoid. Anyone got any help to offer?"

I finished my food and put the plate on the floor by my chair. A tall, black man sitting three chairs down from me raised his hand. The leader nodded to him.

"Hey, Paranoid. Welcome back, Man. My name is T.R. and I'm a grateful recovering alcoholic and addict. I have an allergy to those things. Every time I use them I break out in the back of a police car."

Everyone in the room laughed.

"But seriously," the man said, "I had a tough time getting clean and sober during my first ten years with this program. I came back after binges, pissing and moaning that the program wouldn't work for me, and finally old Hardy over there pinned me up against a wall and asked me if I had ever worked the 12 Steps."

Hardy and T.R. exchanged grins.

"'Fuck no,' I said. 'I don't need that shit.' 'Fuck yes,' Hardy told me. 'You want to get sober and clean and stay sober and clean, then you work the steps. Otherwise, count on an early death and the total loss of everyone and everything that holds any value for you.'"

This T.R. looked so polished and refined. I'd swear he was a college professor, not a street brawler. But right now he sure sounded like a street brawler.

"So Hardy, he gets a hold of me and walks me through the steps. Man, I hated everyone I ever knew. I didn't have any education, nothin'. That was twenty years ago. I worked the steps and I got over hating people and I got over thinking I was a pathetic victim and I started making a life for myself. You can go to all the meetings you want, man, but if you don't work those steps and heal the childhood shit that got dumped on all of us, then you ain't gonna stay clean. If you wanna get clean and stay clean you gotta work the steps. I'm willing to help anyone work those steps. When I got sick and tired of BSing myself, I was able to see what was keeping me dirty. I thought I was too damn smart to work the steps. The only people who don't get sober in this program are the ones who are too damn smart for their own good. I learned in these rooms what the word NUTS really means. I'm nuts when I'm Not Using The Steps. And that's all I'm going to say."

Others seconded T.R.'s ideas. The leader told Paranoid to talk to people after the meeting, with the idea of getting a sponsor. More men spoke. One man's mother had died earlier in the week and he wept because he had been able to tell her he loved her before she died. I felt sadness as he talked but I couldn't tell you why. Another man had just learned his wife had terminal cancer. He wept, and several other men also wept as they talked of losing loved ones. This was a very macho place. What was happening seemed incongruous to me.

After the meeting, I watched to see what Paranoid would do. He went up to T.R. I strained to hear what he was saying. T.R. shook his head and hugged the burly former linebacker. The two went to the back of the room and got some food and coffee and settled in for a while.

"Will he be okay?" I asked Hardy.

"He will be if he'll work the steps."

"What about T.R.? Was he as bad as he says he was when you met him?"

"Worse. He was on parole and had a rap sheet as long as my arm, and that's a long arm," said Hardy. "No one was safe around him. He was as angry as any human being I've ever known. But, as he worked through his anger and came to understand why he was using drugs and alcohol, good things began to happen. We urged him to go back and get his GED. Then we used some pull and got him into a community college in the East Bay. He got a job and worked his way through. Went on to get his bachelor's degree, then a master's, and now he's finishing his doctorate."

"You're kidding. I was betting he was a college professor. Was I right?"

"Sort of. He's a researcher at Stanford. When he gets done, he may well teach. He's smart enough. He comes back to this meeting every week, all the way from Palo Alto. Wants to give back what he's gotten here. And look. He's doing just that right now."

I shrugged.

"Maybe you'll do an article someday and get out the truth about these self-help groups. A lot of people think they're just for the scum of the earth, you know."

I nodded hoping Hardy hadn't been reading my thoughts. I'd believed for as long as I could remember that self-help groups were for losers. I followed Hardy up the stairs and out onto the street. He took me home and invited himself in. He pulled out a small tablet from the inside pocket of his sport coat. "Here's my cell phone number. Call me anytime. Make a list of three things you'd like to get done today. Cross each one off as you do it. Eat a good meal this evening, and get a good sleep. I'll call you first thing in the morning."

"Ah, that won't be necessary."

"Ah, yes it will. You'll see."

With that he was gone. I went into my living room and looked at how shabby and shallow my life looked on the material plane. I wasn't very far above Paranoid Robinson. I still didn't see alcohol and drugs as a major problem in my life, but I could see parallels between Paranoid's career losses and mine.

I walked down Van Ness to the small grocery store and picked up some sandwich makings, fruits, fresh asparagus, coffee, fresh cream, butter, milk, potatoes, and a small beef roast. I wrote a check for everything. I had enough in the bank, with a couple of dollars to spare. I decided to make myself a nice dinner later in the day. I couldn't believe how clearly I was thinking, how fresh the air in the city smelled, and how good it felt to be out in the sunshine.

I walked home, put the food away, went to my living room and made out my list as Hardy had ordered me to do. It was the first time in my adult life that I had followed orders without feeling deep resentment. Number one on my list was *get groceries*. I scratched it off. Number two was *organize and type first part of article, i.e., the interview with EG*, and number three was *make a list of people to interview next week and make phone calls for appointments*.

And so I began my article on Elizabeth Grayson. I typed my impressions of EG's children as a result of viewing the talk show tape. As I wrote, my hatred and anger toward my own mother poured out of me uncontrollably. I tore up at least a dozen sheets of paper, knowing that Ed Wainwright would have given me the boot immediately if I tried to submit any of them. I took a break and lied down on my bed with "the" book. The memories of the past several days began to flood over me. I wondered why I felt such hatred toward my mother but could sit and talk civilly with Elizabeth Grayson. She was every bit as evil as my mother. Her children sounded more like me than me. And yet, I felt there was far more to EG's story than her children were telling. I thought about the confrontation Madge and I had the night before. She said things to me that my aunt and grandmother had told me years before. I never spoke to my aunt and grandmother after they defended my mother. Yet I knew I would speak with Madge again. I needed Madge's friendship. How could I so badly need a person who so offends me?

I shook myself loose of my answerless questions and went back to reading "the" book. I took the quiz at the end of the chapter I read and realized that I knew very little about who I was. Everything I felt I knew about myself was what I had been told by others. Unexplainably, a memory popped into my head. Because of the memory bubble, I was able to look at something my father did to me when I was young. If I said I liked a certain food and it was something he didn't like, he would tell me that I didn't like it. I wanted his approval so much that I made up my mind to not like that particular food. I remember eating a cottage cheese salad at a friend's house and telling everyone how good it was. My father ridiculed me in front of the rest of the family and shamed me for liking a food he thought was disgusting. EG's book said that giving up our own tastes and preferences to please or be acceptable to another was a symptom of codependency. I wondered if there were foods I might really like that I'd never eaten because my father didn't like them. These were the types of questions EG asked her readers to think about. I wondered, and promised to pay more attention to my tastes in food. EG suggested that her readers try a wide variety of foods to see if they are living in their own tastes or the tastes of others.

When I read that line, I did something totally out of character for me. I got up out of my chair and went back to the grocery store to buy some cottage cheese and two fresh peaches. The salad I ate when I was ten was made with fresh peaches. Peaches weren't really in season, so I paid a pretty stiff price. As I walked back to my apartment, the memory of that experience came back to me totally. The shame I felt because of my father's words was burned deeply in my memory, and I felt the heat of my shame as I walked.

When I got home, I decided to make a small salad and try it right away. I peeled a peach and sliced it. I put a glob of cottage cheese in a bowl and poured the peach slices over it. I shook a teaspoon of sugar over the cottage cheese and fruit. I sat and ate slowly and with true pleasure. It was delicious. Just as delicious as the first salad had been.

"I've been deprived of this stuff for years because my father didn't like it. Shit! How many other things have I bought like this?"

I sliced the second peach and poured it and some sugar over another glob of cottage cheese. It was cool and refreshing and delicious. This insight was awesome. Madge told me I would learn wonderful new things if I allowed myself to get sober and work the program. This was a first for me. It was the first time I truly opened my mind and allowed new thoughts about old things to enter my being.

A softer picture of Elizabeth Grayson and her children began to unfold on paper as I remembered EG's admonition not to think of her children as "crazy." I explained to my readers that everyone in the Monahan family had been harmed by addiction and that I would be giving them information that would explain how good people can end up totally estranged from the people they love and who love them most in the world. I took a few quotes directly from the talk show tape. I addressed each statement with responses from EG. The first page of the article began to take positive form.

I finished a page-and-a-half in fairly quick order. I felt that a book might actually be possible. I immediately stopped that feeling. A book wasn't my job right now—a magazine article was. In many ways, writing a short, concise piece is far more difficult than writing an all-inclusive book. Determining what must be included and what must be left out was probably the most difficult task facing me. Suddenly I had a clear understanding that I would know what should and should not be included. I felt confident of this knowledge and couldn't possibly have told you why.

I crossed off item number two on my list and got out the list of names EG had given me. I called her ex-husband, Matt Monahan. When his answering machine picked up, I explained who I was, what I was doing, and asked him to call me because his view of things was very important to doing a balanced article on his ex-wife and children. "Damn, that was tactful of you, Mr. Howard." I complimented myself on what seemed to be an unusual amount of tact and diplomacy. Tact and diplomacy were never my strong suit, so having this much was notable.

Next I called Margarita Sanchez-Lopez. "Oh-oh," I thought. "A radical feminist, if her name is any indication."

Sanchez-Lopez was EG's original alcoholism counselor. In the notes beside her name, EG had noted that MSL was a "step Nazi" who was as tough and uncompromising in her work with addicts and alcoholics as any human being can be. But EG had added that MSL was compassionate, loving, and deeply caring about helping people out of their addictions.

I felt a little leery about talking with EG's original addictions counselor, but I called anyway and was surprised to find her at home.

"Ms. Sanchez-Lopez?"

"Yes."

"My name is Evan Howard and I'm doing an article on Elizabeth Grayson and her family."

"Yes. Hello, Mr. Howard."

This was going surprisingly well.

"I'd like to meet with you as early next week as possible. Mrs. Grayson said she had already contacted you about the article."

"She did, indeed, and I'll be glad to meet with you. When would you like that to happen?"

"When are you available?"

"Actually, I have to come into the city tomorrow. I could come early and meet with you before I meet a friend for dinner."

Chapter 10

This was great. I thought I'd have to make another trip to the East Bay for this interview. I was counting the time and train fare I would save.

"Where could we meet?"

I certainly didn't want her to come to my apartment. It was bad enough Hardy saw what he saw of it. "Would you be up to meeting me at the Japanese Tea House in Golden Gate Park?"

"That would be lovely. What time?"

"Three o'clock?"

"Three o'clock it is. How will I know you?"

"I'm kind of short, dumpy, graying. I'll be wearing a white shirt, tan pants…"

"… and shoes with no socks, right?"

"Right. So how will I know you?"

"I'm kind of short, dumpy, graying. I'll be wearing a white shirt, navy pants, and shoes with socks, and I'll probably have a navy sweater thrown over my shoulders."

"Our descriptions match most of the population of San Francisco," I said with a laugh. "I'll see you at three at the tea house." I think we knew we would each recognize the other. I liked this woman. I honestly looked forward to three o'clock the next day.

Next I tried to call EG's children. When I spoke to her oldest son, he ended up hanging up on me—told me something about the stupidity of wasting print on a bitch like his mother. My conversation with her other son was similar, except he didn't hang up. He wanted to tell me everything he said on the talk show and then some. I asked for an appointment and he told me the conversation we had just had was it. He didn't want to waste another ounce of breath on his trashy mother. I was about fried emotionally by the time I called EG's daughter. I told her who I was and what I wanted. She agreed to meet me late on Monday afternoon near City Hall. She had to file some papers there and would be free to talk to me about 4:00 p.m. I felt anxious about the negativity of my conversations with EG's sons, so I did what I always did when I had to deal with uncomfortable feelings—I put something in my mouth.

I finished my second bowl of cottage cheese salad with great relish. Not once in my entire life had I ever questioned anything my father said or did. Not once had I felt any anger toward him. My mind seemed to go into overdrive searching for an explanation for why my father would have taught me something so untrue. I wasn't wrong in enjoying that first cottage cheese salad and I wasn't wrong for enjoying the second one either. Still, I felt torn apart by a force I couldn't understand. I felt as though I had just betrayed the most important person in my world. I had always believed that I loved my father unconditionally and that he was a true saint for having put up with my mother for so many years. For the first time in my life I was feeling doubt about the parent I had always been most sure of and sure about.

And then I did what I've always done when it came to my father. I decided that there must be something wrong with me for having taste buds that like cottage cheese and peaches. It would be quite a while before I would understand and accept how controlled I had always been by my father's stern, judgmental way of being. For right now, this fact was too painful to look into further. I scratched number three off my list and went to my bedroom, where I slept for the rest of the afternoon.

When I awoke, I walked outside my door and watched the fog moving over the city. It was breathtaking to watch. When finally it began to descend on me, I returned to my kitchen and made a wonderful meal. When the potatoes were mashed and the roast was ready to slice, I walked over to Madge's door and knocked. My heart jumped when she opened the door.

"I made a roast, mashed potatoes and asparagus for dinner. Can you join me?"

"I'd love to," she said. "I was just trying to think what I would do for dinner."

"Good. Come over in ten minutes. Bring some soda or juice with you. I forgot to get something to drink."

"Will do."

***

Chapter 10

I used the ten minutes to set the table using some nice china my mother had set aside for me years earlier. I washed it and dried it and set two places at my broken down kitchen table. I actually found some napkins in a drawer and put out a couple of nice water glasses. At least I had ice cubes and water to offer my guest.

Madge knocked on the door and walked in. She had a bottle of sparkling grape juice. She took two juice glasses from my cupboard, filled them and set them next to the larger glasses of ice water. I felt good about the meal I had prepared. I sliced the meat and set the dishes of potatoes, asparagus, and gravy on the table. Last came the platter of meat.

The two of us looked at the food and enjoyed the good smells that rose from the table. Madge took my hand and bowed her head.

"Loving Creator, we thank you for our friendship, for the bounty on this table, and for this moment of sobriety in my life and the life of my good friend, Evan. We ask that you keep both of us safe, sane, and sober. Amen."

Madge looked at me, not for affirmation, but for permission to dig in. I nodded and she lunged for the mashed potatoes.

"I love mashed potatoes but don't do them very often. They're sooo fattening," she said with her mouth full. "Your gravy is perfect."

I ate some of everything and thoroughly enjoyed my handiwork. "Damn, it's good to be cooking again." I wondered why I had let go of one of my favorite pastimes. Madge continued to eat.

Soon the small roast was nearly gone. The potatoes and gravy and asparagus were totally gone. And so was the lovely grape juice. I noticed that the sparkling juice teased the tongue in exactly the same way good wine did. The juice enhanced the food—the food enhanced the juice—and eating dinner with a friend was a thing of wonder. Although we said almost nothing to each other as we ate, the experience was clearly enriched by the oohs, aahs, and slurps of appreciation. We were both hungry for food, but I was absolutely starved for human companionship. I didn't want to let Madge go home that evening. I asked her dozens of questions about the process of sobriety, and she gave me encouragement and hope.

We cleaned up the dishes together and sat and watched an old movie on my beat up TV. I couldn't remember the last time I had an evening so pleasant and comfortable as this one. When Madge left, I turned off the TV, took EG's book into the bedroom, set the alarm, and settled down to read about emotional disconnectedness and its effects on human beings. I read only part of the chapter before I was gone once again into the very welcome world of sleep.

***

The next morning I was awakened by the ringing of my phone. I tried to shut it off by pushing in the alarm, but nothing happened. For some reason I was startled into wakefulness and tried to orient myself to the phone's location before it quit ringing. Few people ever called me, and no one ever called at the crack of dawn.

I got to the phone before it quit ringing.

"Hello."

"Is this Evan Howard?"

"Yes it is," I replied.

"My name is Matt Monahan. You left a message on my machine yesterday."

"Yes, Mr. Monahan. I'd like to interview you for an article I've been assigned to do on your ex-wife, Elizabeth Grayson."

"Well, you know we haven't been married for almost twenty years now. I don't see what I could possibly tell you about that woman now."

"To be honest, Mr. Monahan, it's really important to get your side of this story. Your children are going on national television and they're quoting both Mrs. Grayson and you about things that were said or done in their childhoods. It's very important to get at the truth of what was said or done, and the only way I can do that is to talk with each of you individually."

"Hmmm..."

Chapter 10

"Mr. Monahan, I come from a similar background so I have a lot of empathy with your children. But I'm a journalist, and I know there are always more sides to any story than just the obvious perspectives. And I need to tell you that if the article goes well, it's possible I'll be doing a book on Mrs. Grayson and all the people in her life. I'll be taping my interview with you and will use it more widely in a book if I'm permitted."

"Hmmm..."

"Mr. Monahan?"

"Yes, I'm here."

There was a long silence, then he continued.

"When Elizabeth divorced me, Mr. Howard, I got rid of all the pictures of her I could find. I can hardly remember what she looks like, so I don't see how anything I'll say to you will be of any help."

"But surely you have opinions on what happened in the home you and Elizabeth created. You lived together for more than twenty years before you divorced."

"Well, I'll meet with you, but only once. And if I think you're sticking your nose in where it doesn't belong, I'll tell you so."

We set up a time on Tuesday morning. He gave me directions to his home in Marin County, told me to be there promptly at nine a.m. and hung up. I wrote on a sticky note to call EG later in the day and ask if she could meet with me again either later Tuesday or as soon after as possible. I didn't think how I'd get to Matthew Monahan's home in Marin County. I just wanted to get back to sleep. After checking my alarm and making sure it would go off at the proper time, I crawled back into bed. I tossed and turned. Some of the things Matthew Monahan said troubled me. As with everything else I experienced in those two weeks, it would take me a long time to figure out my feelings. I was running into familiar people with every turn of this assignment. I felt another surge of anger toward Ed Wainwright for putting me in this situation. But I wanted sleep more than I wanted anger, so I dozed off. A half hour later I was awakened again—this time by the alarm clock.

I felt as though life was not being fair and I felt angry and anxious. "No one should have to get up twice on any given day," I told myself. I promised to make that a new law if and when I ever became CEO of the world. With that, I began my routine and braced myself for another round with Hardy.

CHAPTER 11

Hardy picked me up for the men's meeting. Paranoid was there and looking a little better. T.R. was right there with him. After the meeting, the four of us stopped at a nearby coffee shop.

Paranoid cried about his sorry mother, his sorry father, his sorry career, his sorry sad self. He had achieved the heights that millions of men in America longed for, and all he could do this morning was sit and cry about his sorry life. That irritated me and I said so. Hardy and T.R. sat back like sages of old and let us go at each other for about ten minutes. Finally, T.R. tapped Paranoid on the shoulder and told him he had been sitting on the pity pot long enough and now it was time to start getting into the positive.

Hardy tapped me on the shoulder and said I'd been self-righteous enough and now it was time to get into the positive. Paranoid and I looked at each other with that "I hate them" look that juveniles give each other when they're being corrected by their parents. The waiter filled our coffee cups again. Hardy asked me what issue I'd like to heal most in my first months of sobriety.

"Huh?" I answered.

"You heard me. What hurts you more than anything else in your life? That's what we'll work on healing first in your sobriety."

"Nothing hurts me."

Paranoid looked at T.R. and then at Hardy and then at me. "What the fuck's the matter with you, Man? All us addicts and alcoholics are self-medicating against something or other. We don't put ourselves in the gutter for no reason, you know. We self-medicate because we're hurtin'."

"I'm not self medicating."

"The hell you ain't. If you were drinking every day, you were self-medicating. Now I know you may not know what you're hurtin' over, but you're hurtin' over something. I learned that my first week in AA years ago."

"Yeah? So why are you still out drugging and drinking if you're so damned smart?" I thought it took a lot of nerve for this derelict to be criticizing or trying to educate me.

"'Cause I haven't had the guts to admit what's hurting me more than anything in the world. Every time I come back from a slip, someone always says to me, 'Are you ready to work on your most painful issues now?' And I always think I am, but then when it comes to writin' it down and talkin' it over with anyone, I just can't do it."

"So what's your big issue that you can't talk about?"

"I'll talk about my fuckin' issue if you'll talk about yours."

Paranoid and I were right in each other's faces, and I hated where I was. He was backing me into an emotional corner, and something in me sensed I would not be able to escape or save face.

"I'll have to think about it. I don't think I'm in pain. I like having a drink after work, that's all. Why does something painful have to be involved?" I asked.

"When people socialize with alcohol, they have a drink or two and that's it," said Hardy. "They may not think about a drink for weeks or until they're invited to another social function. But when you've got to have a drink every day, when you've got to have a couple of joints, then you're medicating something. That's just how it is, Evan."

A feeling of comfort came over me when Hardy said my name. He was talking to me with respect and caring. I hadn't gotten a lot of that kind of attention in my life. I felt liking for this tall, gray-haired, remnant from early America. And then I felt distrust. Usually there was a smack on the head or a put-down after compliments.

"Tell you what," said T.R. "How about we put the two of you up against each other? You can be soul brothers in sobriety. You're both coming in the same week. Let's see if you two can strengthen each other's sobriety through a special friendship that includes ol' Hardy and me. I'd kind of like that myself. I loved Paranoid when he was playing and I used to read everything you did when you were at the *Chron*, Evan. Never thought I'd be sitting at a table having coffee with the two of you. Never thought that at all."

"You can bet your ass I never thought about meeting you, T.R." Paranoid smiled at T.R. He appeared to be anything but paranoid. In time I would learn that Paranoid was way ahead of me in expressing his feelings, but way behind me in reasoning and deduction. If T.R.'s experiment worked out, it would certainly be one of the stranger friendships in the history of the world. The idea of being one-fourth of T.R.'s circle of friendship interested me. Maybe I could write a book about this weird group of men.

"What are you thinking about, Evan?" Hardy asked.

"I was thinking if this friendship thing works out, I might write a book. I could call it Little Men. It might outsell Little Women."

"I doubt it," Paranoid laughed and slapped me on the back. Everyone laughed, and we got down to some serious talk about learning to feel feelings and heal wounds from childhood.

Hardy asked me what my greatest resentments involved. I was able to say I had some anger at my mother because she was so selfish and self-centered and cared for no one but herself.

"Okay," said Hardy. "Now we've got a beginning. Paranoid—what do your greatest resentments involve?"

"Man, I can't talk about that."

"About what?" T.R. asked.

"About my problem."

"Are you afraid we'll reject you, Paranoid?" T.R. leaned toward the huge man sitting across from me. He gave him a look of caring and concern that seemed genuine. "Would it involve your sexual orientation or something terrible that happened when you were a kid that you don't think you can talk about?"

"Well...yeah...both."

T.R. turned to me. "Evan, one of the most sacred things about 12-Step recovery is the need to be honest and not have it go beyond the people who are told. What Paranoid says stays with us. Do you understand why that's so important?"

"I guess it's kind of like when a source reveals something to me about a story. If I tell who told me, then people will soon come to distrust me and will never tell me anything again."

"That's part of it. But see," said Hardy, "we've all been liars all our lives. We've lied most to ourselves. So when we finally come clean about something very important, we have to know our secret is safe with the people we've told. Now, the time will probably come when we're no longer ashamed of who we are or what we've done or things that were done to us. Then we can tell anyone our secrets. But it has to be our choice to disclose these secrets to the world. So will you swear to never tell anything that any of us disclose to each other?"

"I can do that," I said. I raised my right hand as though swearing on a bible.

"Good," Hardy said, and gave a knowing look to Paranoid.

"I know the rules," he said. "I promise."

T.R. told about the constant beatings and sexual abuse inflicted on him in his childhood by an older brother. He talked about the saving love he got from his grandmother and how that was the only thing that pulled him back from attempted suicides over twenty years of hard drinking and drugging.

112

Chapter 11

Hardy talked about the loneliness and isolation of being an only child of a school teacher mother and accountant father who didn't believe in showing feelings of any kind. He told us all his physical and intellectual needs were met, but none of his spiritual and emotional needs.

"I don't ever remember being touched or hugged. I don't remember ever getting a compliment from either of my parents. I grew up in an emotional vacuum, and I thought there was something terribly wrong with me because I felt emotions. Both of my parents verbally shamed me for crying. My soul suffered terrible neglect, and I didn't know how to connect with any human being. I grew up without a conscience and was only able to develop one by healing the childhood wounds through the 12 Steps of Recovery. The first girlfriend I had was almost suffocated by my neediness. I didn't know that at the time but I do now. Never got near another woman until I got into recovery, because I knew I'd kill myself if I was ever rejected by a woman again."

By this time Paranoid was sobbing. T.R. reached across the table and touched the hand of the former football star. For my part, I looked around to see how many people were staring at us. To my surprise, no one was. Out of curiosity I asked, "Paranoid, are you feeling T.R.'s and Hardy's pain? Is that why you're sobbing so?"

"Naw, man. I got beaten by my old man and molested by my mother and sister. And to top everything off, I'm gay."

"Oh sure," I said. "That'll be the day when the biggest linebacker in the NFL is gay."

"Man, you don't know much of anything, do you?" The speaker was T.R. "The NFL is a great place for a gay man to hide. So is the priesthood and the ministry. I've been living in the San Francisco area for most of my life, and I've learned never to be surprised at who is gay and who isn't."

"So, Paranoid," I asked, "which hurts more? The abuse or being gay?"

"I don't know, man. I just hate being me."

Paranoid's words hit me like a bolt of lightening. I knew in that flash that I had never liked being me.

All three men looked at me. I would learn later that they clearly saw that I had recognized my greatest pain at that moment. My personal self-loathing had been projected onto anyone and everyone, but it had never occurred to me that I had spent a lot of energy trying to make others look or feel as inferior as I felt.

There was a sharp pain in my chest. It wasn't like the pain that involved my heart during my first few days without alcohol. I shook and fought tears. Hardy leaned over and talked very quietly to me.

"Are you feeling sadness, Evan? I know I've felt deep sadness for wasted years, wasted youth, and God knows what else has been lost. Is that what you're feeling?"

I shrugged my shoulders and put my head down on my arms. I didn't think I could stand the pain, and said so.

"Oh man, I didn't mean to cause you to hurt like this," said Paranoid.

"You didn't cause him to hurt like this, Paranoid," said T.R. "We do this stuff to ourselves. We just don't know we're doing it to ourselves."

I told the others I needed to leave because I really did need to leave. I needed to get home and figure out what was going on inside me. Hardy asked me to write about what I just felt. I said I would try to do that. I rushed out of the coffee shop and back to my apartment. I got inside the door and had another anxiety attack. I hadn't had one for a couple of days and this one was even less welcome than my earlier attacks. I sat down in the shadows of my living room. Finally, I ordered myself to calm down. I looked at the clock and realized that I needed to put some questions together for my interview with Margarita Sanchez-Lopez. As important as that preparation was, I also took time to write down my thoughts on what happened to me when Paranoid said he didn't like being him. I knew Hardy would call me on his assignment.

Chapter 11

I wrote about the bolt of electricity that seemed to hit near my heart as Paranoid spoke his truth. I wrote about recognizing my own self-disdain. I wondered if this is what happens when one man's truth joins up with another man's truth. I hated this new awareness. I wondered if disliking myself caused me problems in the same way Paranoid caused himself problems. I actually wrote a question to myself that I would have to answer sooner or later. "Am I medicating my feelings of dislike for myself in the same way Paranoid does?"

The question troubled me. I wasn't gay or a criminal. I made some notes about how I felt about myself, and I thought about the cottage cheese salad. Was the shame I felt for having liked that first salad so many years ago similar to Paranoid's feelings about his sexuality? Could shame be connected to something as simple as a cottage cheese salad and be as painful to bear as shame connected to what the world thinks of a person's sexuality?

"Wouldn't that be a pisser," I thought, "if I'm trying to kill myself because I liked a cottage cheese salad and Paranoid is trying to kill himself because his father beat him and his mother and sister molested him. What's that make me?"

I didn't have time to answer, but I would soon be with someone who would help me understand that Paranoid and I were suffering the same pain and for the same reasons. Paranoid and I took separate paths to self-loathing but we ended up in the same smelly place.

I put my interview materials into my briefcase and took off for Golden Gate Park. I needed the sunshine and I needed to be with people. This would be a major breakthrough day for me—but I wouldn't fully understand for years just how major it was.

***

I reached the Park in good time. I watched rollerbladers and skateboarders as they rolled and maneuvered their way through unbelievably tight places and in the most graceful, elegant ways. I thought that some of these people must be world class in their sport. I wondered why they weren't on television or in a road troupe.

"Why aren't they performing for crowds in arenas?" I asked myself. I wondered if I should become a sports agent and sign up some of the performers. My thoughts wandered to how much we might make together. And then I caught myself. This was an example of the intellectual scheming I had done for years on end, and none of it ever amounted to anything. Again I saw myself as stupid, inept, and uncreative. "There are guys who would come in here and turn all this artistry into something, but I'm not one of them." I wondered why I wasn't more creative and daring. Why was my success so limited while all around me I saw others being extremely creative and successful? Fortunately, a stroke of common sense hit me. I got myself back into reality and I headed for the Japanese Tea House.

I stood near the hostess station and looked at the outside tables to see if Ms. Sanchez-Lopez might have arrived. I certainly felt dumpy and gray, and I hoped I'd recognize someone who described herself in the same way. I didn't. I looked straight at her that day. Fortunately, Mrs. Sanchez-Lopez was very in tune with that day's happenings. I felt a little tug on my shirt sleeve.

"Evan Howard?"

I turned and looked down at a tiny little woman with the brownest eyes and the nicest smile I had seen in a long time.

"Yes. Mrs. Sanchez-Lopez?"

"I'm very glad to meet you. Ah, can we dispense with the Mrs.? I prefer to be called Margarita if you don't mind."

"I don't. Please call me Evan."

"Okay, Evan. Let's get a table and talk."

When we were seated, I looked at Margarita Sanchez-Lopez. She was not quite five feet tall. Her hair was dark with just a little gray woven into the waves which surrounded her face perfectly. I decided she was pretty. As soon as she opened her mouth, I realized she was a presence to be reckoned with.

"So…what kind of a reporter are you now that you're doing magazine reporting, Evan?"

"The same kind of reporter I was at the *Chron*, Margarita."

Chapter 11

"Really? I always thought you were depressingly cynical and pessimistic. I'm not sure I want to have my words picked apart the way you took interviews apart in your newspaper life."

I immediately became defensive.

"My work was thought-provoking."

"It certainly provoked a lot of thoughts in me. I could almost feel the anger in your column when I picked up the paper. The paper was always singed around your column."

"I have a lot of righteous anger. The world is a nasty place."

"Maybe. Maybe not," she said. "I hope you'll be more open minded in doing this story, Evan. I was assured by Elizabeth that your editor is very fair and objective and that's the only reason I'm here meeting with you. I know Elizabeth's children have gone national, but there's a lot about their birth family they refuse to look at or understand. I've known their mother for more than twenty years and I've even tried to work with them on a couple of occasions."

"I didn't know that."

"Oh yes. I've also met their father and I've tried to communicate with him a couple of times also. My contact with them happened years ago, but I'm notorious for thorough progress notes on my sessions with clients, and I'm here to tell you there was nothing new said on that talk show. There hasn't been a single new thought in Elizabeth's children's heads in twenty years. The notes I made on the Monahan family twenty years ago are intact, and Elizabeth has allowed her treatment records to be opened. I thought I was going to have to walk a tightrope protecting confidentiality for those kids. They spoke their minds twenty years ago. They're speaking their minds today. None of it is favorable to Elizabeth.

"I also have a journal from the time of Elizabeth's treatment that will be helpful. Something told me Elizabeth would do great things if she got sober and stayed sober, and I kept records of some of our conversations. You understand that I can't and won't reveal anything that her ex-husband or children said or did in their private sessions with me."

"So you kept notes of your therapy sessions?"

"The state requires documentation of treatment in rehabilitation centers. If you want to talk to me about things that occurred during her 28-day treatment program, I can refer back to that documentation. But I think the most revealing information I have concerning Elizabeth's first marriage, and the family that came from that marriage, is contained in notes I wrote of conversations we had outside of therapy. Elizabeth kept in touch with me. I kept letters she wrote and I kept copies of letters I wrote to her. Sometimes I'd be so touched by things she told me she was learning that I wrote about it in my journal. Even though I was her original addictions counselor, she shot way ahead of most of us in many ways in just a few years."

The waitress brought our tea and sweet rice cakes. Margarita filled our cups and helped herself to some of the sweets. I tasted one of the cakes and decided I'd rather eat plastic. I sipped the tea and enjoyed its warmth as it slid into my middle. I looked at the person opposite me.

"How old are you, Margarita?"

"What?"

"I know this may seem rude, but I met Elizabeth and I know she's close to seventy. She's amazing. I couldn't have guessed her age if my life depended on it. I know the two of you have known each other for twenty years and that you were already a therapist at that time. Frankly, it helps me to have some idea of a person's age in doing an article like this."

"Let's just say I'm over fifty."

I whistled.

"What?"

The "what" was a demand for an explanation and I knew I had better give one.

"I would never have guessed. Tell me, are you in recovery from alcoholism too?"

"Yes, I am. I'm also in recovery from addiction to marijuana and work. And you can add relationship addiction to my list of difficulties, too."

"Relationship addiction?"

"You heard me. Relationship addiction. That's what makes Elizabeth's work so exciting. She's developed a simple program that enables people to become healthy, happy individuals without a need to be joined at the hip to other people. When she came into recovery, the relapse rate for alcoholics and drug addicts was off the chart. The first week she was there she began understanding how to utilize the 12-Step recovery process in a totally new way—a way that would drastically reduce the relapse rate in addicts. To be truthful, most of us working in the field thought she was off her nut. One person, Dr. Walter Johannson, listened to what she was saying. He told us that she was going to revolutionize the treatment of addictions in this country. We all thought he was crazy, too. She had a bachelor's degree in political science. She was knowledgeable enough, but most of us 'professionals' saw her as just another alcoholic or addict.

"Who's Dr. Johannson?"

"He's dead now. One of the greatest, most caring doctors the world has ever known. He lived long enough to see Elizabeth's first book published. He was the medical director of the Phoenix Program. He was a very quiet, gentle man, but when he caught fire about something or someone, you couldn't shut him up. He had special talks with Elizabeth while she was in treatment. At first we wondered if maybe the old goat was falling for his patient, but it wasn't that at all. Both Walter and his wife worked together to get Elizabeth's first book published. The three of them became fast friends right to the end."

"I know about the Phoenix Recovery Centers. They're no longer in operation, right?"

"Right. HMOs have done everything possible to avoid paying for treatment of alcoholism or drug addiction in this country. Most of the reputable programs here in northern California have gone belly up, and Phoenix was one of those. I understand treatment programs all across the country are not doing well because treatment still isn't a priority. In-patient treatment is pretty much limited to the wealthy. Dr. Johannson kept his Phoenix

Center going for years. I think he spent his own money keeping it going. He didn't have children—he had his treatment center."

I asked Margarita for permission to start my tape recorder and to ask the questions I had written up for her. She nodded. I asked her name, credentials, and to explain how long she had known Elizabeth Grayson. This part went well. She met Mrs. Grayson more than twenty years earlier. Margarita was an alcoholism counselor when EG first entered treatment.

"I watched Leslie Wilder's show with Elizabeth's children, and I have to tell you, there are discrepancies between what they say is true and what Phoenix records and my notes and memories clearly show. But I'm not here to correct them. I'm here to tell you what I know about Elizabeth Grayson. It happens that I had some experiences with her children and I don't have to rely on my memory to recall them. Dr. Johannson knew how difficult family relationships can be for people recovering from addictions, so he insisted that all our notes and observations be included in the patients' files. I believe you'll find that most of her children's claims will be easily debunked by the official records of her treatment."

"Are you saying her children are liars?"

"I'm saying they have some very distorted views of what went on twenty years ago, and that perhaps their perceptions of other things concerning their mother may be equally distorted. I'm going through my DVD of the Wilder program, and I'm putting material from her file beside their statements on the talk show. I hope you will look at the original file with me and set the record straight for Elizabeth's sake."

I felt uncomfortable with what Margarita was saying.

"We all have erroneous views of things that happened in childhood and in our adult lives, Evan. Part of becoming a mature, integrated adult is the sorting out of what is true in our past and what was erroneously perceived. Our minds are very limited as children. We see things from a very, very limited perspective, and we are all wrong about many, many things."

"Are you calling EG's children liars?" This time I almost spit the question in her face.

"I guess you didn't hear what I just said. I'm saying Elizabeth's children have either serious misperceptions of things that happened in their growing up years and about their mother's rehabilitation, or maybe they are what you say—liars."

"Could it be that you're just too close to Elizabeth to be objective?"

"I am close to Elizabeth. I'm probably not objective, but I'm not talking from personal opinion, Mr. Howard. I'm going strictly by documents created by several professionals and myself during the first years of Elizabeth's recovery. The documents afford as objective a look at a person's life as is humanly possible. None of us knew Elizabeth very well during her 28-day treatment program. We wrote what we saw and what we experienced with her and with her children and husband. We were professionals, Mr. Howard. We wrote the truth to the very best of our ability. We were in no way emotionally involved with Elizabeth at that time. Our goal was the same with every client—to help them get free of addiction or alcoholism." Margarita Sanchez-Lopez was visibly angry. She snapped a sweet rice cake between her teeth.

I could tell that I had again pushed the envelope a little too far, and I wondered why I had become so emotional and so angry at a stranger who was good enough to take time from her day to help me do my job.

"I'm sorry to have upset you, Margarita."

"Do you have some issues with your mother, Evan? If so, perhaps someone else should do this story."

A panic attack set in. Water began to pour from my forehead. My armpits were quickly soaked. I felt glued to my seat. Margarita handed me some tissues from her purse.

"I've got to meet someone soon, Evan. I hope you'll meet with me as soon as I get through the DVD of the talk show. I'll show you why the rift between Elizabeth and her children is so frustrating to so many people. Will you meet with me?"

Margarita rose from the table. She picked up her purse and the last sweet cake from the plate. She took one more gulp of tea as she headed out of the tea house. "Call me tomorrow, Evan.

121

We'll set up a meeting later in the week. And please be in a better mood."

I paid the bill, feeling like I was being stiffed since I had drunk just about half a cup of tea and eaten half a bite of a tea cake. Feelings swirled through me as I walked toward the entrance to the park. I decided to walk home—no small task since I was miles away. Some of my anxiety dissipated as I walked, but discomfort stayed with me. My feet started to hurt so I caught buses and cable cars to Van Ness. I saw very little of the passing scene as I walked and rode the miles between Golden Gate Park and my apartment near Van Ness and California Streets.

"Do you have issues with your mother, Evan? Perhaps someone else should do this story." I heard Margarita's words over and over in my mind. I wished with all my heart that I could get someone else to do this story, but there was no reasoning with Ed Wainwright. My economic life was on the line and I felt myself disintegrating internally. The sun was going down as I neared my apartment. I turned toward Polk Street and one of the delis. I ordered a giant sub and a large soda to go. I went to my apartment to eat, think, and write.

The fog was rolling in. I closed my door behind me. I put my food on a plate and sat myself in front of the television set. Something told me life would never again be the same for me. I longed for a drink to smooth out the chaos within me. I took a bite of my sandwich and called Hardy. I told him about my meeting with Margarita and her challenges to me. I expected consolation and commiseration.

"You're going to find that this woman is right, Evan. There's no doubt you have incorrect perceptions about your parents and what went on in your childhood. I've learned that we keep ourselves in pain because we hold onto childish thinking. What we thought happened in childhood is always quite different from what really happened. In the little time we've spent together, it's clear to me you have very serious issues with your mother. Maybe the best thing you can do is go to your boss and tell him you can't do the article because it's too close to your own pain."

Chapter 11

"I can't do that, Hardy. I have to have that job. It's the only thing I have."

"You can do anything you put your mind to, Evan. There are plenty of jobs you can do to keep the rent paid and food on the table. You don't have to have that job. I can get you ten other jobs tomorrow."

"You don't understand. I have to have *this* job. I'm a journalist. I'm not going to work in a fast food joint or drive a cab like those losers in AA."

"You're a drunk and a drug addict before you're a journalist, Evan. You will do great things in journalism once you've gotten hold of your recovery. If you decide to stay with this job, I'll do all I can to help you stay sober through writing the article, but you'd better realize you're going to go through a lot of pain. Elizabeth Grayson's story sounds much like your mother's story."

"Except that Elizabeth Grayson is a decent human being. My mother wasn't."

"What if you're wrong about that? What happens to Evan Howard if he finds out he's wrong about his mother?"

"Evan Howard isn't wrong about his mother, I assure you."

"All I can do is ask that you open your mind and your heart to new information about everything, Evan. That's what recovery is all about. We step out of old thinking and old decisions and into a life of truth, honesty, and respectful self care. We have to be honest everywhere in our lives. If you're going to get sober and stay sober, you need to begin that road to honesty, and the first person you need to be honest with is yourself. The next person has to be your boss. We've talked long enough, Evan. Finish your meal and then get yourself to bed. Your body is exhausted. God loves you."

And with that he hung up. I finished my sandwich and went to bed. I heard nothing until my alarm went off the next morning.

CHAPTER 12

My alarm rang at seven and I sat up immediately. My mind was clear and I had no doubt as to where I was. For years, I had awakened in a fog. I couldn't remember not waking up in a fog. I know I never got out of bed immediately. Usually I rolled over and slept for another hour or two. For all those years, I swore to everyone who ever challenged my tardiness that I was a night person and couldn't help it if I was late. Getting up at seven with a clear head felt more than strange. Not in a negative way. I wondered if perhaps I was losing my ability to sleep in. And then I noticed there was a shaft of sunlight falling onto the rug in my living room. I could see it's brightness from my bed. I wondered if sunshine had ever come into this apartment before. If it had, it was news to me.

"Observing and having fuzzy feelings about a ray of sunshine on a rug is just way too feminine for me," I thought. "Just what the hell is happening to me?" And then I remembered my conversation with Hardy about perceptions. "Maybe," I thought, "I haven't seen things that were right before my eyes. Maybe I was wrong about my mother like I was wrong about cottage cheese salads." And then I felt rage. I did not want to be wrong about her. I threw myself back on the bed and hit my head on the headboard. I screamed from the pain and I hit my pillow with my fists. I had hated my mother for so long that I couldn't imagine not hating her.

Hardy's words about honesty played through my mind again. "I honestly hate my mother," I told myself, "and that's the truth." I felt safe and secure in my hatred and anger at my mother. It was all I had ever known and the familiarity of it was reassuring. I rolled over and sat up again. I felt the lump on my head. I had apparently hit an edge. There was blood on my fingers. I went to the bathroom and washed the cut and then applied antibiotic ointment. I did the rest of my bathroom routine and then returned to my bed.

I picked up my meditation book. Hardy told me to begin the day with meditation. I agreed I would do it at least until the article was completed. The reading was on forgiveness.

"Oh barf," I thought. I slammed the book on the nightstand.

Hardy told me that I needed to spend some quiet time apart with my "higher power" every morning. Since I needed my wits about me to keep my job, I tried not to curse the meditation and any idea of a higher power. I only had to follow Hardy's crappy suggestions for another week-and-a-half and then I would be free of this stupid recovery stuff. I picked the book up and read the reading again so I could prove to Hardy that I was sincere about "getting better." I'd heard that expression in the meetings. The reading said our first need is to forgive ourselves and that we can't forgive others until we're able to forgive ourselves. I heard that kind of reasoning in at least two of the meetings I'd attended. It didn't make any more sense to me on this day than it had when someone else was saying it. I shook my head and moved my body out of inertia.

I got up to go about my day. Just as I finished dressing, there was a knock on my door. Madge let herself in and hollered from the kitchen, "How are you this morning?"

"Feeling better. Had a good night's sleep," I said, as I wandered into the kitchen. Madge was pouring coffee into two mugs from the carafe she had brought from her apartment. I decided not to tell her about the lump on my head. I didn't want any mother-henning today.

"Glad to hear it. What's the schedule for today?"

"I have an appointment with EG's daughter at four this afternoon. She's going to be in the city and agreed to meet me near City Hall. I do know what she looks like. Mrs. Grayson gave me a picture from happier days."

And then it dawned on me that I hadn't checked my answering machine since very early the day before. I went into the living room and hauled it up from the floor next to the couch. There were messages. The first was from Matthew Monahan. I was to call him at my earliest convenience. The second message was from Jeff Monahan. He had changed his mind and wanted to talk with me. Madge was sitting in my lounge chair and listened intently to the messages.

"That should be an interesting interview," she said.

"Very," I answered. "I hope EG's ex hasn't decided to back out of meeting with me."

"I do, too," said Madge. "Need help with anything?"

"Nope."

"Got a meeting lined up for today?"

"Hardy ordered me to meet him at the AA club off of Union Square at noon."

"Good."

"Not good. When the hell am I supposed to write this article if I'm in these damned meetings all the time?"

"How much time did you spend drinking every day, Evan?"

"What's the point?"

"The point is you spent hours every day drinking. You can spend one hour and the time it takes to get to and from the meeting, in not drinking. The time you'll save will be plenty to do any writing you have to do."

"Fuck trying to make any points with you 12-Step Nazis."

"Have a nice day, Evan. I love you." Madge hugged me and left. I finished my coffee and looked in the refrigerator to see if there was anything edible and appealing. There wasn't so I headed out the door for the little grocery on Van Ness to pick up some donuts, a paper, and more coffee. On the way I checked my billfold and realized I was running low on money. I decided

126

to buy some staples so I could eat for the rest of the week. I picked up ground coffee, eggs, Bisquick, milk, some cooking oil, imitation maple syrup, and a large melon.

I struggled with two plastic bags of groceries. My mother taught me to always pick the biggest melon if they're all the same price. Trudging two long San Francisco blocks carrying the biggest melon in the store, along with a half gallon of milk, a large box of Bisquick, and a large can of coffee, not to mention a Monday edition of San Francisco's morning paper, was more of a chore than I bargained for.

"Just another reason to hate good ol' Mom," I thought. I made it back to my apartment, cut up half the melon, whipped up a batch of pancakes, and sat down to a very satisfying breakfast with the first pot of fresh coffee my apartment had seen in years. I read the paper as I ate, and I felt like I had my act together better than just about anyone. There was a feeling of empowerment filling me that I hadn't felt since my early successes as a journalist. The feeling didn't come from writing a Pulitzer prize winning article. It came from going to the store and making myself a decent breakfast. It frightened me that I was recognizing accomplishment like a kid does. I wondered if I'd be getting gold stars from Hardy. I ate the food as if it came from the finest French restaurant in the city. I felt a comfort from being in an apartment I'd always thought of as beneath me. I skimmed most of the paper and read some of the comics. I actually chuckled at a couple of them.

And then I remembered the messages on my answering machine and got out the list of phone numbers EG had given me. I dialed Matt Monahan's number.

"Hello."

"Mr. Monahan? This is Evan Howard."

"Yes. I got to thinking about how you would get here. I'm not easy to find, so I thought I'd better give you some better directions."

I heaved a sigh of relief. I needed to talk to EG's ex-husband.

Matthew Monahan gave explicit directions to his home and he warned me I would need to drive there because he lived far from public transportation. I then asked him when we could meet.

"This morning would be good for me."

This presented a problem because I had no car and hadn't driven for years. I tried to explain my situation in a way that wouldn't put Monahan off.

"I'm one of those San Franciscans who doesn't own a car. I doubt I can make it out this morning. Would tomorrow morning be all right?"

Matt Monahan guessed it would be all right. As soon as I hung up I called Ed Wainwright's office to tell him of my dilemma. He was in his office, which surprised me. I expected to leave a message. Instead Ed came on the line.

"Evan, how are you doing?"

"I'm doing all right, Ed. I've run into a bit of a problem. Elizabeth Grayson's ex-husband has agreed to an interview but I have to go way up in Marin County to interview him. He says there's no public transportation near his home. I don't have much money on hand and I don't do credit cards. That means I can't afford a cab clear up there and I can't rent a car. Could the magazine help me out on this?"

"When do you need a car?" Ed asked.

"He wanted me to come this morning, but I told him I didn't think that could be worked out. He agreed to tomorrow morning."

"You can borrow my car and still make it up to Marin this morning if you want."

"Your car?"

"My car," Ed said.

"Thanks, Ed," I said. I felt confused. Why would a man who told me what he told me last week offer to loan me his car this week? "Actually, I have to meet someone for a meeting at noon today and I don't want to have to cut an interview with Monahan short. I have a feeling he's going to shed a whole new light on this article."

"You may be right. What meeting do you have at noon?"

I felt like telling Ed it was none of his business, but my mouth wasn't paying very careful attention to any of my rules and regulations about disclosing my comings and goings. "My neighbor, Madge, has been badgering me for years to go to some of those 12-Step Recovery meetings with her. I've been trying some of them out and I met this pushy old coot who's trying to take me under his wing and 'get me well'." I said the words "get me well" with all the sarcasm I could muster.

"Interesting," Ed said. "Is it helping?"

"Helping what?"

"Nothing. Let's just talk about tomorrow morning. I'll see to it that there's a car here for you. Get down here early enough so that you have most of the morning to do this interview."

"Okay, Daddy." There was no reaction to my sarcasm.

I told Ed that I didn't know if I'd be in the office today, and that I had also gotten a call from Jeff Monahan and that he, too, had changed his mind about being interviewed. With that, we hung up. I dialed Jeff Monahan's number. It rang several times. I expected to get an answering machine.

"Hullo?"

"Yes. I'm trying to reach Jeff Monahan, Elizabeth's Grayson's son."

"That's who you've got," the voice said. It sounded as though the speaker was asleep or drugged.

I explained who I was and that I was pleased he was now agreeing to meet with me. I asked when that could happen.

"I don't know," Monahan said. "Give me your number and I'll call you back."

I gave him my number and resisted the temptation to tell him he had called me just yesterday and must still have my number somewhere. I asked when I might expect his call. He said he'd call back in a half hour or so. We hung up. I called Matt Monahan back and firmed up the interview for the next morning. As much as I dreaded meeting Elizabeth Grayson, I looked forward to meeting Matt and Jeff Monahan. I felt I understood them better than they probably understood themselves.

I went into the living room and sat down at my trusty type-writer. I began to write about my conversation with Margarita Sanchez-Lopez and her belief that the Monahan children view their mother through their father's eyes. I felt this was an impossible concept to justify because EG's children were in their forties and certainly could see their mother from their own perspectives. This is the exact point I tried to make during my meeting with Margarita that prompted her to question my relationship with my mother. Suddenly I began to feel a flood of anxiety in my mid-section. My heart began racing, sweat began to pour from my forehead. I lied down on the couch and hoped the panic would pass. It did, but I felt a pain in my chest that lingered after the pounding subsided. I took a deep breath and sat up. The episode had lasted a mere five minutes. I thought perhaps I was suffering heart failure. I promised myself I'd get to a doctor and have myself checked out. Finally the anxiety passed. I felt all right. I sat up and got back to work.

Once again I typed about Margarita's beliefs concerning the Monahan family. This time I listened to the tape recording. When I got to the part where I was challenged, I heard Margarita say that all human beings have mistaken ideas about the people in their childhoods and the events of childhood. I heard her say that Elizabeth Grayson had made a valuable contribution to human understanding when she blueprinted what psychologists now call the three sets of senses that make up the human navigational system. As I listened again to Margarita, the first part of EG's book finally made sense to me. Margarita explained how EG recognized during her first week in drug rehab that people who got well through 12-Step recovery work became intuitive and began to make better choices in their lives. I typed Margarita's words verbatim:

> Elizabeth's first AA meeting was a Promises meeting. Somehow she was able to focus in on the eleventh promise that says we will intuitively know how to handle situations that used to baffle us. She met with Dr. Johannson and asked why

that happens. He told her he didn't know, but what he did know is that professionals working with alcoholics and addicts were missing something very important. Dr. Johannson felt something was missing from traditional addiction treatment because the relapse rate was unbearably high. He challenged Elizabeth to find out what the missing element was and to write a book about it. After years of observing people who got recovery and people who constantly relapsed, Elizabeth figured out what made the difference.

People who got well, reattach to or became friendly with their emotions, their feelings. In American society, men are taught to NOT feel anything that might cause tears. We teach our male children to NOT cry, to NOT be soft lest they be considered feminine. On the other hand, we teach our female children they must be sensitive in order to nurture our babies properly. We also teach them that nice girls NEVER get angry. And then we teach our female children that their emotions are what make them inferior to men. Whether you're male or female in this society, a huge number of people have been taught to either shut down emotionally or to be ashamed of their emotions. We systematically disconnect our children from the emotional parts of self. Our emotions give us our most direct connection to the spirit part of the Universe. We disable our children in one way or another almost from birth. If we blinded our children or did something to stop oxygen from going to the brain so they became learning disabled, we would face criminal action. And yet we force our children to disconnect from

some or all of their emotions and wonder why so
many of our children become sociopaths.

I reread Margarita's words several times and decided there
was no need to edit anything. EG had said that the most important page in her book on emotional disconnectedness was the
page that laid out the human navigational system. I got the book
and turned to that page. She listed the body senses, the intellect's
senses, and the spirit's senses. My mind and hand wanted to reject the term "spirit" but I couldn't find another word to put in
its place. I tried "soul" but that had an even more religious con-
notation for me. EG explained in the early pages of her book that
all humans have a body, a mind, and a spirit, and she acknowledged that many people would mistakenly view anything of the
spirit as "religious." She stressed that when she writes of the
"spirit" she's talking about what modern psychology calls the
unconscious or subconscious. EG emphasized that it is the part
of every human that contains the programming picked up in
early childhood that rules all of the adult's attitudes, behaviors,
choices, and relationships.

I included details regarding the human navigational system
in the article. I felt it was important because it was the core of
knowledge that had propelled its author into national and inter-
national prominence.

The Human Navigational System

Healthy human beings, what professionals
call authentic, self-actualizing people, are balanced in the use of their physical, mental, and
spirit senses.

The Body's Senses:

Seeing • Hearing • Touching •
Tasting • Smelling

Mental Senses:

Reasoning • Deducting • Analyzing • Remembering • Organiz-
ing Information

Chapter 12

<u>Spirit Senses</u>:
Emoting • Sensing • Dreaming •
Imagining • Intuiting

I popped the tape I did with EG into my machine. I went into my notes and found the spot on the tape where EG talked about her theory. I typed her words:

> You see, Mr. Howard, we have strict laws in this country to protect people who have physical disabilities. If we are without the advantage of one or more of our physical senses, we are truly handicapped in life. Unfortunately, it's only recently that humanity has begun to help the physically disabled and to treasure the gifts they bring us in other, non-ordinary ways. Today we have laws in this country to protect people who are not able to have full use of their mental abilities. When someone can't read or organize information systematically, we understand how difficult life becomes for them and we have laws in place to help them. When one has limited intellectual ability, we protect them with a very specific set of laws. What we fail to understand in American society is spirit disability. Many people have very high IQs but are not attached to their spirit senses, which are the source of common sense. I think many of us know people who have near-genius IQ and no common sense.
>
> If you work long with alcoholics or addicts, you can quickly pinpoint the age at which they began drinking and drugging. If they started medicating at age thirteen, they are emotionally arrested at that age. That's why so many people in early recovery act like teenagers. They get giggly and worry about what some good-looking person is saying or doing, etc. People who began

abusing substances in their adult years are often baffled by the behaviors of people coming into recovery who began their substance abuse as teenagers.

This society has little or no recognition of those who are cut off from one or more of their spirit senses. We set people up for addictions and then we despise them because they are so emotionally immature.

I played the talk show tape in my mind again. If her children had knowledge of EG's concept of emotional disconnectedness and how it affects anyone touched by addiction, there was no indication of that knowledge anywhere on the talk show tape. I wondered what they thought of her book or if they had ever read it.

EG stated to me, and in her book, that our spirit senses are our deepest connection to the process called life. According to her, these senses are what give human beings their centeredness, their sense of being part of the Universal whole. EG insists that the spirit senses are the electronics of the human navigational system. I inserted a paragraph to this effect into the draft of the article. In her book, EG called human beings who are separated from any or all of their spirit senses codependents. I quoted her book:

A Codependent Is...

...a person who represses, ignores, denies, detaches from, or disowns his/her feelings, emotions, imagination, dreams, and intuition. A codependent is partially or totally separated from the core of being which is called spirit or unconscious. The codependent person does not have the use of the deepest part of the human navigational system.

Chapter 12

Codependency Is...

> ...the attachment of a codependent person to something outside of his/her self which allows the person to feel attached to life. The person can be attached to another soul, group, gang, cult, cause, profession, job, substance, or thing[s]. The codependent hopes to be made whole through this attachment and may actually feel whole in the beginning of the attachment. Some of the things codependents look for in their exterior at-tachments include: being taken care of, finding a worthwhile identity, being fulfilled, being com-pleted, being released from the psychic/emotional pain that comes from being separated from the core of self.

Another panic attack flowed through me. How many people had told me to get out of my intellect and into my feelings? Was this what they were talking about? Was I separated from certain senses and was this why I drank alcohol? I tried to shake the thoughts away. I told myself that I drink because I like alcohol. Every teenager I had ever known in my teen years lived to be able to drink legally. Everyone I worked with as an adult drank. "Hell," I thought, "those are my best memories."

The phone rang. It was Jeff Monahan. He asked if he could meet with me when I met with his sister.

"Well, I don't know," I said. "I'd have to ask her."

"No you don't. She said you were meeting by City Hall. She won't mind me coming by. I work close to there. What time are you meeting?"

"Four o'clock."

"Good. I'll see you then." I would figure out later in the day that Jeff Monahan had taken over the interview arrangements. It apparently didn't matter what I wanted from the interview. Young Mr. Monahan wanted to meet me when I met with his sister and that was that. I made a mental note to ask Madge or Hardy or Margarita why I felt angry with Jeff Monahan. But for now I needed to calm myself. I sat quietly in the chair and felt the shaking in my mid-section. My body settled down. I had heard all my life about a mind/body connection and I had no problem with that idea. But this mind/body/spirit connection … now that idea was fearful to me. I didn't want to believe anything Elizabeth Grayson wrote or said. I didn't want to believe or accept anything Ed Wainwright or the people in the 12-Step groups were saying. Most important, I did not want to believe anything my mother ever said could be right or true. She had made my life painful in every way, and there was no way I could let her be right about anything. No way.

I tried to bury myself in my writing and it worked for almost two hours. I had a couple of pages laid out when the phone rang.

"Hello?"

"Good morning, Evan. It's Hardy."

"Yeah?"

"Just calling to remind you about the meeting off Union Square. You still coming?"

"I guess so, although I'm really rolling on this article. Maybe I should just skip the meeting today."

"No, no, Evan. You go to meetings when you feel like going and you go to meetings when you don't want to or when you think something's more important. I'm not far from your place. How about meeting me at the corner in twenty minutes and we'll hop public transportation?"

"Okay. Twenty minutes."

I hung up the phone and read through what I had written. It needed a lot of polishing. Reluctantly, I set my work aside and prepared to meet Hardy. I felt pushed and angry. I was angry at myself because I didn't have the strength to tell Jeff Monahan that I would decide whether it was all right for him to join my meeting with his sister. I was angry because I didn't have the strength to tell Hardy I wouldn't meet him and I wouldn't go to his damned meeting. In all my adult life I had never had problems telling people to butt out or to get out of my face. I felt like a little boy who would get scolded if he didn't meet the teacher on time. As I left the apartment, I slammed the door behind me.

Chapter 12

A neighbor was working in the yard below. He jumped at the slamming door and then gave me a look that would wither a lion after a female in heat. I had seen that look before and I felt another anxiety attack coming on. Yep. I had seen that look before, many times. Where had I seen it? I had not seen it on my mother's face, and yet that's where my first thought went.

I shook the thought out of my head and went down to the street to meet Hardy. I hated the things I was feeling. I hated my mother and now I hated Jeff Monahan and Hardy, too.

CHAPTER 13

Hardy was on the corner impatiently looking at his watch. He muttered something about twenty minutes being twenty minutes and not forty minutes. He hailed a taxi, which got us to the meeting exactly on time. It was in an office in one of those dark, old, rundown buildings that the Chamber of Commerce and elected officials try to hide from the tourists. It was just a couple of blocks off Union Square. The windows were streaked and dirty. Union Square was filled with lovely trees and benches surrounded by upscale hotels, restaurants, and shops. We were on a seedy block off of Union Square where there were no trees and the sidewalks and building fronts were in desperate need of repair. The meeting was on the second floor of the building.

There were fifty or more people sitting in folding chairs. Some of them were eating lunches picked up from nearby sandwich shops. A large number of them were wearing three piece suits and carrying briefcases. I noticed that some of the women were dressed to the nines—clearly they were successful and proud of it. Suddenly everything seemed out of context for me. I felt disoriented. We were sitting in a seedy meeting room in a seedy building, and the room held one of the strangest mixes of people I could imagine. There were a few construction workers eating their lunches from metal boxes with thermos jugs. There

Chapter 13

was a derelict, leaning against a wall, listening to everything that was being said. But the most disconcerting thing to me was the presence of the "elegant people."

Several of them disclosed some of the most intimate information a person can disclose. One man, clearly successful financially, talked about his years in jail for killing a family while driving drunk. One woman, who admitted to being an attorney, talked about years of promiscuity before getting into treatment for alcoholism. She said she had to heal the wounds from years of incest from her father in order to stay sober. One after another, people talked about horrendous experiences and how their lives had changed for the better because they got into recovery. I didn't realize that all of these stories were being told for my benefit. When the leader asked if there was anyone new to the program, I had raised my hand and said I was new and didn't understand why one has to go to meetings for so many years when all one had to do was stop drinking or drugging. As a journalist, I was fascinated by what these people were saying. In one way, this group was much more to my liking than was the Sunday morning men's meeting. That meeting included a high percentage of people I considered losers.

After the meeting Hardy and I walked down to the street. Paranoid Robinson walked up to us. He was clean shaven, had on new clothes, and a smile.

"Hey, brothers," he said.

My mouth dropped.

"Hey, Bro," he said. "Miracles can happen. Your mouth's hangin' open, Mr. H. I'm out job hunting. T.R. staked me to the clothes, haircut, shave. I haven't done anything, no drugs or alcohol since I saw you all yesterday morning. I'm on my way to a couple of employment agencies right now."

"Have you had lunch, yet, Paranoid? If not, join us." Hardy headed across the street toward a dimly lit deli in another seedy building off Union Square.

"Ah, I'm kind of low on money, Hardy," I said. "If it's okay with you, I'll skip lunch today."

"Don't worry about the money. It's more important for you both to get on a healthy eating schedule. My treat today. You'll have plenty of chances to pay back anything you get in these first weeks of recovery."

With that he moved us into the deli. We seated ourselves. Hardy passed each of us a menu that had years of grease and grime on it. He told us the deli served some of the best corned beef sandwiches in the world. I hadn't had a corned beef sandwich in years. I actually began to drool. The 12-Step meeting went on long enough for the regular lunch crowd to clear out, so a waitress was available right away. We all ordered corned beef sandwiches. When they came, the smells were almost more than I could stand. Fresh pumpernickel bread loaded with thinly sliced corned beef. I slathered horseradish mustard on mine and dug in. And then I took a bite of the large dill pickle that came with the sandwich. My stomach was in heaven.

"You're right. These are incredible. I'll have to remember this place," I said.

"A dear friend of mine who's dead now introduced me to this place," said Hardy. Neither Paranoid nor I took much heed of what Hardy had just said. We were too busy filling our faces. When I finally got enough of the sandwich to allow me to think of something else, I remembered something.

"You know, my mother introduced me to corned beef years ago. I remember going to a deli somewhere in the city. I don't remember where it was, but it was almost as good as this. My mother loved corned beef sandwiches and she loved them piled high with shaved meat."

"Ah," said Hardy. "So you do have at least one good memory of your mother."

"Yeah," I said. "But that's about it."

"Well guys," said Hardy, "I've got a meeting I've got to get to. What are your plans for the rest of the afternoon?"

Paranoid was going job seeking and I was going to the library near city Hall to do some research until my appointment with Stacy Monahan Jansen and her brother, Jeff, at four. Hardy seemed satisfied with our answers and dashed off. I got a refill on my soda and Paranoid had another cup of coffee.

"Ol' Hardy's the best," said Paranoid.

"I think he's a pain in the butt. But I have to admit, he's been good to me. I don't like being obligated to anyone the way I'm getting into debt to him."

"What? For a couple of meals?" Paranoid looked at me in disbelief. "Shit, I've burned folks in AA, NA, and CA for thousands of bucks. What're you into Hardy for? A few meals? Some doughnuts? Shit, if you're gonna get prideful, do it over something bigger than a bag or two of food."

I finished the last of my sandwich and had to agree that a few meals weren't worth getting a knot in my underwear. I swallowed the rest of my soda and sat back in my chair, wishing I had the money for another sandwich for dinner. This meal comforted me. I wanted to stay in this place and smell the smells. I had heard people talking about comfort food and I thought they were full of bull. But I had to admit I got real comfort from this food.

"So how long have you gone without a drink, Bro?"

"I had my last drink a week ago tomorrow."

"What drugs do you do, Bro?"

"I don't do drugs, Bro." I answered snidely, and Paranoid read exactly what I was thinking.

"You drink alcohol, you do drugs, Bro. Alcohol is an anesthetic. You can cut an arm or a leg off a person if you pour enough booze in the body. Don't go gettin' high handed because you only drink alcohol. Being a drunk ain't one damn bit better than bein' an addict no matter how many old time AAers tell you different. You're a fuckin' druggie and that's all there is to it."

"You may be right, Paranoid. You may be right. I don't want to argue with you or anyone else. I just want to relax a little and let this good food settle. Do you mind?"

"I don't mind a bit. Sorry if I upset you."

"You didn't upset me. How are you doing? Really. You look like a different person today. You look a lot like you did in your playing days."

"Yeah. Every time I come back into the program there are people who help me get back on my feet. They clean me up, feed me, and I do real good for a few months, and then I start lyin' to them and fuckin' them over. I don't wanna do that this time. I don't wanna hurt any more people in my life."

"I'm lucky," I said, "I don't have anyone in my life to hurt."

"Yes you do. Hardy'll hurt if you go back out. T.R. will hurt if you go back out. I'll hurt."

"Bullshit."

"You sound just like me ten years ago, Mr. Smartass. Don't do to yourself what I've done to myself. I've always told myself that nobody cares and I don't care about nobody. Biggest pack of lies anyone's ever fed me."

"Let's talk about something important."

"Okay." Paranoid leaned toward me and listened intently.

"Can you get a good lay if you're not drinking or drugging?"

"Uh huh. Been a week since you had a drink, huh? You can always tell. The juices are flowing again. Man, I'm telling you, if you've never had sex sober, you've never had sex." Paranoid was grinning from ear to ear. "Matter of fact, Bro, that's one of the things I miss most when I go back to druggin'." Unfortunately my addiction is even more powerful than my sex drive. I'm telling you, if you ain't had sex sober, you ain't had sex at all."

"Yeah. Well I'm starting to feel horny. How do you pick someone up in those meetings? I wasn't good at picking women up in bars while I had booze to help me so how in the hell will I ever score sober?"

"Don't worry about that. Healthy women won't come near you for at least a year. Take care of yourself, Bro, and stay away from the women. If one comes up to you before you're sober a year, run for your life. They're sicker than you are. Just take care of yourself and leave the women alone."

"I'm not going back to drinking, ever," I said.

"Don't say that, man. Just say you're not going to drink just for today. You can't handle forever. No one can."

"Bullshit."

"You like that word, huh, Bro?"

"It fits all this crap better than any other word." I pushed back my chair and stood up. "I've got to go to the library and do some research. I'll see you."

"Yes you will, Bro. Yes you will."

I left the restaurant and got my bearings. I decided to walk to the library. I had a couple of dollars in dimes on me for the copy machine. I knew I'd be able to duplicate the materials I needed for the article and take the copies home for study. It was almost two. I'd have plenty of time to pick up some of the materials referred to in E.G.'s book and to get some materials that Ms. Sanchez-Lopez told me about. I'd be able to meet the two younger Monahan children and still get some work done on the article in the evening hours.

I walked through the city, and was almost painfully aware of the people walking toward me. The sidewalks were full of people on every block. I wondered if people walked around the city like this every day. If so, it was news to me. It occurred to me that I almost never was out and about in the city during the day. If I went to the office, I rode the cable cars and they were always full of tourists. I accepted crowding on the cable cars and could deal with it. I was not happy that the same crowding took place on the sidewalks of the City by the Bay. Several people bumped me and I wanted to punch someone for being in my way.

"I really hate people," I thought to myself. "I really hate people."

I trudged on to the library and went through the massive revolving door. Armed security guards checked my case for weapons. The city had been on high alert since the day in November of 1978 when an angry Dan White killed the city's mayor and a gay supervisor. It would never go back to the wide open, fun loving, ass-kicking city it was before November of '78.

I went to the computer and dug out the reference numbers of the materials I needed. I was in my element. I was a good reporter and I thoroughly enjoyed the research aspects of my work. I found the books and periodicals I needed and took them to an open copy machine. I had everything I needed in less than an hour. I began reading. Interesting stuff, but I doubted much of it.

Stacy Jansen had told me she might be a little early for our appointment. So at three-thirty I laid out the xeroxed pages and clipped each group together. I carefully marked each set by author and book title. When the packets were safe in my briefcase, I shut it, took a deep breath, and headed toward city Hall for my meeting with EG's two younger children.

***

I got to the designated bench about ten minutes to four. A woman and a man were seated. I hesitated because neither of them looked like the teenagers in the picture that EG had shown me. I realized that I hadn't looked closely at the faces of EG's children when I watched the video with Ed and Madge. I felt their pain and then got into my own pain. Both of the people on the bench were graying. Both looked tired. They were busy talking together and I wondered if perhaps two accidental bench sitters had wandered into my picture. I stood to the side of the bench for a minute or two. Both looked toward me at once. The woman spoke.

"Mr. Howard?"

"Yes."

"I'm Stacy Jansen. This is my brother, Jeff Monahan."

I shook their hands. The two moved apart on the bench and made room for me in the middle. I put my briefcase on the ground and took out my stenographer's pad containing the questions I had prepared. I set up my tape recorder and made sure it was running properly.

"First, I want to thank both of you for agreeing to talk to me. I know this is a painful situation for you."

Chapter 13

"It used to be painful, Mr. Howard," said Jeff Monahan. "We're so totally used to our mother's neglect that it's no longer painful. Today it's just irritating."

"Please call me Evan. I feel we're contemporaries in age, and maybe in some of our experiences."

"I doubt that, Evan. I don't believe anyone could have had a mother so selfish and self-centered as our mother was, and still is." Stacy Monahan Jansen was visibly angry and clearly not in a mood to hear about my woes with my mother. I felt empathy toward her and I felt anger at the same time. I had met Stacy's mother, and I had felt her genuine love and caring toward her children. I heard EG acknowledge errors she had made in her first-marriage home. I heard from their mother what I had longed to hear my mother say. I knew on every level of my being that their mother wasn't nearly as self-centered and selfish as they seemed to think. She certainly wasn't the witch they believed she was, at least not in my mind. I had to pull myself back from these wandering thoughts. I realized that both were talking to each other about the wickedness of the woman who had given birth to them. I wasn't really needed for this conversation. I could watch it again on the tape that my boss had given me.

"I've watched the tape of your appearance on the Leslie Wilder Show, so we're kind of plowing old ground here. Our time is limited, so I'd like to ask you some questions that will clarify certain points for the article I'm doing."

"We understand," Stacy said.

"How long has it been since you saw your mother in person and talked with her?"

Jeff answered first. "I haven't seen her since about a year before she supposedly got sober. I saw her briefly at Stacy's wedding, but I didn't speak to her or acknowledge her."

"Did she try to speak with you?"

"Yes. But I wanted to make it clear that she is no longer a part of my life, so I just walked away."

"And you, Stacy?"

"I haven't spoken to my mother for more than eight years. I don't want her near my children. She destroyed us and I'm doing everything in my power to protect my children from her. I don't want her telling them distortions about our childhood. She's totally unwilling to apologize for the total destruction of four people."

"Four people? I thought there were only three children."

"We include our father in her path of destruction. He was never anything but gentle and quiet and caring," said Jeff.

"As you know, I've already interviewed your mother. She understands that you want some kind of total apology for the ruination of your childhood home, but she also says that your father was just as responsible for all that happened in your growing up years as she was."

Jeff stood up and hovered over me. He looked at me with pure hatred. Jeff Monahan looked like his mother. He had looked most like her when he smiled as we shook hands. At this moment he looked like he was ready to hit me, but I didn't feel fear. Mostly I felt the heat of his frustration. I noticed he was beginning to get paunchy in the same way I was. His clothes were a little less than perfect, just like mine. He was my height. He had a strong chin and was probably very handsome when he was younger. In my altered state of sobriety, I could see the lines on his face. The look in his eyes was loneliness. I recognized his loneliness because I had seen that same look in my mirror several times over the past week. It occurred to me that Jeff Monahan and I shared the same loneliness and the same hatred of our mothers. I didn't get to think much about this possibility because Jeff literally screamed at me.

"What is it with you people? My father did nothing to harm us, do you hear me, Mr. Howard? Nothing! She was evil, she is evil, and if you're going to do another apology for that bitch, I'm out of here right now." Jeff Monahan had risen and was leaning over me.

I put my hands up to calm him. I needed to be able to quote these two people in order to give the article honest balance.

"Please understand—I'm a journalist. I have to present all sides in this article and I really need to get your input. If a question angers you, please understand that I'm asking it because I need to get your views on something. I'm not taking your mother's side. Believe me, I'm not taking your mother's side in this article."

Stacy nodded understanding. Jeff sat down hard on the bench. He was clearly unhappy. I tried to get the three of us back on track.

"Do either of you remember any good times with your mother?"

"None," Jeff said.

"That's not true. We had a lot of good times. Mother was a good cook and we always had dinner together as a family. There was never any fighting at the table. Holidays were wonderful when we were little. And I remember having a kind of fairy tale life until I was about eight years old. Something happened then, because Mother became furious with Daddy. I remember her having some outbursts before that, but I also remember understanding why. Our father was not emotionally available to any of us, and I remember asking him a question that he brushed off and Mom—ah, Elizabeth—admonished him for not hearing me and answering me. He just walked off, whistling as he always did."

"You say your father was not emotionally available?"

"He never loved her." Jeff said it while looking at the sidewalk between his feet.

"How do you know that?" I asked.

"We all knew that."

"But your mother loved him, as I understand it."

"Actually," said Stacy, "I think he loved her to the best of his ability, but it was never enough for Mother."

"Then why aren't you angry at your father? I don't understand."

"She was the smart one. She could have gotten out and not put us through years of drunkenness and her insane outbursts. She tortured us and put all of us through years of her alcoholism." Jeff's voice was bitter. He was still looking at the sidewalk between his feet.

"If your father didn't love her, wasn't he obligated to not marry her in the first place? I'm sorry, but there's something wrong with this picture. What was your father's responsibility in all of this?"

"Look, our father was raised in a very unemotional family. His people were extremely cold and distant. We all had difficulty connecting to him, but he was there for us in a lot of ways. He was dependable. He cleaned up the vomit when she threw up. He put up with her harangues. He held that house together. He wasn't the one who ranted and raved."

"I've been told that your mother never lost a job, never missed cooking a meal, that she did all the other things mothers did in those years. Is that a lie?"

"No, probably not. But she started drinking when I was six," Stacy said with clenched teeth. "And then she wasn't there for us anymore. She abandoned us."

"Didn't your father abandon you, too?"

"No. Don't you get it, Jerk?" Jeff shot me another of those withering looks. "Dad has always been the same with all of us. She changed. She went crazy. He never got angry. He never yelled. He never changed one bit in all the years we were growing up. She started drinking when I was six and she got angrier and angrier, meaner and meaner. We were all afraid of her. In fact we were all afraid of her long before she started drinking. We couldn't wait for her to leave."

"Ok. I'll make note of all this." I went back to my list of questions. I did not like being here. I just wanted this interview over. "Do either of you remember your father telling you that if you had problems when you grew up it would be your mother's fault because she was the active one, she was the doer?"

"Yeah," they answered in unison. "So?"

"Could it be that you were led to believe at a very early age that your mother was the sole source of trouble in your life?"

"What kind of a question is that?" Stacy asked. She was bone thin. She dressed conservatively. She wore a long skirt, plain blue shoes, a high necked blouse with a short jacket. The clothes appeared to be of good quality. Stacy looked like her

148

mother as well. She actually looked closer in age to her mother. Her eyes looked weary. And there, again, was the lost and lonely look. Margarita Sanches-Lopez had told me that Stacy's husband was a good person who had contacted Margarita for counseling because he was deeply troubled by his wife's alienation from her mother. She said he was most concerned because Stacy wouldn't allow their children to see their grandmother.

"I need to verify that this statement was made to you when you were little."

"Well it was," said Stacy. "Our father could see the handwriting on the wall."

The two regaled me with more horror stories from childhood. I dutifully made notes. It was almost five o'clock when we parted company. I headed for my apartment and for an evening of pounding the old typewriter. The most important element in my interview of EG's children was verification that their father had told them their adult problems would be caused by their mother.

I reached the apartment just as the fog rolled over Van Ness Avenue. I turned on the light in the kitchen. I took out another ancient can of soup and began looking for the can opener. There was a knock on the door.

"Hi, Evan. How are you?"

"I'm fine, Madge."

"Hey, I happened to be down by Union Square and I picked up some corned beef sandwiches at one of my favorite delis. I thought you might enjoy one. Wanna join me for a bite of supper?"

I told Madge about my experience with Hardy. I asked if it was the same deli and she said it was. She told me that lots of 12-Step people go there.

"It's one of my favorite places in the whole world, Evan. I take it you won't mind having more corned beef for dinner."

I followed her to her apartment. Everything was set. It looked like a feast. She had placed the sandwiches on real plates. There was a bowl of coleslaw and some fresh dill spears. I helped myself to some of each. Madge poured soda into glasses and we sat down to eat.

"Mind if I say a blessing, Evan?"

I nodded.

"Higher Power, we thank you for this food, for all the hands who helped bring it to this table, and for the friendship the two of us share. Amen."

My amen got caught in my throat. I felt overwhelmed by thankfulness as Madge said her prayer. I choked.

"What's wrong?"

"I don't know," I said. "I feel teary-eyed. I had lunch with Hardy and I remembered my mother taking me for a corned beef sandwich somewhere in the city years ago. I was probably in the first grade. I remembered how good it was, and all of a sudden I felt very emotional. And now it's happening again. If this is the kind of stuff that happens in sobriety, I don't like it."

"Eat," she said. "And then we'll talk."

I ate my sandwich with the same pleasure as I had earlier in the day. We ate without a word. I felt safe and cared for here in Madge's kitchen, with this most delicious food. When we finished we just sat quietly and enjoyed the pleasure of each other's company and the joy of good food. Finally, Madge began to clear the table. She started a pot of coffee and I told her about my wish for enough money to buy another sandwich to take home with me for dinner. I told her how strange it was that she had bought sandwiches with me in mind as her dinner guest.

"Evan, I'm going to tell you something and I don't want any razzle-dazzle mental games because what I say flies in the face of your view of life on Planet Earth."

"Okay," I said.

"It was no accident that I brought you your heart's desire from earlier in the day. These things happen to good people all the time. When we're trying to be in the spiritual and to do the right thing, good things happen to us all the time. It's called grace, God's blessings on a good life… whatever."

Discomfort was immediate. I rolled my eyes back in my head.

"I asked you not to make fun of what I said, Evan. And there you go doing it."

"I'm sorry. I wasn't making fun of what you said."

"You were, dammit. You gave me that 'here she goes again' look, rolling your eyes, and generally acting like a five-year-old. You do it all the time. I just bought you a lovely meal that your heart really wanted, and you can't respect me long enough to just listen to something I want to say that's important for me and might some day be important to you."

"I'm sorry, Madge. I'm sorry. I do appreciate this meal and I'm trying to appreciate all you've done for me. I can't stop all my feelings. I'm new in recovery."

"That's the only reason you haven't been thrown out the door, Evan. No one is asking you to stop your feelings. But you can change your behaviors. The stuff you've believed to this point in time got you a one-way ticket to skid row, so I'm asking you to stop rolling your eyes and acting disgusted at stuff that's gotten me and a lot of other people to very good places in life."

"I'm sorry. I'll try. But I don't think I know how to stop rolling my eyes."

"You can stop rolling your eyes if you choose to stop rolling your eyes."

I was tempted to roll my eyes again, but I didn't do it. I was proving her point and I hated both of us for that.

"I got something special for us for dessert." Madge went to the refrigerator and brought out a box from a bakery I had never heard of. "This is one of my most favorite things in the world. It's called a bee sting."

She placed a large, round roll on a plate in front of me. The top of it was loaded with toasted almond slices, covered with brown sugar and a glaze. The roll was cut in half horizontally. There was a thick layer of Bavarian creme between the halves. Madge brought me a sharp steak knife and a fresh cup of coffee. She served herself the second bee sting. I waited and watched her cut the dessert. She inserted a fork into the pastry and then inserted the point of a sharp knife straight down to the plate. She sliced off a bite-sized portion and lifted it on the fork to her mouth. She appeared to be in the middle of an orgasm as she slowly chewed the delicacy.

I followed her example. It was the most delicious sweet thing I had ever eaten. Again, we ate in silence. Mouthful by mouthful, I felt deep sadness as I came to the last piece. I wondered at the deliciousness of the dessert and the moment. I was beginning to understand what Hardy had told me about enriched experiences because my senses were no longer anesthetized. The coffee was as delicious as the rest of the meal had been. I was in heaven. I felt safe and cared for.

"So," Madge said, "tell me about your day."

"Most of it was good. I made arrangements to go out and meet with EG's ex-husband tomorrow. And I got together with her younger children late this afternoon."

"How did that go?"

"It was pretty much a repeat of the talk show. A couple of things came out of it that trouble me. The interview I had with Jeff and Stacy Monahan bothers me."

"Really?"

"The first thing they told me shocked me. Both kids told me that their father was emotionally unavailable and that he never loved EG."

"If that's true, why aren't they angry at their father for marrying their mother when he didn't love her? Why are they so angry at their mother and not at him?"

"The son said that she was the smart one and she should never have married him or should have gotten out when she realized he wasn't emotionally available. I said it was my understanding that EG didn't understand until after she got out of the marriage that her husband never loved her. And then there was the second thing. EG told me that her husband had told the children often that if they had problems when they grew up, it would be EG's fault because she was the active one, she was the doer. The kids admit he told them that, and they say he was absolutely right. I guess what bothers me is the fact that it doesn't seem fair for one parent to blame the other parent for their children's future problems."

Chapter 13

"Bingo! You see, Evan, you're already getting better. It isn't fair to tell little children that their future problems will be because of their father or mother. Yet that's done all the time. The problem is, those kids will go to the grave believing their mother is evil because they picked up the message with one-hundred percent pure emotion very early in life. So early that it becomes gospel. And the message came from a person who was critical to their development. Everything we internalize as little children is put in with pure emotion. It takes an atom bomb to change early childhood beliefs, but that's what the 12-Step Process enables us to do. If EG's kids ever get into a recovery program, they may be able to change that erroneous piece of information. Otherwise, they'll never be free of hating one-half of their selves."

"One-half of their selves?"

"The half that comes from their mother. If we hate one of our parents, we're in trouble because we hate one-half of our self. If we hate both of our parents, we will have serious problems."

"Hmm." I poured a little more coffee for myself and Madge, and tried to think about the point she was making.

"I hate my mother. Does that mean I hate half of myself."

"It does. The half of you that comes from her."

I almost rolled my eyes but stopped myself. I'm not sure I did it out of respect for Madge or out of fear that I'd never get another corned beef sandwich or bee sting. But I heard her. I was being criticized, and my first feeling was shame. Madge may have read what was going on inside me. She came over and put her arms around me and hugged me. I cried and Madge rocked me.

"Stop hating yourself, Evan. Stop hating your mother. You are a good person no matter what you've come to believe about yourself." When my sobbing stopped she pushed me back and held my face in her hand. "You're just a little boy who needs his Mom and his Dad. We never get past needing our Moms and Dads."

I nodded and blew my nose on my napkin. I don't know why I wasn't more embarrassed about crying. I don't remember crying in front of anyone since before I went to kindergarten. For some reason it seemed okay. I wiped my eyes and then helped clean up the dishes. We were both silent. I felt safe in this apartment with my old friend Madge. We sat and had a little more coffee and then I excused myself and went home to read and write for most of the evening. When my back began to ache, I watched the late news and then turned into bed. I took enough time to thank my Higher Power for corned beef sandwiches and the bee sting. And then, with no warning, a wall of pain washed over me. I cried as hard as I've ever cried in my life. I don't know how long the tears flowed. I didn't know what was happening to me. I couldn't stop the tears and I couldn't stop the pain. Somehow, I drifted off to sleep—as deep a sleep as I've ever had.

CHAPTER 14

I awoke bright and early the next morning, feeling clear in my head and relatively free of physical pain in my joints. I remembered everything that happened the day before. I even knew exactly where I needed to go this morning. I showered, shaved, and dressed, then made a pot of coffee, heated a leftover pancake in the microwave, slathered it with butter, a sliced banana and syrup, and sat down to what seemed to be a royal feast. I picked up the paper in front of my neighbor's door. I'd done that many times, but I always kept it neat and put it back in front of the neighbor's door when I finished with it. My radio got the morning news station perfectly. I had a feeling of wellness that was exhilarating. I didn't have to hit the radio or curse the paperboy for not delivering the neighbor's paper. When you've done these things repeatedly for years, it feels odd to not hit and not curse. My being was confused and uncomfortable, but I wasn't in deep pain. I wondered how long it would be before something mean and ugly would crop up to ruin my day.

I ate my food, scanned the paper and listened to the news. The world hadn't blown up overnight, so I felt it was safe to wander down California to Market Street and pick up the car Ed Wainwright had promised me. I brushed my teeth, combed my hair and looked at the person staring back at me in the mirror.

The eyes of the person I saw looked different, I thought. Better. But the loneliness was still there. The terrible loneliness that had been with me all my life. I always thought I covered it well. On this day, I realized I had only fooled myself. I had seen the same loneliness in the faces of dozens of people in the past several days. That loneliness was everywhere—on the faces of people I passed on the street, in the little grocery store near my apartment, at my office, in some of the people at the 12-Step meetings, and in the faces of Elizabeth Grayson's younger children.

I headed toward the office with a vague feeling of dread. I would be meeting Elizabeth Grayson's former husband a little later in the day. There was no reason to fear him. The two younger children clearly adored their father. Elizabeth Grayson herself hadn't really said anything negative about him. In the past, the feeling of dread that was overtaking me would have been dealt with swiftly. A couple of shots of good bourbon and it was bye-bye dread. I got off the cable car at Market Street and headed toward the office wishing I could have a drink. I could feel human if I just had one or two shots. I shook the idea off. Progress was being made on the article. I knew enough about Matthew Monahan to understand that boozers would probably not be welcome in his home. His interview was critical to the completion of the article, so the thought of booze quickly lost currency.

True to his word, Ed was at his desk and had his keys at the ready. He took me to the garage and gave me a quick lesson on operating his car. It was a beauty. Brand new. Leather seats. A Mercedes. I'd never driven anything more than a beat-up clunker. When I was at my peak at the *Chron* and people saw me driving that clunker, they called me eccentric. When I got fired from the *Chron* and people saw me driving that clunker, they called me a failure. I told Ed I would have the car back shortly after noon, and headed toward the Golden Gate Bridge and Marin County. I placed the directions to the Monahan home on the passenger seat. I was confident about the first two-thirds of my trip north. I had taken the same route many times during my first years at the *Chron*.

Chapter 14

Matt Monahan lived a little north of Muir Woods—an ancient stand of redwoods that was preserved to honor the man who is generally credited with beginning America's environmental movement.

The car was wonderful. Quiet and powerful. I felt the thrill of being able to escape the city, to see places only reached by automobile. I thought about skipping my interview with Matt Monahan and just driving on to the Canadian border and beyond, and then I thought about the twenty dollar bill that had to carry me until payday. That, and the half-tank Ed had given me, would probably get me near the California-Oregon border. After that, I'd have to call Ed for a tow.

"Nope," I thought. "Do the interview and get this heap back to the garage without a scratch and you will be one step closer to saving your sorry ass."

I turned the radio on and found my favorite news station. The world still wasn't falling apart. I heard about traffic jams around the Bay Area. Fortunately, Highway 101 in Marin County was reportedly trouble-free this morning. I was going away from rush hour traffic. Life was quiet and I felt powerful. I thought about Hardy, T.R. and Paranoid. I laughed out loud at the incongruity of our four beings. If I was writing a script for the most outlandish soap opera on television, I couldn't have come up with a stranger mix of personalities. But, I wasn't writing a soap opera. This was real life, and these were real people, and I was one of them. The experiences of the last few days had given me a glimpse of myself as the world viewed me. I was a cynical recluse who might have fit nicely into one of Charles Dickens' plots. I thought about my childhood dreams. I always fantasized about saving the world through my writing. I was sure my life would be filled with beautiful women and grateful men. The reality of what I had become would have scared me in my childhood years. I had become my own worst nightmare.

In a little under an hour, I was pulling into a small dirt road north of Muir Woods. I watched carefully for the mail box that had been described in detail for me. I found the green box with the right number and turned into the driveway it marked. The house was set far back from the road. It was a simple old house, very small and very plain—quite a contrast to Elizabeth Grayson's house. Matt Monahan had given me clear directions on where to park the car. I pulled in next to a small foreign compact car. The light blue paint was dull and quite thin on the top of the hood, the fenders, and the roof. A picture of the man I would soon meet was taking shape in my mind. My imaginary Matt Monahan looked very much like my own father. It struck me that my father and Elizabeth Grayson's first husband drove remarkably similar cars. I hadn't been in contact with my own father for several years. Still, it wasn't difficult for me to believe that my own father's car probably looked much like the car next to the Mercedes. I realized that I was starting to stereotype Matt Monahan. This could be a dangerous practice to a journalist, and I tried to shake my most recent thoughts out of my mind.

"Stop judging," I told myself. "Wait and see before you brand this person in any way."

I noticed a curtain move in the front window as I walked toward the porch. Another car pulled in and parked on the other side of the Mercedes. A man about my own age got out of the car and followed me toward the porch.

"Mr. Howard?"

"Yes."

"Bud Monahan."

"Oh, yes."

"I hope this is all right. My father told me you were coming out. I think we all want to make sure you get a clear picture of what our mother did to us. When we talked earlier, I wasn't sure if I wanted to be part of this article you're doing. But then between talking with Stacy and Jeff and then Dad, I decided it would be best to at least try to help you understand things from my perspective, too."

I nodded and reached for the doorbell. The door opened before I could push it.

"Good morning, Mr. Howard."

"Mr. Monahan. Good to meet you."

Chapter 14

Matthew Monahan looked amazingly like my own father. The facial features were different, but the carriage of his body, the slippers, and the worn cardigan were my father all over. I felt a shiver run through me. Bud Monahan brushed his hand across his father's shoulder. In my father's house, that was the equivalent of a hug. I wondered if it was the same in this house.

"Let's go in the kitchen. I've got some tea water going. Would you like some tea, Mr. Howard?"

"That would be fine," I lied. I wanted a good stiff drink, because creepy feelings were cropping up all over the place. I felt confusion and familiarity all at once. I didn't know then that I was feeling these things, but I was able to analyze my feelings in the Mercedes on my way back to the city. I seated myself at Matthew Monahan's kitchen table. I pulled my tape recorder and note pads out as tea was poured into three cups.

"Mr. Monahan, there may be some questions you wouldn't wish to answer in front of one of your children."

"Nonsense. My children have understood their mother since they were very young. Bud is certainly mature enough to handle anything I might say at this point in time. He's probably going to read the article at least once."

Bud chuckled and gave his father a knowing nod.

I shrugged my shoulders and decided to proceed with questions that were direct and, I hoped, revealing.

"I'd like to begin with your courtship and early marriage."

"Fine."

"It's my understanding that you were both deeply involved in your churches and that you both agreed to go to pre-marital counseling in your church. Is that correct?"

"It is."

"And in at least one of those counseling sessions you stated that it wouldn't matter if and when Elizabeth got pregnant, that the timing of your children's conceptions was up to God?"

"I may have said something like that, but I didn't expect her to get pregnant right away."

"When Elizabeth came home from the doctor's a few months after you were married, did you become extremely angry because she was pregnant?"

"Let me tell you something, Mr. Howard. That happened, but it was more than forty-five years ago. Elizabeth got her little feelings hurt and has never been able to get over it. Don't you think it's time to let go of that and grow up?"

"Did you apologize to her for having said one thing before you were married and then doing something exactly opposite after you were married?"

There was no answer. Both men looked at me as though I was insane.

"I never owed Elizabeth an apology, Mr. Howard. She owed much more than that to me and I never got it."

"How is that, Mr. Monahan?"

"I believed that Elizabeth and I shared the same religious principles and values. This sharing was extremely important to me. I could overlook the fact that Elizabeth's religion wasn't quite as enlightened as mine. I felt real love for Elizabeth when she agreed to marry in my church and to raise our children in that religion."

Matthew Monahan had my attention totally. I wondered where he was going and what EG had done that she never apologized for. Bud Monahan was totally focused on his father and the story he was telling. I made a mental note to write about the devotion the younger man apparently felt for the older man.

"Shortly after we were married, Mr. Howard, Elizabeth confessed something to me that destroyed my feelings for her. I was totally conflicted because I had taken vows to her and would have to live with her sin for the rest of my life. At least that's what I believed at that time."

I nodded and resisted the temptation to ask him to hurry up and get to the point.

"Elizabeth told me that she had permitted a young man that she was enthralled with to touch her breast. She had been improperly touched by a man before she married. She let it happen and then had the gall to tell me about it."

160

Chapter 14

"And you felt that by not telling you about it before your marriage, she betrayed you?" I was dumbfounded by the man's sincerity and conviction about the rightness of his attitude.

"I'm sure you're 'modern' in your thinking, Mr. Howard. Today young people sleep with whomever they wish and their future partners have to accept their youthful promiscuity. But I assure you, Mr. Howard, Elizabeth stated she was a virgin to me and to our minister. Getting upset because I didn't stick to something I said in the pre-marital counseling sessions is truly the pot calling the kettle black."

"Let me get this straight. Because Elizabeth confessed that a man she had dated had touched her breast, you feel she totally betrayed your trust. Is that correct?"

"Think about it, Mr. Howard. I believed we shared the same values, and within weeks after our marriage she told me that we didn't share the same values about the sacredness of marriage and sex. She was flawed, deeply flawed in this regard. I married a woman who was not pure and she lied to me about that."

"Couldn't you have gotten your marriage annulled, Mr. Monahan? That would seem to have been a wise move on your part since you felt the marriage bond had been broken by a lie." I was shocked at the wisdom of this question and actually wondered where it came from.

"Unfortunately, I was very young and naive. I thought that once you exchanged vows with someone in the church, only death could part you. Twenty-five years later, Elizabeth disproved this belief for me. She filed for divorce. I filed for annulment and got one. I don't spend a lot of time thinking about what might have been. What is, is."

I looked at Bud Monahan. "Do you have any feelings about what you're hearing?" I asked.

"As a matter of fact, I do. I never knew until this moment exactly why my father didn't love my mother. It all makes sense now. I always knew he didn't love her. I'm not sure I agree that having been touched on the breast by a man is a good reason for trashing a woman, but I understand my father and know what a disappointment that must have been to him. As you're probably beginning to figure out, my mother can be quite stupid and hurtful. Why would anyone hurt my father by telling him such a hurtful truth?"

Bud heaved the last words toward me and I smelled stale alcohol on his breath. His hair was oily and unwashed. His eyes were tired and lonely. He was wearing a plaid flannel shirt just like his father's.

"Elizabeth has never apologized for marrying me with that sin on her soul, Mr. Howard."

"Have you told her what the real core of the problem was for you, Mr. Monahan? I've interviewed Mrs. Grayson and I honestly don't believe she's aware of your feelings in this regard."

"Why would I speak to her of this ever? There was nothing she could do to change the facts. She was tainted. I had never touched any other woman and never would have. Marriage is sacred. You young people think so little of sex and sexuality, but I was raised to be sexual only with my wife and never with anyone else. I thought Elizabeth believed that, too."

I looked at the man who was speaking so directly, so unabashedly about the ultimate betrayal of his life. He truly felt that his wife was unworthy of a marriage with him because she had allowed a man to touch her breast in the heat of youthful passion. A man she had met before she had met and married him. I began to write notes. I wanted to observe my surroundings and look more closely at the subject of my interview.

"Did you remarry?"

"Yes. I did. I'm married to a wonderful woman. She's not of my faith but she's respectful of all that I believe. She's visiting some friends in New York right now. I'm sorry you won't get to meet her."

Matt Monahan was probably close to six feet tall. He was extremely thin and looked much taller. He never quite looked me in the eye. As I made more notes, he walked over to the stove and turned the burner on under the tea kettle. He started a conversation with his son about his wife's trip and expected return. Bud stood and moved nearer to his father. He was a slightly shorter version of Matt Monahan. They seemed comfortable with each other.

I cleared my throat and both turned to look at me. "Could I ask some questions of you, Bud?"

"Yes." The younger Monahan sat down across from me. When I looked directly into his eyes, a tactic I had learned early in my journalism career, he shifted his eyes away exactly as his father had done."

"Do you think the problems between your parents have caused you any difficulties in your adult life?"

"None of us believe that Dad caused our adult problems, Mr. Howard. I've been married three times and lived with three other women. None of my relationships have ever worked out and we all know why."

"I'm sorry to hear that. Do you believe your parents' divorce set you up for broken relationships?"

"I believe my mother set me up for failed relationships."

"I asked your brother and sister this question and I need to ask it of you. Do you recall your father telling you when you were little that if you had problems when you grew up it would be your mother's fault because she was the active one, she was the doer?"

"I don't know if it was put exactly that way, but I've always known that. And yes, I probably heard that from my father. I know I told my brother and sister the same thing. You have to understand, Mr. Howard, my mother began to drink when I was ten years old. Before that she would go ballistic every few weeks."

"Did she go ballistic at you?"

"I know she yelled at my father a lot. And we were all afraid of her."

"Actually, I tried to protect my children from her anger." Matthew Monahan had reseated himself at the table. He pushed a fresh cup of tea toward me.

"Every Saturday she taught catechism at our church to children who couldn't go to the church school. All of us scrambled to get her house cleaned so that she wouldn't kill us when she got home."

I suddenly flashed back to Saturdays in my childhood home. My mother worked on Saturdays to help supplement my father's income. My father told me and my siblings that we'd better get everything spotless or our mother would kill us when she got home.

"I hated her and her cleaning. The house was more important than any of us." Bud Monahan's face twisted as he spoke of his mother. And you know, every damn woman I've ever met seems to be just like her. They always have these lists of things they want you to do. I've just decided there aren't any women on earth who can just let you be who you are. They've always got to get you organized or worse—enslaved."

Suddenly another wise question occurred to me, and again I wondered where it came from.

"Mr. Monahan, did you ever use the threat of Elizabeth's anger to get things done that you wanted done?"

"What do you mean by that?"

"I just wondered if you ever used the fear your children developed toward their mother to get things done that you wanted done?"

Matt Monahan stood and leaned over the table. He actually appeared menacing.

For some reason he didn't frighten me. "I've known people who used the threat of another to get things they wanted. Did you do that to your children?"

"I don't know what tree your barking up, Mr. Howard, but I don't like your tone. I loved my children. I was saddled with a very difficult woman—a woman who had lied to me, to our minister and to God."

I realized that two of the Monahan children were males and this was their role model. Could it be that they hated their mother in the same way he did? Did his daughter hate her mother in the same way the males in her family did because she didn't want to be closed off from their friendship? I made a note to check with Margarita Sanchez-Lopez to see if there was any research available that might give me the answer to this question.

I drank my tea and asked permission to call them if I had further questions. They told me I could. I turned off the tape recorder and packed my briefcase. I thanked both of them, shook their hands and went out to the Mercedes. Then I remembered something very important and went back to the house. I rang the bell. Both Matt and Bud Monahan answered the door.

"I thought of something else I need to ask. All of your children have been divorced or have lived with people outside of marriage, Mr. Monahan. Do you hate them as you hated their mother because she allowed a man to whom she wasn't married to touch her breast?"

"No, Mr. Howard. I pray for salvation for my children. Their mother set them on this path. It isn't their fault. They really didn't have a chance, did they?"

I shook my head and nodded and turned toward the Mercedes. I had just had one of the most interesting and disturbing interviews of my professional life. In time, I would understand that I had just had a moment of clarity in my personal life.

The joy of driving the Mercedes was gone. I returned to the city feeling awful. I returned the car to the garage and the keys to Ed Wainwright. He asked how the interview went and I told him it went well as far as I could tell. And then I went home and threw up.

CHAPTER 15

My stomach settled down, but a feeling of anxiety surrounded me. I sat at my kitchen table and gave serious thought to going down to the little grocery and picking up a bottle. I even thought about picking up some orange juice so I'd be drinking something healthy. And then I thought about having only twenty dollars in my pocket. If I didn't finish the article, that would be all the money I would have for a very long time. I dismissed the idea of going to the grocery and decided to call Elizabeth Grayson instead.

I punched the number in and listened to the phone ring. Denise Kinzler answered. "Graysons. This is Denise Kinzler. May I help you?"

"Yes, you may," I said. "This is Evan Howard. I've just completed interviews with Matthew Monahan and all of his children. I have some questions based on those interviews that I need to pose to Mrs. Grayson. As you know, I'm on a deadline. Would it be possible for her to see me either later today or early tomorrow?"

"Hold on. I'll ask her."

I took a deep breath and realized that I felt cheered by the voice of Denise Kinzler. I pictured the face that went with the friendly voice. She was way out of my league, but I felt myself warm to the idea of getting to know her. And then I stopped that thought. "She'd never give you a second look, Howard. You're a jerk who lives in a roach-infested one-bedroom apartment. She's so out of your league that you've got to be crazy for imagining she'd ever give you a first look much less a second one."

"Evan?"

"Yes?"

"Is there any chance you could come out later this afternoon? Elizabeth is seeing some clients until about three. She could meet with you at about three-thirty."

"That would work very well. Would you be able to pick me up at the BART station?"

"I'll plan on it. I'll be there at 3:15. If you get there earlier, go to the place where I picked you up the last time."

I thanked her and hung up. Regardless of how hopeless dreams of Denise Kinzler might be, her voice and cooperative spirit were medicinal to me. I looked forward to seeing her. My wish to socialize with Denise made me acutely aware of the reality of my negative bank balance. This prompted me to think that I might be able to save a couple of bucks if I could connect with Margarita Sanchez-Lopez while in the East Bay later in the day. I dialed her number. She answered.

"Hello."

"Margarita, this is Evan Howard. I've interviewed Matthew Monahan and all three of Elizabeth Grayson's children. I need to talk with you about possible research in certain areas, and I also have more questions I need to put to you about the family as you saw it when Elizabeth first came into treatment. I have an appointment with Mrs. Grayson at 3:30 this afternoon and wondered if you might be able to meet with me this evening."

"I think I can manage that. I'll be through about five or five-thirty. What say I pick you up at Elizabeth's and we grab a bite to eat somewhere in Walnut Creek? You can quiz me there or quiz me back at my place. I have to pick my grandson up about eight o'clock from a class at the community college. I can drop him back at my place and then take you to BART to catch a late train to the city, or you can stay at my place and go back in the morning. It's up to you."

"I'm not sure how I'll feel this evening. It's been a grueling day. If it's all right with you, I'd appreciate it if you would just come by Mrs. Grayson's, if that's all right."

"That's all right, Evan. Don't worry about what you'll be doing this evening. We'll play it by ear."

With that she hung up. I gathered everything needed for the follow up interviews, stuffed them in my battle-worn briefcase, and then grabbed my copy of EG's book. I headed for the BART station on Market Street. The depressed feeling that came with me from Marin County was lifting as I headed to the East Bay. I wondered if I was being hormonal—depressed in male company, elated in female company, especially female company named Denise Kinzel. The ride to Walnut Creek was pleasant. I read some and studied people some. After arriving I went to the bench to wait for my ride. I made notes of the questions I needed to ask EG and Margarita. The sun warmed me. I felt a warmth that was more than just rising body temperature from being in the sun. I remembered the feeling of caring and security that visited me for twenty-four hours in the Grayson home. I searched my thinking and feelings to see if I was playing mind games with myself. I felt pretty sure my thinking and feelings were genuine. I had indeed, been in a very safe, very caring place for twenty-four hours. I felt a lump catch in my throat. Had I ever experienced this feeling before? There wasn't time to answer the question. Denise Kinzler pulled up in the convertible and looked absolutely stunning. Now my hormones really kicked into overdrive and I had no doubt as to what I was feeling. I just hoped there weren't any visible external signs. I used the old briefcase to cover myself just in case.

"Hi, Evan. How are you doing?"

"Fine."

"Just fine?"

"What do you mean, just fine?"

Her question seemed intrusive. My physical elation at seeing her evaporated.

Chapter 15

"In 12-Step Recovery, when someone new to the program says they're fine, we know it really means they're Fucked up, Insecure, Neurotic, and Egocentric. Is that what you are?"

"I'd have to say that is a very accurate description of me. Especially after my interviews with Matt Monahan and EG's three children," I said. "I want you to know I don't appreciate being analyzed through the use of some cutesy 12-Step slogan. I feel I'm a fairly complex human being who can't be reduced to a sentence or two."

"Good. You're making progress already. We know good things are beginning to take hold when someone can admit they're not totally perfect and together. And," she looked me in the eye, "the defensiveness leaves after a while. As you begin to love yourself, you don't take every little statement so personally."

As beautiful as she was, she was really pissing me off. I said nothing more. It was actually a relief to feel dislike for Denise Kinzler and I accepted it as I always accepted negativity. I once again felt normal.

We arrived at the house and pulled into the circular driveway. This time I took a good look at what could be seen of the outside of the house. It was painted soft beige with white trim. It was a very large house but not garish. I had always dreamed of having a house like this one. We walked in through the garage. This time I knew exactly where I was going. Denise left me in the hall. I visited the bathroom and got settled in the family room just as I had done during my first visit. EG came in a few minutes later. I stood and she walked toward me with open arms and hugged me. I returned her hug and was thrown off guard by the spontaneity of our greeting.

"Would you like something to drink?"

"Soda would be fine."

She went to the kitchen and returned with two cans of soda and two glasses with ice. I took my can and glass from the tray while she took care of her drink. I set the glass on the table next to the piece of colored glass that had fascinated me a week earlier. A pain shot through my chest as the light from the window behind me danced through the piece of glass and into my eye.

"Is something wrong, Mr. Howard? You don't look so good."

I turned away from the piece and collected my thoughts.

"I interviewed your daughter and younger son yesterday afternoon. I interviewed your ex-husband and older son this morning. I need to ask you some follow-up questions."

EG nodded.

"I don't exactly know how to phrase this…"

"Mr. Howard, I don't think there's anything you can tell me that will shock or hurt me more than what's already happened with my first-marriage family."

"Okay. When I started to ask Mr. Monahan about the hurt that came out of his raging at you when you told him you were pregnant with Bud, he said that you had wounded him far more seriously prior to that and have never apologized for wounding him so."

EG looked at me curiously. "What? What in heaven's name was he talking about? I take back what I just told you."

"He told me that only days, or perhaps a week, after your marriage you confessed that you had allowed a man to touch your breast in the heat of passion."

I could see EG searching her memory.

"I remember telling him that I didn't want to have any secrets between us. I was terribly naïve, Mr. Howard. I wanted ours to be the perfect marriage and I thought that meant being up front with my husband about everything."

"Mrs. Grayson, as far as Matt Monahan was concerned, the rest of your marriage was a farce because you had sinned before marriage and had not been honest with him or the minister before you married."

"The minister asked us if we were virgins, Mr. Howard. I believed I was. I don't think I even gave the little bit of petting I did with my first love a thought. I certainly didn't think I was lying. My God, Mr. Howard, I told both Matt and the minister that I had been incested by my father. Is that what he's held against me all these years? I remember telling him about being touched on the breast and I remember what he told me in return."

"What?" I checked to make sure the tape recorder was running and noted the number on the counter so that I could quickly refer back to this part of the interview.

"Matt knew that I had been molested by my father. When I told him that a boyfriend had touched me, he said that considering my background, he was surprised that my history with men wasn't worse. Now that I think back on that conversation, that was a very judgmental thing to say, wasn't it? He believed I was a fallen woman, didn't he?"

"He told me that you had betrayed him, your minister, and your children, and even more importantly, God."

"Everything makes sense, Mr. Howard. I'm understanding what never made sense to me before." With that EG broke down. She reached for the tissue box on the table. She held a tissue before her eyes. I could see her shoulders shake. I knew she was in pain. I was paralyzed. I wanted to help her but I couldn't move out of my seat. Tears welled up in my eyes. No matter how I felt about my own mother, I understood how hopeless Elizabeth Grayson's situation with her first husband was. Once she admitted her "sin," she was forever cast into hell in her husband's mind. He would never let her out and he would teach her children to keep her there also.

We sat in silence for a full ten minutes. Finally EG caught her breath.

"If it hadn't been for the children going on national TV to air their hatred of me, I would never have known, much less understood, what really went wrong in that family. As painful as this is, Mr. Howard, I see your work as a gift. I know that I'll work through this pain. I have my husband, my friends, and my support groups to get me through this. I don't know if my children or Matt have anyone outside of themselves to help them deal with the disappointment I've been to all of them."

"I don't understand, Mrs. Grayson. Don't you see how ludicrous this all is? For God's sake, to trash someone because of a minor youthful indiscretion is absurd."

I realized I was yelling when EG's head went back and she rose out of the chair to get farther away from me.

"I'm sorry. But the whole thing is absolutely absurd."

"No, Mr. Howard, it is not. My first husband has a set of values that are hard to live up to for most of us, but they are his values and he's entitled to them just as you are entitled to your values and I am to mine. Before I got into 12-Step recovery I would have been right over there with you, feeling self-righteous and superior to what I would have called Matt's 13th Century morality. I would have been in the camp of all that is really wrong with the world. I've learned to live and let live. If I allow others to have their value systems, then I have a right to my own value system."

I didn't understand a word she was saying to me, but I made note of it on the counter because I knew I would have to decipher the message somehow for the article. And then I remembered another point Matt Monahan had made.

"Mrs. Grayson, Mr. Monahan told me that he's able to forgive all his children's sexual sins because they come from you and didn't have a chance of being pure sexually. How do you respond to that?"

"Again, thank you, Mr. Howard. I used to wonder why my children could live with whomever they wished without the benefit of marriage and still be wholly accepted by their father. You just helped me understand why Matt can accept anything they do that he ordinarily considers immoral. Of course he can accept the sins of his children because he doesn't believe they had any other choice coming from their sinful mother. It all makes sense to me now." Again the tears flowed.

I couldn't take another minute of this interview. I excused myself and went to the bathroom. When I came out, EG was staring at the glass piece on the table.

"I think I can finish the article from your perspective, Mrs. Grayson. Margarita Sanchez-Lopez is going to pick me up here at about 5:30. In the meantime I'd like to sit in the garden and work on my notes and listen again to the tapes with your children and ex-husband, and this tape with you."

"Whatever you need to do, Mr. Howard. I'll be in my office working. Please feel free to come back if you need anything."

I worked diligently to sketch out this part of the article from the tapes. I was able to sit at a shaded table. A gentle breeze blew past me. I looked up and saw the western face of Mount Diablo. My family used to picnic on this side of the mountain. The last thing I wanted to do was think of my family. I was so tired of family. EG's family. My family. Any family. I was so tired of family crap. I couldn't believe that a man would trash any woman for the reason Matt Monahan had.

My generation was so loose sexually that EG's description of 13th Century morality fit Matthew Monahan's moral code, at least in my mind it did. I felt anger toward EG's ex-husband. I wrote "I hate self-righteous, judgmental bastards."

I figured it was getting close to 5:30. I packed up the old briefcase and went back into the house. I wandered down the hall that Denise Kinzler always took to go to her office. I passed a lovely living and dining room that looked out onto the pool. The ceilings soared and then fell to tall sliding glass doors that spread beautifully across the entire outside wall. The glass doors were folded back into storage areas in the walls. The house seemed to be wide open. The same breeze that cooled me on the patio outside the family room, flowed into these rooms. I walked past the front entry hall and into the hall that lead to the offices. I peaked in the first door. It was a small office, bright and cheery. It too opened onto the pool deck. The room was dark except for the light that came from the outer wall.

I moved to the next door in the hallway. This room was somewhat larger than the first office. The furnishings were light and cheerful, just as they were in the first office. EG was sitting at the desk. When she looked up I could see she had been crying.

"I am so sorry to have brought you this pain, Mrs. Grayson."

"You didn't bring me this pain, Mr. Howard. I brought this on myself. Me and my damned big mouth."

173

"Excuse me?"

"When I look back on things I did in that marriage, Mr. Howard, I have to wonder how intelligent and sane I was. I didn't have to reveal to Matthew that someone touched my breast before I ever met him. What was I thinking? I was so terribly naive. I am more angry at myself than I've ever been because I opened my big mouth unnecessarily then, and kept it shut when Matthew was telling the children that if they had problems when they got older, it would be my fault because I was the active one, I was the doer. I helped him hate me and I helped him teach the children to hate me. I'm paying the ultimate price for my own big-mouthed stupidity."

I was dumbfounded by her ability to assess her own behaviors so negatively. I wanted her to stop letting her ex-husband off the hook.

"Mrs. Grayson, your husband is the bad guy. Why are you excusing him?" My voice was getting louder again and I could see her moving back again. "I'm sorry. I just can't stand here and let you take all the blame for everything that went wrong in that marriage. Your ex-husband was a self-righteous son-of-a-bitch who put his so-called moral standards ahead of any human consideration. He didn't care about you and he didn't care about his children. He destroyed the most important thing in their lives and that's their relationship with their mother."

"Matthew Monahan was responsible for fifty percent of the destruction of that marriage and that household, Mr. Howard. I was responsible for the other fifty percent. My children are adults. They're now responsible for any relationships they might have with their mother. I have said I am available for a relationship and will apologize for my fifty percent of the harm done them. They have said that's not good enough. The truth is, Mr. Howard, they're not in enough pain or haven't been pushed to think about the truth of their parents' marriage. They may never be."

EG looked past me and nodded. I turned and saw Margarita behind me.

"I let myself in. Goodness! What's this all about?"

Margarita walked by me. EG came from behind the desk and the women hugged.

"You don't look so good, Elizabeth. What's going on?"

"Mr. Howard will explain. I don't want to go through the news he brought me again. But I do want to tell you something more, Mr. Howard. If it wasn't for my first-marriage family, I wouldn't be doing the work I'm doing today. I've been able to help many families who suffer from the same problems I experienced in my first-marriage family. The pain of loving and losing my children propelled me into the work I'm doing today. Please don't forget that when you write your article."

The women hugged again.

"Elizabeth, call me if you need anything. You know I'm available at any time."

"I just may take you up on that, Margarita."

"We're going to dinner. If you need to talk, leave word on my answering machine and I'll get right back to you."

"Have a good dinner. I'll be all right. I just have to work through another layer of understanding of my own stupidity. Please—don't let this bring you down, Mr. Howard. And be careful how you word this part of the article. My children aren't crazy. They just had parents who were a disastrous combination."

Elizabeth Grayson saw us to the door. I waved to her as Margarita pulled away from the house. She waved back. My heart hurt for her.

CHAPTER 16

Margarita asked if I liked Mexican food. I said I did, and she drove to a lovely place on Main Street in Walnut Creek.

"If you want to go back to the city, we're very close to the BART station, Evan. I'd really like to urge you to stay the night. I have three bedrooms. My grandson is in the second bedroom and you can have the third. There's so much I want to talk to you about for this article."

I nodded and said I'd think about her offer. We were quickly seated near the fireplace. The hostess asked if we would like a cocktail before dinner. Margarita said she'd like a diet soda. I resisted the urge to order a margarita and asked for water with ice and lemon.

"This is a first," I said. "It's my firm belief that when you're at a Mexican restaurant you have a Mexican drink."

"I used to live my life that way, too. And I'm Mexican-American." Margarita looked at me in the most direct, straightforward way. "After I made a fool of myself dancing on the tables of almost all the Mexican restaurants in the Bay Area, I finally realized that drinking like a Mexican brought out the worst in me. My drink of choice was the margarita ... naturally. It's made with grapefruit juice so I thought I was being extremely health conscious in my drinking."

I chuckled. She was so lively and animated that she seemed like a tonic to me.

"Let's order and then you can tell me about your interview with Matthew Monahan."

The waiter came and took our order and I settled back into the leather of my chair. It squeaked with that wonderful squeak that comes with strong, sturdy leather. I loved the smell of the leather mixed with the smoke from the fire. I felt safe and was almost moved to tears.

"So—what's the big bombshell that came out of your meeting with Mr. Monahan?"

I retold the story, being careful not to embellish it with my own anger and upset. When I was through, Margarita sat in silence. I waited for a reaction from her. I could see her working through the new information.

"Wow! "

"That's it? Wow? I used to think I knew what a 'pregnant' pause was, but you 12-Step people have mastered pregnant pauses to the nth degree. What is it with you people? Can't you just allow yourself to let go with some normal human reaction?"

"No, Evan, we can't. That's how addicts live their lives all the time. Knee-jerk reactions are the primary symptom of jerks."

"Can I quote you on that?"

"You can. "

"So what do you think?"

"I think we all have a new and deeper understanding of what really happened in Elizabeth's first marriage."

"I've got a million questions about this, Margarita. Elizabeth says it was her big mouth and openness that destroyed that marriage. I say it's Matthew Monahan's small mindedness and intolerance that destroyed it."

"You're both right."

"Goddammit! Who in his right mind would trash an entire marriage because his wife was touched on the breast by someone long before he ever met her?"

"Matthew Monahan would and did. He feels she wasn't truly a virgin before she married him. Worse, he believes she lied to him and their minister about it. You may see Mr. Monahan's attitude and behaviors as small minded and intolerant, but he and millions of other people believe he has a very strong case against his ex-wife. This really is a large piece of what has been a very confusing puzzle up until now, Evan."

"You and Mrs. Grayson say you understand everything so much better now, but I have to tell you, I'm more confused than ever. I have to write a magazine article in less than a week and I'll never be able to include the whole story. It will take a book to explain all of this to reasonable people." It was dawning on me that my work on this article would be much more complex than I originally thought.

"Let me simplify things a little for you. Take or leave any advice I give you, Evan, but don't go into detail in the article about what the 'sin' was. Save that for the book. Just tell your readers that there was a major difference in the value systems of Matthew and Elizabeth and that neither of them understood the difference existed in the other."

Margarita's suggestion did simplify things.

"That's a very good idea," I said. "But I want everyone to understand how unfair this whole thing has been to Mrs. Grayson. Why did Matthew Monahan go ahead with the marriage when he knew that Mrs. G. had been molested by her father?"

"You know, Evan, everyone calls her Elizabeth. I notice she calls you Mr. Howard and you always refer to her as Mrs. Grayson. Why's that?"

"I can't speak for her, but I wouldn't feel right calling her by her first name."

"Hmmm. That's interesting."

"Are you analyzing me?"

"Of course."

"Stop it, please. My mother analyzed everyone and I hated it."

"Tough. I'm a therapist. I like you and plan to get to know you better and I'll probably analyze you for some time to come. But to speak to your question about Elizabeth's father having molested her—I suspect that a minister or some other important person told Matt Monahan that Elizabeth had no part in that sin because she was just a young child. I'm just guessing, but I think it's a pretty good guess."

I shrugged my shoulders and began accepting the reality of Matthew Monahan's value system.

"I need to ask you if there's any research about families like Elizabeth's. Everyone in the family admits that Matt Monahan told the children that their problems in adult life would be caused by their mother. For some reason that seems wrong to me, but both Matthew Monahan and the children look at me like I'm crazy for questioning this issue."

"We've known about parental alienation in the divorce process but I don't think much attention has been paid to it when it begins as soon as a child is born and goes on unabated. Elizabeth was made the family scapegoat. It's probably the most common dynamic in dysfunctional families. There are hundreds of books on the subject of scapegoating. If you want to go back to my place afterward, I'll loan you one of the best books on the subject ever written."

"That would take care of deciding whether to go back to the city tonight or in the morning," I said.

Margarita had ordered *nachos grande* for an appetizer. She suggested that I not eat the chips and salsa but wait for the nachos instead. I obeyed.

When the nachos came we both dug in. They were superb. I could have made dinner out of the nachos. The meats and cheeses blended perfectly with fresh salsa and sour cream on hot crisp corn chips. I couldn't get enough. I considered myself a connoisseur of spicy foods, especially spicy Mexican foods. I had never had anything that pleased my taste buds more. Margarita ate her fair share, but for the most part, she watched me enjoy mouthful after mouthful. I looked up at her as I worked on a particularly large chip piled high with the other ingredients.

"You like that, huh?"

"Uh-huh," I grunted as I reached for my next portion.

"You'll like dinner equally well."

Finally, I satisfied enough of my appetite to take a breath and involve myself in conversation with my dinner companion. Suddenly I experienced another feeling of panic. I realized I was eating like a pig with almost no money in my wallet.

"I can't pay for this, Margarita. I'm flat broke. I've about enough for carfare back into the city."

"It's my treat. I never intended for you to pay for dinner tonight. I'm happy that someone is working on getting the truth about Elizabeth's family out to the world. When you write the book, you can take me out to dinner. How will that be?"

"*If* I write the book. I'm supposed to be objective, Margarita, but I'm struggling with an urge to belt Matt Monahan and his offspring. I do not understand how Mrs. Grayson can say and feel the things she does. I'll concede that I can accept her husband hating her, but what's the matter with her kids?"

"Haven't you ever felt hatred against one of your parents, Evan? When we start to hate someone in our early years, and we feel that hatred with one hundred percent pure emotion, it can stay with us for a lifetime and never change. We think that the person is hateful and the only thing that will change our belief is an emotional atomic bomb. Elizabeth's children haven't been hit with an emotional atomic bomb. Their father bails them out of every problem they've ever had, and when he does, he gives them the same message he always has: 'If it wasn't for your mother, you wouldn't have gotten into this trouble.' As long as they can blame Elizabeth for all their problems, they will never have to look to themselves as the true source of their difficulties."

Dinner arrived. I asked for a diet soda and that was quickly delivered. The meal was just as Margarita promised—absolutely delicious. She explained to me how food tastes so much better after one gets free of alcohol and drugs.

"Alcohol is a drug and drugs dull all the senses, Evan. Body, mind, and spirit senses."

"I met a guy named Paranoid Johnson at one of the 12-Step meetings people have been dragging me to. He told me I've never had sex if I never had sex sober. Is that the same thing?"

"Same thing," Margarita said as she filled her mouth with food. We talked little until our meal was finished. We both cleaned our plates.

"Want dessert?"

"I couldn't eat another bite," I replied.

"Coffee?"

"No thanks."

Margarita asked for the bill. When it was paid, she handed me some mints that came with her receipt on the little tray. I popped them in my mouth. I wondered how much weight I would gain in a year if I ate like I'd been eating over the past week. It occurred to me that I really didn't care if I gained weight. I wanted the feeling of being fed and cared for to go on forever. I had to admit that meals with 12-Step people were awesome.

Margarita dropped her billfold into her purse, searched for and found her keys. She pushed back from the table and I followed suit. I walked behind her to the parking lot. Unthinkingly, I opened her door for her. She thanked me and smiled. She slid into the driver's seat and I closed the door. I got into the passenger seat and laid my head back on the headrest.

"Thank you for that meal. I have to remember this restaurant. The food was delicious. I don't know if I can stay awake long enough to get all the information I need from you to finish the article."

"You're welcome to stay the night. We can go over any questions you have in the morning. I'll get out the reference books on dysfunctional families and scapegoats tonight. Tell you what—I'll pull them out the minute we get to my place. You can get to sleep early. If you wake up early you can begin to study the books where I mark them. I'll be up about seven. We'll have a couple of hours to talk before I take you back to BART and I go on to my office. How's that sound?"

"Sounds great. I promised someone I would call this evening and let him know how things are going. May I use your phone?"

"As long as you're not calling outside the U.S."

"He's in the city."

"That's fine."

We pulled into a parking space behind a row of townhouses. I followed Margarita into the back door of her townhouse. She turned on the lights and I moved into a lovely garden room. It was filled with beautiful plants that showed tender and loving care. The room was filled with rattan furniture. Windows surrounded the room on three sides. Wide French doors opened into the kitchen. Margarita explained that she had it designed to suit her height and her style of cooking. The cabinets were white. Beautiful pieces of pottery were placed to show them in their best light. I could see that Margarita was proud of the place she had put together for herself. I thought about my apartment and wondered if I might live in a beautiful home twenty years down the road if I really stopped drinking.

Margarita showed me the rest of her home. She led me to the guest room, laid out towels, soaps, a tooth brush and toothpaste, and a razor. She handed me a pair of pajamas.

"I'm putting you to a lot of trouble."

"Not really. I have several grandchildren in their teens or twenties. They come often, and they never remember to bring everything they need. I buy bags of razors and toothbrushes at my wholesale club. And I keep plenty of toothpaste and soap on hand. I bought the pajamas as a birthday present for my ex-husband, but we split two days before his birthday. It's funny. I've never shed a tear over these pajamas. Somehow I knew they were meant for other people who would come into my life at a later date. Like you. Make yourself comfortable. I'll get those books. Need anything else?"

"Just the phone."

"There's one right there on the night stand."

I punched in Hardy's number.

"Hello."

"Hardy, it's Evan."

"Well hello there. Glad to hear from you. Where are you? I thought you'd go to the meeting with me this evening."

"I'm out in the East Bay at the home of Elizabeth Grayson's first alcoholism counselor. I'm doing more research. I've had an awful day. I interviewed Matthew Monahan and his oldest son this morning. They told me some things that put a whole new light on this article on Elizabeth Grayson."

"Good things?"

"No. Troubling things."

"Hmmm."

"Hardy…"

"Yes?"

"I need some male input. I'm all screwed up about this stuff. I think EG got shafted badly, but I'm supposed to do an even-handed article. When this thing started out I was totally on the kids' side. Now I'm in EG's corner, and I want to blast her ex-husband and her kids and she's telling me not to do that."

"Sounds like she's a fair person who loves her children."

"Goddammit. Are all you recovery people crazy? Don't you people understand when someone is doing you dirt?"

"Yes, Evan, we do. But as responsible, healthy adults we have to look at our part in setting up situations where people can do us dirt. But this isn't the time for us to be arguing. I appreciate hearing from you. I left a message on your answering machine asking if you'd meet me for the meeting tonight."

"I'm staying here overnight. Margarita—that's EG's first alcoholism counselor—is putting me up. She took me out for a Mexican dinner, and frankly, I'm so full I can hardly keep my eyes open. She's going to give me some reference books. I'm going to go to sleep and get up early to do some research in the books. She said she'd meet with me over breakfast and take me down to BART around nine."

"Would you like me to meet you at the BART station?"

"I would. I'll give you a call when I'm leaving here. And Hardy…"

"Evan…"

"I forgot my meditation book so I won't be able to do the routine this evening."

"Yes you will. Hold on."

Hardy got his meditation books and read two readings to me. One was on fear and the other was on forgiveness. When he finished reading, he told me that just about all our struggles come from fear and most of our peace and serenity come to us through forgiveness. I nodded my head and yawned.

"Get a good sleep, Evan. I'll see you in the morning."

Margarita was standing at the doorway. I turned as I hung up the phone.

"My temporary sponsor. He's six-feet-eight. Told me I have to call him every day or else. I have to call him right before we leave here tomorrow. He's going to meet me in the city and try to help me understand you crazy 12-Step people."

"Sounds like just what you need."

"You don't know what I need."

"Yes I do. And right now you need some sleep. Ordinarily I wouldn't recommend that you go to sleep right after a big meal, but you look exhausted."

"I am exhausted. I'm sick of unfairness. I'm sick of intolerant people. I'm really tired of working to get ahead and always falling behind."

"Get some sleep," Margarita said. She turned and left. I used the bathroom and turned down the spread on the bed, crawled under the covers and turned off the light. I fell asleep quickly and dreamed of *nachos grande.*

***

Margarita predicted I would awaken early and she was right. I lay in bed, and through the window on the east side of the room, watched the gentle arrival of daylight. There was no motivation to move. The room felt homey. It was tastefully decorated in a way that was neither too feminine nor too masculine. There were soft stripes on the upper walls. Enameled white wainscoting divided the upper walls from the lower walls. Below it, the walls were painted a soft, solid green. Everything in the room was pulled together. I felt the room probably reflected Margarita's state of being. As this thought occurred to me, I felt a knot form in my stomach.

Chapter 16

"For God's sake, Evan, you've been in the world of psychology too long. If you get through this article, you need to find a healthier, saner job."

That said, I rolled out of bed, went to the bathroom, brushed my teeth and crawled back into bed with the materials Margarita had given me the evening before. Hardy's admonition to begin my days with prayer kicked in and I muttered something to my Higher Power to help me do this day well and free of alcohol and drugs. That was the most I could do with prayer. I then picked up a book on family dynamics. Margarita had attached sticky-note sheets at the places she believed would be most helpful.

I began reading about scapegoats and a family dynamic called well-one/sick-one. I could see clearly how EG's family fell into both patterns. I made notes and referred back to places on my taped interviews that verified what the book was telling me. I became engrossed in this new information. It explained everything. I was beginning to understand that neither Matthew Monahan nor Elizabeth Grayson ever intended to destroy their family or their children as individuals. And yet they did. They set up a family that would either stay enmeshed and in pain forever, or it would explode if the scapegoat decided to leave. The latter is what happened when EG left. She built a new life without her ex-husband and children, but her first-marriage family was still united in the need to keep her as the family scapegoat. No matter what she did to gain mental, emotional, and spiritual health, her family needed to keep her frozen in time. In their minds and hearts, she was their worst enemy and no one could convince them otherwise.

Progress toward understanding the Monahan family and EG was dramatic. I felt empathy for everyone concerned, most of all for EG's children. I looked at the clock. More than two hours had passed. I got out of the warmth and comfort of the guest bed and into my rumpled clothes. I put everything I had been working with into my battered briefcase and headed downstairs. Margarita was sitting in the sunroom. The room was lit naturally through the windows on the east. She didn't look up when I entered the room. I could see she was reading some meditation books. I stood silently while she finished her readings.

"Good morning," she said as she looked up at me. "Sleep well?"

"Very well. More important, I read through most of the materials you gave me on scapegoats and well-one/sick-one. There's no question that the Monahan family is a text book case of both of those dynamics."

"I've known that for over 20 years. Glad you're reaching understanding so easily. Another thing you need to understand is that this type of dysfunction is as common as rain during the monsoon season."

"That common?"

"That common."

Margarita got up and went into the kitchen. I followed. She signaled me to sit on a stool at the bar where I could watch everything she was doing.

"Eggs, bacon, toast, and juice?" she asked.

"Great."

She went to work and carried on a conversation without missing a beat. "Any further questions?"

"Yes. Was any of the information about scapegoats and well-one/sick-one given to the Monahans?"

"I can tell you that the entire family met with me and the resident family therapist when Elizabeth was in treatment, and they were given good information on their family dysfunctions. It wasn't as technical as what you've read, but it was clear, concise, and to the point. Please note—those books I gave you are well over twenty years old. We knew it then and we told everyone involved about it. Matthew Monahan couldn't accept what we were telling him. Therefore, none of the children could accept what we were saying. How do you want your eggs?"

"Over easy. Thanks."

The breakfast was put together as if constructed by a world class short-order cook. She put both our plates on the bar, then came around and sat beside me. I poured orange juice into our glasses. Margarita picked up her glass and toasted.

"To the truth and the person who is writing it."

"May God help me," I said.

She looked at me curiously.

"I have no idea what I meant by that," I said as I broke my toast in half and began eating. "To be honest, I have no use for God and religious crap." Margarita nodded. I couldn't tell if she agreed or disagreed with me. What's more, I truly didn't care.

We ate in silence. I couldn't believe how hungry I was. Again, every bite was delicious.

"I don't understand why I'm so hungry all the time."

"You will, in time."

More silence. Finally we finished. We both had cleaned our plates.

"Did you ever hear how scapegoating came about?" Margarita asked.

"No."

"Back in ancient times, I think in Mesopotamia or Phoenicia—one of the original civilizations— the population was so small they couldn't afford to do away with too many people. So when someone committed a crime, they would be put on trial. If they were convicted of murder or some other outrageous crime, they would have to bring a goat to the justice center and the goat would be put to death. I'm not sure, but I think the goat would get tortured for lesser crimes. This was no small punishment in those days. One's wealth was highly invested in the number of animals they owned. So, the society didn't lose a pair of human hands, and the animal would be feasted upon after it was slaughtered."

"Wow. That's really interesting, but kind of sick. I think people should have to pay the consequences for their crimes," I said.

"Wow," she said back. "Isn't that a novel idea?"

I said nothing.

"Back to the Monahan family, Evan. Our society is completely saturated with a deep-seated belief in the scapegoat. Listen to the news, listen to criminals, politicians. Go to divorce courts. Everyone blames something outside of themselves for their problems. And yet, the truth is every one of us is responsible for everything that is in our lives. We may have wounds from childhood, but so does everyone else. We may be predisposed to addiction. We aren't responsible for the original wound, or being born an addict, but it's our responsibility to heal the wound and/or addiction and then stop the harmful attitudes and behaviors we developed because of the original wound or addiction. That's what 12-Step recovery and most therapies are about."

I got out my tape recorder and asked her to repeat what she had just told me. She did, and I made a note to include her words somewhere in the article or the book.

"I've got to get ready for work. Put the dirty dishes in the dishwasher, will you?"

I nodded. "Where's your grandson?"

"Asleep. Will be 'til noon, probably. He's a teenager, you know. That's a dysfunction all by itself."

She disappeared. I cleaned up the kitchen and hoped it would meet her approval. I ran some hot dishwater and wiped the counters. When I finished I went back to the garden room and played back what had just been recorded.

Margarita breezed into the room looking very professional. Dark suit, soft colored coordinated scarf and pin. Very together.

"Okay. Let's hit the trail. I'll drop you at BART and then head to my office."

"I promised to call my sponsor. He's going to meet me at the station."

"Do it."

I called Hardy and told him we were leaving. He told me not to worry. He'd have reading material with him and wouldn't mind waiting a while for my arrival. I hung up and turned around to see Margarita looking over my handiwork.

"The kitchen looks wonderful. Thank you."

I blushed. I was grateful she said nothing more. We drove in silence to BART.

"Don't hesitate to call me if you have any questions, Evan."

Chapter 16

I thanked her again and felt sadness as she pulled away. More than anyone I had met in the course of the last ten days, Margarita Sanchez-Lopez touched my heart most deeply. It wasn't the man-woman thing. I felt that with Denise Kinzler, and I knew clearly what that was. Margarita felt like a true friend, maybe like a loving older sister. She kidded me and challenged me. I thought a lot about that on the way into the city. I couldn't remember ever liking a woman who challenged me before.

Hardy was at the BART station as he promised. We went to an open discussion meeting together in the heart of the financial district. The subject of the discussion was blaming. Afterwards we went for a bite to eat. I amazed myself by eating another full meal, thanks to Hardy.

"Hardy, how do you ever pay back all the kindnesses that people in these 12-Step programs do for you?"

"A little at a time, you give to new people coming in as you've been given to. You see, Evan, people did this for me when I first came in. They don't need or want the kindness paid back to them. So when you get some time in sobriety and get back on your feet financially, you'll see yourself walk through the doors and your heart will tell you how to pay back all that was done for you. Don't worry about it. Just don't drink, get to meetings, listen to your sponsor, work the steps, and watch the miracles happen."

"To be honest, Hardy, I don't really want to work those steps. That Fourth Step terrifies me."

"It does everyone. Don't worry about that now. You've got to get your article written. When that's done, we'll dig in and get you working the steps. You'll be amazed at how good a person you really are underneath that addiction of yours."

I heard what he said and discounted it mentally. I knew there was nothing good about me and never would be. Hardy ordered another glass of soda for me and a cup of coffee for himself. When we finished, he headed for a home somewhere in the city and I returned to my apartment. I spent the rest of the day wrestling with the article. In the evening Madge and I put a dinner together between our two refrigerators, and she took me to another meeting on blame. I wondered if there was a conspiracy against me.

That's how the next couple of days went. Hardy and Madge made sure I was fed and I worked six to eight hours on the article. I certainly had the beginnings of a book. It was good to focus on the dysfunctional Monahan family. I struggled with feelings of empathy for Elizabeth Grayson because I saw so many characteristics of my own mother in her. I fought my empathy for Elizabeth and I didn't understand why. I told myself constantly that my family wasn't the Monahan family. After all, none of us stayed together. I hadn't talked to my father or my sibling in years. In my mind, we weren't like the Monahans at all.

I completed the article in the time allotted, and had it on Ed Wainright's desk at the appointed hour. Now all I could do was wait. I went home to do that. I wasn't home more than an hour when my childhood friend called to say there were only a few minor changes to be made. I got out my copy and agreed with two of the changes and argued about the third. In the end, he agreed to allow the third point to stand as I had written it. All three involved semantics.

And so it was done. I felt an enormous weight lifted from me. I was free to be me again.

CHAPTER 17

This Chapter Written By Martha Bullock
Publisher of *World of Psychology Magazine*

I write this epilogue so that you, the reader, can be fully aware of how this story actually came about and how it seems to have ended. Many people were involved in the building of this story. After Evan Howard submitted his article, a group of us met to discuss what came out of this project and to support each other because the outcome appears to be painfully far from our goal. We thought we were conspiring for good and truth. Instead, we may have nearly cost a man his life.

A little over two months ago, Elizabeth Grayson's children appeared on a national television talk show. I saw that program. Elizabeth Grayson is one of my dearest friends. Beyond being my friend, Elizabeth has done ground-breaking work in the field of emotional development in human beings. Much of what Elizabeth's children said on the talk show was not true. You see, I was in the same treatment center that Elizabeth was in more than twenty years ago. I don't rely on my memories from that time. Professionals confronted Elizabeth, her husband and children during her stay. In family group therapy, her now-ex-husband was told that he had problems as serious as Elizabeth's.

He vehemently denied that any of his family's problems could be laid at his door. I also remember the professionals telling my dear friend that things might never heal with her family—that they may never be able to let go of their scapegoat.

After the talk show, I met with my editor, Ed Wainwright. We discussed the possibility of having an article done to rebut at least some of what was said on that television program. During our meeting Ed told me his best writer was Evan Howard, but that Evan's drinking was overtaking his good sense and his writing abilities and he was about to fire him.

"Well," I said, "isn't this interesting. We, you and I, Mr. Wainwright, were very close friends of his mother, Angela Howard."

"Yes," Ed said, "but I've never mentioned that Angela and I came to know each other in our adult lives. I mean, he has always known that I knew Angela when we were kids. But he has no idea that she became one of my dearest friends in 12-Step Recovery."

You see, dear reader, Angela Howard died of cancer and her son, Evan, refused to have anything to do with her. On her death bed, Angela got me and Ed to promise we'd look after Evan and help him if we could. I owned a magazine and Ed was the editor. When Evan got fired from the Chron, Ed managed to bump into him at his favorite watering hole. It was always our hope that someday Evan would recognize his difficulties with alcohol and seek help for it. Ed offered his childhood friend a job and Evan accepted. There were reasonable stipulations, of course.

It soon became clear that Evan knew almost nothing about his mother's life after she divorced his father. He's worked at this magazine for almost five years and has said not one word to me. He believes the job came from his friend Ed. If he has any idea that his mother and I knew each other, he has never given any indication of it.

We met on the Monday morning after Evan gave the article to Ed. The meeting was in the magazine's board room. We needed to assess the results of our conspiracy. My secretary has transcribed the conversations recorded at that meeting:

Chapter 17

May 27, 2004

Meeting was called to order at 10:00 a.m. by Chairman Martha Bullock.

Mrs. Bullock: Okay. Let's summarize what's happened so far. The closest friends of Angela Howard and Elizabeth Grayson have joined an effort to get justice and understanding for both of them. Ed, what's your assessment of this project?

Ed: As you all know, I was on the brink of firing Evan Howard when Mrs. Bullock came to me and asked if we might do an article on Elizabeth because many questions were being raised by people in the mental health field regarding Elizabeth's Grayson's qualifications. Elizabeth's work was being questioned because her family was so divided. It occurred to Mrs. Bullock and me that maybe we could win two battles with one article. We decided to give Evan another chance and assign this article to him, making it very clear that he either did the article and did it right or the job was gone. That's what happened. I called Elizabeth, Madge, Hardy, and Margarita and the rest is history.

Mrs. Bullock: Not quite. How did he do?

Ed: The article is excellent. I haven't heard a word from him since we hammered out a few changes on Friday.

Madge: He's drinking. I checked with his favorite liquor store and he bought several bottles yesterday afternoon. I knocked on Evan's door. There was no answer.

Hardy: I thought we were doing some bonding. He was as hungry as anyone I've ever seen come through the doors. We ate together a lot. He said he was enjoying the freedom from hangovers. He was getting a lot of clarity in his thinking.

Elizabeth: He may have been getting too much clarity.

Margarita: I met with him last Wednesday evening and Thursday morning. He stayed over at my house. I gave him as clear a lesson on well-one/sick-one and the scapegoat syndrome as is possible. If he was connecting it to his own birth family, he didn't show it.

Denise: His hormones were coming back to life, I can tell you that. I think he would have asked for a date if he had been able to put together another week of sobriety. He was already trying to flirt.

Madge: I saw him at least once on the Friday, Saturday, and Sunday weekend before this current weekend. We had some meals together and went to meetings. The rest of the time he was either with Hardy, Margarita, or he was holed up in his room typing. He did have interviews with Matt Monahan and all the children, and he followed up with Elizabeth.

Ed: He brought the first draft in on Friday. He was right on schedule. That was a remarkably positive sign considering his work habits of the past two or three years. He faxed a copy of the article to Dr. Hudson in Los Angeles. Dr. Hudson assured Evan he'd assess the Monahan-Grayson situation and get a written answer to him by Saturday afternoon. Everything went as scheduled. That's a first for Evan in a long, long time.

Hardy: The last time I saw him he said he was exhausted. That was Friday. He said he was bringing the final product in. He said something about getting it past the "mother superior."

Ed: That's me. Anyone who feels like authority to Evan becomes "mother superior." Dr. Hudson responded, and we put his comments into the article. Evan said he'd done his job and that's the last I saw of him.

Margarita: I want to know if Evan Howard learned anything at all about his own mother and his own life over the past two weeks.

Ed: I think the best thing we could do here is take time to read the article and then try to assess whether we accomplished anything.

Tape recorder is turned off so that attendees can read Evan Howard's article. The article is entered into these minutes as a matter of record.

Chapter 17

The Hated Mother: An American Family Tragedy

by Evan Howard

World of Psychology Magazine Senior Staff Writer

Elizabeth Grayson is a noted author, lecturer, and counselor. She is highly respected as the person who has helped focus American society on the perils of emotional/spirit disconnection in humans. In her work as a psychologist, Elizabeth Grayson has developed a program of recovery from spirit disconnection that has substantially cut relapse rates for alcoholics and addicts. Her program has positively impacted people involved in domestic violence situations. The Grayson Model of the Human Navigational System has revolutionized the socialization of American children.

When I began work on this article, I faced what seemed to be a dilemma. Despite her good works, Elizabeth Grayson appeared to have two very distinct personalities. If you talk with mental health professionals, she is considered a national treasure. She is beloved by many she has counseled. I have spoken to many of these people and was discomforted by the fact that there were few statements made by any of these people that could be considered even remotely negative. The worst I heard was, "She confronts lies and incongruity with all the charm of a cobra." This was from a man who claims she saved his life.

When I spoke with the people who should love and treasure her the most, I got quite a different story. The three people to whom she gave birth despise her and feel she lives a life of grave hypocrisy.

Many people were interviewed for this article. It's my job to give you the views of as many of the players as space permits and to then allow you to decide what is true and what is not.

When I watched the tape of the Leslie Wilder Television Talk Show, I felt great empathy for Mrs. Grayson's children. But I learned long ago that there are always at least two sides to any story and this one was no exception. There are several sides to this story. I found elements in it that apply to my family and most other families I know. You, the reader, may experience similar awareness as you study this very visible American family.

Elizabeth Grayson has been in recovery from self-diagnosed alcoholism and drug addiction for more than twenty years. She put herself into a treatment center in 1984. She has given me full access to the people who treated her and to the records that were kept during her confinement. Some of the people who worked with Mrs. Grayson during her time at the treatment center are now deceased. However, the records are intact so that much of what Mrs. Grayson and her children say happened during her treatment can be verified. In addition, Mrs. Grayson's primary therapist in the center is still alive and very interested in helping with the telling of this story. Margarita Sanchez-Lopez made herself available to me for the purpose of this article. Mrs. Grayson agreed to the release of Margarita Sanchez-Lopez's records as well as the release of her records at the Phoenix Recovery Center.

Elizabeth Grayson has three children. Matthew Monahan, Jr. (Bud) is forty-five years old. He is an architect and is three times divorced. Stacy Monahan Jansen is forty-two years old, is married to her second husband and has four children, ages five to twelve. She is a full-time mother and part-time marketing specialist. Jeffrey Monahan is thirty-nine years old, was married once but has no children. He is a biomedical researcher and the baby of the family. The woman he was married to became alcoholic. They divorced, but Jeffrey says he continues contact with her. Elizabeth Grayson's ex-husband, Matthew Monahan, is seventy years old and has been remarried for more than twelve years. He is retired.

I met first with Elizabeth Grayson, and she asked only one thing of me. She asked me to not state or imply that her children were flawed in their thinking. She told me her children aren't crazy and aren't nasty, mean-spirited people. She insists that both she and her ex-husband taught their children that she would be the source of their problems in adult life. She is emphatic that her children were molded to feel and do what they are doing today. This may not become clear to you, the reader, until we get to information given by her ex-husband and her children. But I assure you, you will see that Mrs. Grayson has long understood, at least in part, what tore her family apart.

Elizabeth's Grayson's children made it clear on the talk show that they will accept nothing less than a total apology for all the pain they suffered during their growing up years and for the loss of friendship and caring she's deprived them of as adults. Elizabeth Grayson admits she became alcoholic during her first marriage. She freely admits that she became educated and became professionally employed outside her home during that marriage. Following are the critical points of my first interview with Mrs. Grayson:

Howard: Why can't or won't you accept the blame for what you admit you did so that you can at least have a relationship with your children?

Grayson: I will accept only fifty percent of the blame for the problems and abandonment my children say they've experienced. My children had two parents and their father was just as responsible for creating the home they grew up in as I was. I had no idea what damage was being done in their earliest years when their father made certain statements to them. Matthew would tell the children when they were very little that if they had problems when they got older, it would be my fault because I was the active one, I was the doer.

Howard: Wasn't that a compliment?

Grayson: That's what I thought in the beginning. Later in our marriage, when I was beginning to hate Matthew because I couldn't reach him, I thought they could plainly see what I was going through, and I naively thought they could understand my side of the story. I was totally wrong on that point. They didn't understand what was really being said then, and they still don't see it. I don't think our children understand that they were programmed to feel as they do today. Words spoken to children when they're very young are more powerful than we can understand. And when no one refutes what's being said, children believe the words with all their beings. I've learned from research that statements like this one are common in dysfunctional families and are a setup to put any and all blame on one person. These statements divert blame away from the speaker. A small child listens literally and internalizes such clear messages from powerful, important figures in his or her life. Remember, I stood there silently when Matthew gave them this message. We both taught them that what Matthew was saying was true. I loved Matthew very much and I wanted them to love him, too. It wasn't until I got into recovery much later in life that I was told that we had all been set up for exactly what we've got today. And I was clearly shown how I had helped teach that lesson to them.

Howard: Do you think your ex-husband purposely set out to destroy any affection your children might have for you?

Grayson: No, I don't. I think he wanted to make sure he wouldn't get blamed or shamed, and it's probable he had no conscious awareness that what he was doing might hurt his children. I know that he loved our children. I don't think he was ever emotionally available to anyone in the years we were married. He had a very difficult childhood. I've worked with many people who have been similarly brutalized as children. Many of them are so closed off from their emotions they can never reconnect.

Today, I'm not sure Matthew ever loved me. I felt he shut down when we got married and I don't know why. What I do know is that I spent more than twenty years trying to find the person I dated and was engaged to.

I have a question, too, Mr. Howard. On the talk show, my children claimed that they were physically and emotionally abused by me. They also said that their father was a saint who suffered terrible torment by me. Why didn't Matthew rescue his children? Why didn't he do something to either help me or get me away from himself and his children?

I had no answer for her.

The next person I'll refer to is Margarita Sanchez-Lopez, Mrs. Grayson's first alcoholism counselor. Mrs. Sanchez-Lopez agreed to watch the tape of the Monahan children and to help identify information the children had that might not agree with the records of their mother's treatment and recovery. I asked if Sanchez-Lopez had any knowledge of the statements Mrs. Grayson claimed were made by her ex-husband to their children. I was shown one of Grayson's original progress notes from the treatment center. It was submitted by the head nurse of the rehabilitation center and said:

Elizabeth Monahan was brought to the hospital by her husband from whom she is separated, and her two younger children. She had called two days before, asking if she could be admitted. She said she had to quit drinking and wanted help. I did Mrs. Monahan's preliminary intake. (Attached.) I am putting

this note into Elizabeth Monahan's re-
cord because I observed something that
may indicate serious problems within
this patient's family which could lead to
relapse or estrangement from her family
if she chooses to stay sober and work a
solid program of recovery. While doing
the preliminary intake at the front desk,
I spoke with Elizabeth about her pur-
poses for coming into treatment and she
told me she had tried to quit drinking
and couldn't stop. I asked if she thought
she was alcoholic and she stated she
probably was. Her husband, who was
standing behind her, turned to their two
children and said, "I told you it's al-
ways been her."

This patient will need help in under-
standing that she may be the family
scapegoat and may have difficulty step-
ping out of that role in the eyes and
hearts of her family members.

Signed, Winifred Somners, R.N.

The two younger Monahan children agreed to
meet with me next. I asked them if they remembered the above described situation. They became angry and told me that the people in the
rehab center were always on their mother's side.
They doubted the incident really happened and
wondered what the point of my question was. I
said I was trying to determine if their view of
their mother might come from early childhood
messages that directed them to blame or hate
their mother. The anger that came back at me for
making that statement was extremely uncomfortable. Both of the younger children admit their father told them that their adult problems would be

caused by their mother, the active one, the doer. But they both told me in no uncertain terms that their father was right and that I'd better not try to make their mother look good or their father look bad.

Because I had met Elizabeth Grayson, I found it difficult to understand why these people were so hardened against their mother. They had not seen her for more than twenty years, except at an occasional funeral or wedding of a family member. Both of her younger children stated they had hated their mother long before she went into the rehabilitation center. Jeff Monahan said that the children had wished many times that their mother would die and were always disappointed when she didn't.

The younger children also revealed that they always knew their father not only didn't love their mother but that he stayed as uninvolved with her as was humanly possible. I asked if they knew why and they said they had no idea except that their mother was despicable.

Matthew Monahan, Jr., Elizabeth Grayson's oldest child, said he would not meet with me when I first contacted him. After an appointment with his father was arranged, he decided to meet with me during that interview at his father's home. It was during this interview that a missing piece of the puzzle fell in place. I will use direct quotations from that interview so that you, the reader, will get the full impact of what was said.

Howard: Mr. Monahan, there may be some questions you won't want to answer in front of one of your children."

Monahan, Sr.: Nonsense. My children have understood their mother since they were very young. Bud is certainly mature enough to handle anything I might say at this point in time. He's probably going to read the article when it comes out.

Howard: It's my understanding that you were both deeply involved in your churches and that you both agreed to pre-marital counseling in your church. Is that correct?"

Monahan, Sr. : It is.

Howard: And in at least one of those counseling sessions, you stated that it wouldn't matter if or when Elizabeth got pregnant, that the time of your children's conceptions was up to God.

Monahan, Sr.: I may have said something like that, but I didn't expect her to get pregnant right away.

Howard: When your wife came home from the doctor's a few months after you were married, did you become angry and scream at her when she told you she was pregnant?

Monahan, Sr.: Let me tell you something, Mr. Howard. That happened, but it was more than forty-five years ago. Elizabeth got her little feelings hurt and has never been able to get over it. Don't you think it's time to let go of that and grow up?

Howard: Did you apologize to her for having said one thing before you were married and then doing something exactly opposite after you were married?

Monahan, Sr. (after a long silence): I never owed Elizabeth an apology, Mr.

Howard. She owed much more than that to me and I never got it.

Howard: I don't understand.

Monahan, Sr.: I believed that Elizabeth and I shared the same religious principles and values. This was extremely important to me. I could overlook the fact that Elizabeth's religion wasn't quite as enlightened as mine. I felt real love for Elizabeth when she agreed to marry in my church and to raise our children in that religion. Shortly after we were married, Mr. Howard, Elizabeth confessed to me that she'd done something as a teenager that was totally against my religion. She destroyed my feelings for her. I was totally conflicted because I had taken vows to her and would have to live with her sin for the rest of my life.

Howard: And you felt that by not telling you about it before your marriage, she betrayed you?

Monahan, Sr.: I'm sure you're modern in your thinking, Mr. Howard. Today, young people sleep with whomever they wish and their future partners have to accept their youthful promiscuity. But I assure you, Mr. Howard, Elizabeth stated she was a virgin, not just to me but to our minister. Getting upset because I didn't stick to a minor point I might have made in a pre-marital counseling session is truly the pot calling the kettle black. Think about it, Mr. Howard. I believed we shared the same values and within weeks after our marriage she told me that we didn't share the same values about the sacredness of marriage and sex. She was flawed, deeply flawed in this regard. I married a woman who was not pure and she lied about it.

Howard: Couldn't you have gotten your marriage annulled? That would seem to have been a wise move on your part since you felt the marriage bond had been broken by a lie.

Monahan, Sr.: Unfortunately, I was very young and naive. I thought that once you took vows to someone in the church, only death could part you. Twenty-five years later Elizabeth proved I was wrong in this thinking. She divorced me. I applied for an annulment in my church and got one.

Howard (to Bud Monahan): Do you have any feelings about what you're hearing?

Monahan, Jr.: As a matter of fact, I do. I never knew until this moment exactly why my father didn't love my mother. It all makes sense finally. I always knew he didn't love her. I'm not sure I agree that what my mother did is a valid reason for trashing a woman, but I understand my father and know what a disappointment that must have been to him. As you're beginning to figure out, my mother can be quite stupid and hurtful. Why would anyone hurt my father by telling him such a disgusting thing?

Matthew Monahan, Sr. never once told his first wife what had killed his love for her. It turns out she had no idea what had really happened. I asked for a follow-up interview with Elizabeth Grayson. I related what I had learned from her ex-husband and she was astonished. She, too, stated that everything finally made sense to her. She thanked me profusely. However, her response shocked me as much as her ex-husband's statements did.

Elizabeth Grayson feels she and her family were victims of one of her character flaws. That flaw, in her words, is the inability to know when to open her mouth and when to keep it shut. As I look at her family's tragic situation I understand what she means. She feels her family would have been healthier and happier had she never tried to ease her guilt over her teenage indiscretion. And she feels her children would feel quite differently about her had she opened her mouth and objected when her husband told her children that she would be the cause of their adult problems. In addition, Mrs. Grayson says she spent years trying to get her children to understand her point of view concerning the marriage and divorce. This, she says, simply pushed her children farther into their father's camp.

Margarita Sanchez-Lopez provided a great deal of current research on the family scapegoat syndrome which is common in dysfunctional families. She also provided information that has aided understanding of what happened to the Monahans. Dysfunctional families build coalitions that oppose one or more persons within the family. Elizabeth Grayson says she always felt it was "them against me." Matthew Monahan, Sr. and his children all acknowledge that they united against her.

Chapter 17

Clearly, this family tragedy was caused by a misunderstanding of the true values held by two good people. Neither Elizabeth Grayson nor Matthew Monahan are evil people. But they do come from similar yet distinctly different value systems. The differences in those value systems were not apparent to either party. Yet those differences caused a cataclysmic rift that destroyed the marriage and destroyed relationships that ordinarily are among the strongest forces on earth. The natural love most children have for their mother couldn't survive in the Monahan home. The "sin" that destroyed Matthew and Elizabeth Monahan's marriage may never have been uncovered had their three children not gone on national television to air their grievances. It is only now that the enormity of the differences between Matthew Monahan and Elizabeth Grayson can be clearly understood.

I submitted the final draft of this article to Duane Hudson, Ph.D., professor emeritus in the Psychology Department at the University of California at Los Angeles. Dr. Hudson is highly regarded internationally as a pioneer in the field of family therapy. He has written articles for this magazine and dozens of other publications. We sought Dr. Hudson's input because he is not personally acquainted with Elizabeth Grayson, although he is very aware of her work. We asked him to give us any insight he might have of this situation. Here is the exact text of his written response:

Mr. Howard:
The situation you describe in your article is certainly an extreme case. However, it is in no way unique. I will

try to make my response as brief and succinct as possible.

The Monahan children were born into a home where one of their caretakers had already been judged inferior or immoral. One half of their being came from that "inferior" parent. In addition, their mother's neediness for their father's approval became their neediness. The children might vehemently argue with this but the truth is, they are as needy for their father's approval as their mother was. They saw clearly what happened to their mother and they didn't want their father's wrath directed at them.

Elizabeth Monahan began taking on more and more of the family's emotional acting out, particularly anger. She became the lightening rod for everyone's anger, including her own. They came to hate what they perceived as her inferiority and imperfection. But, and this is a very important point, her angry outbursts were critical to the emotional balance of the family unit. As the years went on, the family began doing a dance. Promises made during the last angry outburst would not be kept, buttons would be pushed, and Mrs. Monahan would explode. More promises would be made, then broken, and this would again be followed by an angry outburst by the mother of the family. Her angry outbursts discharged pent up anger for all. It was the family cycle. Mrs. Grayson acknowledges that busi-

ness would go on as if nothing happened the morning after one of her tirades. This is pretty common in dysfunctional families.

When Mrs. Monahan left the family, she left an enormous hole which no one wanted to fill or knew how to fill. Certainly the new Mrs. Monahan has not filled that hole. The children have tried to find spouses who would do their mother's work but they appear to have been unsuccessful, with the possible exception of the daughter who is married. It's possible either she or her spouse will duplicate her childhood home in some way. She will not do this because she wishes to but because her early childhood programming impels her to.

Why do the children refuse to attempt healing with their mother? The children have frozen their mother in time and now their hate-filled memories allow them to continue to dump their anger on her. It will never end until they deal with all of the errors of both of their caretakers, and there were many. They will then have to deal with their own parts in the destruction of their birth family. As long as they can blame their mother for their problems, they have no reason to change. The Monahan children must ignore the person their mother has become. If they acknowledge who their mother is today, they will have to look at themselves as the source of their problems.

There are millions of families living in this dynamic, Mr. Howard. I believe this work that you're doing will bring great understanding to a large number of people. I hope what I've written will contribute to that understanding.
Sincerely,
Duane Hudson, Ph.D.

Perhaps the pain this family has suffered will bring great good to the world. Elizabeth Grayson told me in our last meeting that there is no way she could be helping the people she's working with if she hadn't experienced the pain of her first-marriage family.

The purpose of this article was to discover how a renowned psychologist, who is much loved by many people, could be so hated by her own children. I believe that has been accomplished. Can peace ever be made between Elizabeth Grayson and her children? Only time will tell. At least they are all alive. If everyone can admit that wrong was done to all of them, and if all of the parties can open their hearts and forgive, healing can happen.

I must make an admission before I finish this article. I resented being assigned to write this piece because I felt about my mother much as the Monahan children feel about their mother. My mother is dead and my father has had a stroke which has left him with difficulty in speaking. I will never know what truly happened in my birth family. It is my hope that the Monahan children will repair their relationship with their mother before she dies. I thought I knew the truth about my mother. Now I'm not sure of anything about either of my parents. I, and probably thousands of others like myself, will never be able to hear

"I'm sorry" or say "I'm sorry" to the person who gave birth to us. We are children of tragedy because we didn't know how to find the truth. We have lost much because our hearts are filled with our fathers' hate.

***

Evan Howard
From my bed in
San Francisco
General Hospital

August 30, 2007

Dear Reader: (If there ever is one.)

I've been told by the powers that be to write a book about an article I recently wrote and which was recently published in *World Of Psychology Magazine*. I worked on the article with every bit of dedication I could muster every day. I did it in slightly less than two weeks without a single drop of alcohol. Now, the powers that be say I need to do the same thing again—only this time a book, not an article. So I've been writing out how I did the article. My friend Paranoid Robinson has been reading what I've written every day. When I got to my last memory of the writing of the article on Elizabeth Grayson's family, Paranoid said he had something he needed to bring me. He brought it to me this morning, and he had Hardy and Madge with him. If I hadn't been in traction and casts from head to foot, I'd have killed all three of them.

No one can be as dumbfounded as I to learn that an entire web of people surrounded me in this painful adventure. I am angry and feel foolish and betrayed that everyone knew what was going on except me. I read the minutes of last Monday morning's meeting at the magazine. Martha Bullock, the owner of the magazine, and Ed Wainwright, the editor, came into the room just as I finished reading the minutes. They explained why I couldn't be told of the conspiracy to get me to write the article on EG and to look at my drinking and my hatred of my mother at the same time. I stared at the bunch of them and I hated them because my accident had crippled me and now I needed every one of them in one way or another.

I remember wondering if there was a conspiracy against me. I also remember wondering if perhaps I had been raised in the same dysfunctional system as Elizabeth Grayson's children had been. That thought was so painful that I could no longer bear it without help. I finished the article, turned it in, got it approved, and then went to the nearest liquor store and bought a week's supply of booze. Unfortunately, I drank most of it in a little over a day. I have no idea how I ended up in the middle of Pine Street right below the Mark Hopkins Hotel on the Saturday night following submission of the article. I'm told the person who was driving the car that hit me was an out-of-town tourist who was totally unprepared for the depth of the hill. Apparently he panicked and couldn't find the brake as he approached me. I'm also told that it was a good thing I was as drunk as I was because I bounced out of the way of further damage, much like a balloon when you bat it away.

Martha Bullock and Ed have apologized for their deceit and have asked me to consider writing "the" book. When I was ordered to write the article on Ms. Grayson, it was supposed to be just about her. Now, they want me to write a book on what I've learned and how I've learned it. The truth is, I will need long-term health care and rehabilitation. I've gotten the care I've gotten through the magazine's health care program. I must have the health care coverage my job provides, and they've assured me an additional year if I do a good job on the book. Well la te da! I hated doing two weeks of enslavement to their conspiracy, and now I have to face a full year of it. I'm told that I'm protected under the group insurance plan for an additional six months if I choose to quit the job right now. My thought is, I'll be able to find a better job with people who won't play games and manipulate. Mrs. Bullock and Ed told me they would respect any decision I make. I really don't want to do a book. I really want to drink and go back to hating my mother totally. I was safe and comfortable there.

My friends Paranoid and Hardy visited me this afternoon. They told me I have nothing to lose by writing the book to the best of my ability. They also reminded me that searching for a job in a wheelchair isn't terribly easy to do. They betrayed me, too. But the most hurtful betrayal of all came from my neighbor, Madge. She never once told me she knew my mother and was a good friend to her. She listened to my complaints for years, and I'm sure every word was carried back to my mother. I don't know why Madge's betrayal hurts me so deeply, but it does. If I write the book, maybe I'll figure that out. If I write the book.

Sincerely,
Evan Howard

PART II

THE BOOK

CHAPTER 1

It's been three months since I blacked out and was nearly killed on Pine Street. I'm back in my apartment. Hardy's taking this sponsorship stuff way too seriously. He's ordered me to do some writing every evening about my days—you know, what I'm thinking and feeling. So that's what you're reading. My Tenth Step journal crap. Hardy doesn't read what I've written, but he asks me to show him that I did some writing from the day before. So I show it to him and grab it away before he can actually see what I've written. He asked me if my father used to make me show him my homework when I was a kid. I told him no, but the truth is my father checked all of my homework with a red pencil. I'm intelligent enough to know what Hardy was driving at. If I told him the truth, he'd have had me do a mini-Fourth Step on shame about writing and showing it to men. So as I'm writing this I have to wonder what the hell I was thinking when I became a journalist. I've always had to show my "homework" to older males who use red pencils. I don't have time to deal with this right now. I have all I can do to figure out how to walk again.

I asked Paranoid to take me to Nob Hill so I could see what happened and where I was when I got hit. I never realized how steep Pine Street is. It must terrorize tourists to come over the top of that hill and not see anything but air straight in front of them. The man who hit me has been in touch. I know he's worried sick that I'm going to sue him. I'm not. I can't. He was injured far more by my stupidity than I was by his car. Hardy says it's real growth that I'm able to see this so clearly and say it out loud. I don't get how that's growth but he just keeps telling me to "keep coming back." God, I hate those trite slogans.

Hardy and Paranoid have been taking me to meetings. I still want alcohol. I still can't say I'm an alcoholic and be comfortable about it. According to Elizabeth Grayson's theory, I'm saying it because I'm a suck-up people pleaser.

I'm going to physical therapy three times a week. I'm able to walk up and down the steps if I hang onto the railing. Paranoid usually takes my wheelchair down and helps me get to where I'm going. Hardy usually carries the chair up the steps when we get back from meetings. They're taking turns nursing me. I hate having to depend on them for anything. Paranoid gets me in and out of the shower. I was never good doing that shower stuff with the guys. I'm still not. He and Hardy tell me to ask myself what I'm supposed to learn through all of this. I'm supposed to write about feelings. I am so frustrated because it's booze's fault that I'm in this situation.

I decided I didn't want to write the book. I started calling newspapers and magazines to see if I could pick up some work. Called old friends in the business and all of them said they don't have any openings right now. I've tried every angle I can think of in the writing business and there are no openings anywhere, not even for freelance stuff. I'm thinking there's another conspiracy going on here to get me to write the damned book. Can Mrs. Bullock's power be that far reaching? Or is it Ed's power that is so far reaching? In the end, I have to consider that I have only three months left on the magazine's health insurance. I used all the money I got for the article to pay my rent ahead and keep a roof over my head. Hardy and Paranoid are feeding me and keeping my cupboard and refrigerator stocked. I have to say I'm truly grateful they're here for me, but I truly hate the feeling of obligation I have toward them. I resent owing them. You'd think they'd know better than to be doing so much since their 12-Step Program tells them over and over that resentments are the most dangerous thing facing alcoholics and addicts. But do they listen? No! What is wrong with this picture? Hardy just laughs at me and says neither he nor Paranoid have any resentment toward me at all.

So it looks like I'm going to have to write the book about Elizabeth Grayson. I had a couple of realizations while I was in the hospital. I certainly didn't go looking for them and I'm only now writing them down. I'd be dozing off or waking up and there would be a brand new thought for me to think about. One night I was dozing off and I saw myself back in our living room when I was a kid. And there it was. That piece of colored glass in Mrs. G's living room. The next time she dropped by to visit I asked her about it.

"Was that glass piece my mother's?"

"Yes it was, Mr. Howard. She loved it and didn't want it to get thrown out with the junk or given to a thrift store to sell. She asked me to take it and if either of her children ever came to the point that they wanted something of hers, I'm to give it to the person who wants it."

I said nothing. I think she wanted me to ask to have the piece. I felt sadness that all that was left of my mother's life was a piece of glass. But I also felt a surge of anger that rippled through my body. I wanted to rage at Mrs. G. I looked at her and realized she was reading everything I was feeling.

"We never meant to hurt you, Evan." It was the first time she had ever called me Evan. And dammit, that caused a bunch of feelings to run through me too. I have no idea what those feelings were or are. I'm feeling them again as I write this. Maybe I'll figure them out as I write the book.

I have to tell you, I DO NOT LIKE feeling feelings. I can hardly stand them and can't stop them. Every time I start to feel something I want a drink. And that gave me my next insight. I'm so helpless. There's no way I can make it to any store to buy myself some liquor. In the hospital I got pain medication only at certain times. A big bulldog nurse informed me that because I'm an alcoholic I would not get all the pain killers I wanted. Now that I'm home, Hardy will only give me pain pills at the prescribed times. And I am not allowed to take any more than the prescribed dose. I don't think it's healthy for other people to be so in control of a person's life. After all, didn't that thing called God, or as the 12-Step People call it, the Higher Power, give us all free will?

And then as I sit in my chair or lie on my bed and think about being on the street in San Francisco or anywhere else, I realize I truly don't want to end up on Skid Row. And I will be there if I don't break this attachment to a bottle of liquid that's a poison. Even to non-alcoholics, alcohol is a poison and people die of alcoholic poisoning every day on Planet Earth. I've been dying of alcoholic poisoning for years, the slow version of that death. That's my reality. Even so, I still don't want to say I'm an alcoholic.

***

I've sat with the above thoughts now for three days. I finally told Hardy that I don't really want to die of alcoholism. He shook my hand and said I was working the first step: *We admitted we were powerless over alcohol, that our lives had become unmanageable.* We talked about my need to say this out loud in a meeting. He called Paranoid and the three of us went to our Men's Meeting that evening. When they asked if anyone was having a problem that might be leading them back to a drink, or something else they needed to share, Hardy punched my arm.

I raised my hand and said, "I need to say that my name is Evan and I'm an alcoholic." We had rehearsed this statement about ten times on the way to the meeting. It still didn't feel right to me but I'd gotten to the point where I knew I wasn't going to be struck with lightening if I said those words. Nevertheless, I felt shame as I said them. The room broke out in applause. How crazy is that? Getting a round of applause for saying you're an alcoholic.

But the entire group glommed onto my admission and made a meeting out of it. That felt kind of special. I was told that I'd joined a very elite group of human beings who admit they have a serious problem and then band together to solve the problem. I heard about coming back, working the Steps and having the one disease in the world that can be arrested by simply not drinking and working the 12-Steps. There were a lot of other messages, but those were the main ones. When the meeting was over, people came up and shook my hand. They leaned down and hugged me. This was really uncomfortable. A room full of men hugging me! Oh God, please save me from huggy AAers.

The last person to come up and shake my hand and then hug me was Ed Wainwright. I was surprised, uncomfortable, embarrassed and very concerned about the ramifications of sitting with my boss in a recovery meeting. He had said nothing during this meeting. I didn't even know he was there.

"I haven't come to this meeting when I've known you would be here, Evan. I didn't come before your accident for obvious reasons. And I haven't come when you've been here since the accident because I knew you'd have mixed feelings about my presence. For some reason, I knew I was supposed to be here this evening and I'm glad I followed my intuition. I've hoped to hear you say those words for years. I love you, Evan. The disease is vicious and I don't want to see another friend or relative die of it.

I was at a loss for words. And more of those damned feelings were running through me. Suddenly I was aware that I was sobbing. Blubbering like an idiot. I was told later by Hardy, Paranoid and Ed that no one could hear me sobbing. It sounded like a gigantic thunderstorm in my head, but apparently I suppressed the sounds my body wanted to make. Hardy and Paranoid stood in front of me and blocked anyone from seeing my breakdown. Ed stood behind my wheelchair and rubbed my shoulders. He leaned down a little and just whispered over and over, "It's going to be all right, Evan. It's going to be all right."

When the wave of emotion passed, the three men stepped back. Hardy brought me a cup of coffee and some cookies. Paranoid brought a couple of chairs over and Ed pulled one up next to my chair. The four of us sat in a circle silently drinking coffee and eating cookies. Paranoid finally broke the silence. "Welcome to recovery, Bro. Welcome to recovery." The other two nodded their heads.

I wanted to start crying again, but this time I was able to stop myself.

Ed said, "You'll get to where you won't fight your feelings, Evan. And when you do get there, you'll be able to treasure your God-given emotions."

I looked at him like he was speaking in Greek. I was aware that I was giving my old friend and boss a look that said, "Are you crazy? Are you insane? Men aren't supposed to feel feelings like this."

He looked back at me as though he'd heard every word that went through my head and said, "Yes. We are supposed to feel these feelings, Evan. That's what God intended, and we've stopped rewriting God's technical manuals for mankind!"

I gave up and just concentrated on my coffee and cookies. All of this was too much for me. Nobody said another word, and pretty soon Hardy and Paranoid took me home. I went to sleep that night and had the strangest feeling of freedom. The feeling was alien but exhilarating. I didn't know what I was actually feeling, but I knew I didn't want it to go away. I was having a feeling that I liked. It was a first in my life.

As I went off to sleep I saw myself working on the book. I was in my office at the magazine and I was happy. I'd never seen myself as happy. I was in that place between being awake and being asleep and I was totally aware of my body and of my feelings. Hardy left me a pain pill that night, but I didn't take it. I left it on the night stand. That was another first in my life.

CHAPTER 2

The sun woke me the next morning. I was feeling the feeling I had when I first cleaned up my apartment and my mind was becoming less fogged. I realized that, thanks to Hardy and Paranoid, I wasn't having a stressful detox from the pain killers. There were plenty of people in recovery who had to take pain killers for one reason or another and they hadn't fallen back into addiction. They all told me that I wouldn't have to go through that terrible process if I'd allow Hardy to keep me on track with the drugs. I was always amazed that Hardy never took a single one of my pills. Not a one. He would tell me that we had two weeks of thus and such drug. He'd count out the pills in front of me when the prescription was delivered. By golly, when we were two days away from running out, he would have me call the doctor for a new prescription. I could look in the bottles at any time and the exact number remaining was always correct. I asked Hardy one time if the day would ever come when I'd be able to help someone with their meds like he was helping me. He said, "Maybe." Truthfully, I really doubt that. I doubt I'll ever be able to have bottles of drugs in my hands and not want to take them all and just check out.

When I saw myself writing in my office as I went off to sleep last night, I promised myself I'd call Ed this morning and ask if it would be all right to do all the writing in my office. I called him and asked his permission to use the space that had been mine.

"It's still your space, Evan. I have to admit that we had some cleaning people come in and thoroughly clean it. A lot of things got thrown out but I think the important stuff is still there. No more pizza boxes piling up, Evan. We exterminated and got rid of the roaches and ants. So if you want to work in your office under those conditions, it's fine with me."

"Geez, Ed. How will I recognize the place?"

"I'll push you there the first time. How will that be?"

I made arrangements for handicap services to pick me up and deliver me to the office the next day. I really felt like a big boy while making the arrangements. Madge Underwood knocked on the door while I was on the phone. I waved her in and she listened as I gave the addresses where I was to be picked up and dropped off and the times for both deliveries.

"Can I believe what I'm hearing?"

"Yes, you can. I'm growing up. I actually said I'm an alcoholic in my men's meeting last night."

Madge flopped herself into my big chair as though in a faint. "Oh, Lord, save us, for I know that it is snowing in hell!" she howled. And then she laughed and jumped up in front of me. "I've prayed for this moment for years, Evan. You were such a rotten little bad ass. I didn't ever want to like you, but I couldn't keep myself from loving you."

"That was love? The treatment you gave me was love?"

"You do not want to experience anger and resentment from me, Evan Howard. Yes, it was love. There were plenty of times when I wanted to smash your ungrateful face. But please note— I didn't."

"Madge, what do I do from here? I mean, I know I'll get the book written. I had some feelings last night that said I can do it. But what happens after that? How do I support myself after that?"

"If you're sober, you can be sure you'll be led to greater and greater accomplishments. Hell, Evan, when you were drinking like a fish and destroying every relationship you had, you still had your most basic needs met. Stay in today. Do today well and tomorrow will take care of itself."

"I wish I could believe you, Madge. Things may work that way for you, but I've messed my life up so badly, God's gonna struggle with coming through for me."

"Am I hearing that you're acknowledging that there is a God?" Madge sat still in the big chair. Everything was silent. She was waiting for an answer. All I could do was feel trapped, so I said so.

"It's questions like that that make me feel backed into a corner, Madge." I struggled into the kitchen and poured myself another cup of coffee. I thought to offer her some, hoping that would take her off point and that she'd forget the question.

"I'd love a cup and thank you very much. Now answer my question. Am I hearing you acknowledging that there is a God?"

I sighed and signaled her to pick up her coffee. I struggled with my cup to the old, beat up sofa directly across from her, trying not to spill the hot brew on myself or anywhere else. "I don't know if there's a God, but there's got to be something behind all of this. I sometimes think God's like the Wizard of Oz—creating all of us with egos and yearnings that drive us crazy but not really having much of a plan for anything. That free will stuff doesn't work for most of us. At least it hasn't worked very well for most of the people I've known over the years."

"We're here to learn how to use that free will for our best interests, Evan. We're here to build a relationship with our Higher Power as we come to understand our personal Higher Power."

"I don't know how I can build a relationship with a being that is so punishing. I deserve what I've gotten. But no kid deserves cancer, or being crippled. How can God allow so many innocents to be killed by criminals or in war?"

"Evan, God doesn't give kids cancer. God doesn't shoot the guns that kill. People do. This planet was created to operate perfectly. Kids who get cancer get cancer because we've practically destroyed our air and waters. The soil of the earth is poisoned

225

and is washing away. God did none of this. We've done it. The hand of man is behind all the things that you see as unjust and unfair." Madge sipped her coffee and waited for her words to sink in.

I felt more uncomfortable than ever. Her argument was so rational and logical. "Can we drop this conversation, Madge?" I was feeling anxious and had a vague sense that my anxiety came from not wanting to give up my anger toward God. For years I'd told myself that a good God wouldn't have given kids the mother my sister and I were given.

Madge relaxed her shoulders and sipped the hot coffee. She then asked her usual question. "So what's the game plan for to-day? Where did you schedule your meeting for today?"

"Ah. I hadn't thought about it yet. I guess I'll call Hardy and see if noon's a go."

"Good. Relax Evan. I've been worried about you for so many years, and now that there's a glimmer of hope, I want to take over and make sure you get it totally. I need to back off and let you find your own way through all of this."

"Thanks, Madge. Now go home."

"I'll go, Evan. But know this. You've burned just about every bridge you've ever had. People will always be waiting for you to fall—even those of us who have stuck by you through the worst of your drinking. They'll always wonder if they did the right thing hiring you or giving you anything of weight. So don't think you'll be able to go back to life as it was three months ago. If you want to make progress in this thing called life, you make up your mind that you need to do everything differently. That includes changing your beliefs, attitudes, and behaviors."

I watched the door as it closed behind her. I hadn't under-stood a word she said. I called and left a message for Hardy, and then I got out my notes and started assembling information that seemed to be important to the message of the book.

CHAPTER 3

I did an outline for the book and looked at the list of resources I'd assembled. I dragged myself over to the broken-down bookcase to look for my college text on writing non-fiction. I supposed that the rules for creating a quality finished product hadn't changed much. I plopped myself down on the sofa and began to scan the book. I wondered if I really took the course, because nothing of what I was reading seemed familiar. I vaguely remembered the classroom in which I took the course, but for the life of me, I couldn't remember who taught the course. Nor could I remember anyone else in the class.

The phone rang. It was Hardy returning my call. He and Paranoid would pick me up for the noon meeting. I promised to be ready to go when they got here. I went into my bedroom and lied down to study the college text. At eleven-thirty they were banging at my door and I wasn't ready. I had dozed off. Neither of them betrayed what they must have been feeling. Hardy asked if I wanted to shave, brush my teeth, or what. I brushed my teeth and combed my hair. I'd given up trying to look dapper and dashing at the 12-Step meetings. There were always plenty of people who looked far better than I did and there were always a couple who looked far worse. I was content with being in between the worst and the best.

Hardy took the wheelchair down this day, and Paranoid helped me down the stairs and into the car.

"How ya' doing, Bro?" Paranoid smiled his big, toothy grin.

"I'm okay. Sorry I fell asleep. I was trying to brush up on the ins and outs of writing a successful book."

"I looked at that book, Evan. How old is it? Thirty years old?" Hardy was driving. He'd bought a new car that was larger. Said he needed it because he was tired of being cramped in his old Toyota. I think the new one was a Chevy. I felt pretty certain he'd gotten the new car to more easily move the wheelchair and me around the city. I wasn't putting anything past these recovery people. They could really be devious.

"Let's see. I think I took that class in my junior year at Berkeley. It's probably twenty-seven years old."

"Well, son, I hate to tell you this, but that book probably has nothing to do with reality today. You're gonna have to learn to use a computer and a word processing program." Hardy turned his head to throw the words to the back of the car. He always talked at me like that when he was driving.

"That's not going to happen. I've done all my work and made a pretty good living on that old typewriter." I was damned if I was ever going to learn to use a computer.

"What are you afraid of?"

Hardy threw the question into the back of the car.

"I'm not afraid of anything. Why does everyone have to do their writing a certain way? Shakespeare wrote out his works. Hemingway hunted and pecked some of the greatest books ever written.

"Well, son, you've got a year to write this very complicated book and everyone at the magazine uses computers. Everyone everywhere in the publishing world uses computers. I'm just thinking you're probably going to have to learn to use one."

With that, we pulled into a parking place in front of the noon meeting room off Union Square. We were late because of me and a lot of uncooperative red lights. Paranoid pushed me into the chair. Hardy held the door open as the wheelchair and I were whooshed to the back of the meeting room by a big black man who might have been just a little bit angry. I sat quietly. Hardy got three coffees and sat down. All of us listened, trying to get the gist of the discussion that was going on. I finally figured out that the subject of the meeting was change. Hardy winked at me. How do they do that—talk about some particular aspect of life and then walk into a meeting on that very subject. It was at this particular meeting that I decided I just might write a book some-day on these very weird and whacky people who quit drinking and drugging and developed this underground movement called 12-Step programs. But that book would have to wait until later. Right now I needed to do the book that Martha Bullock and Ed Wainwright wanted. And just then a wave of panic flowed through me. What if Hardy was right and I had to learn to use a computer and a word processing program—whatever the hell that is. I broke out in a sweat. He'd been right about a lot of things and I didn't want him to be right about this. I've always loathed modern technology. I've never owned a cell phone, com-puter or VCR. I certainly was not going to go against a promise I made to myself years ago to never be victimized by modern tech-nology.

When the meeting was over, we had our corned beef sand-wiches. I asked Hardy if he'd mind taking me to the office so that I could see what I needed to bring with me the next day. Both Hardy and Paranoid said they've love to see the magazine offices, so off we went. Hardy parked in the garage in the build-ing. He'd called Ed Wainwright and said we were coming. Ed said to park in the building's parking garage and he'd take care of the fee. I was very aware that Hardy was using his cell phone to make these arrangements. Once again, I was dumped out of the car and into the wheelchair and pushed onto the elevator. I told them which floor to go to. When we entered the lobby of the magazine's offices, I was amazed at how bright and clean everything looked. I hadn't been there since the day before the accident. I wondered what they'd done to the place.

Ed greeted us. He shook Hardy's and Paranoid's hands and patted me on the shoulder.

"Want to see the offices?" he asked no one in particular.

Hardy and Paranoid said yes. I said no. Either no one heard me, or no one paid attention, because Ed gave us the grand tour. I said nothing but had a strange feeling. I'd worked in these offices for years but there was only a vague feeling of familiarity.

"Have you changed a lot of things around here, Ed?" I asked.

"No. As I told you, we did clean your office."

We arrived at my office just a minute or two later. Ed opened the door and Paranoid pushed me in. I truly did not recognize the place. "What happened? Did you demolish everything?"

"No," said Ed. "We cleaned everything out. Had the furniture polished and buffed. Got you a couple of new chairs. Washed the windows. And...ta da! We got you a brand new computer with all the software you'll ever need on it."

I could feel my face redden. "You're all in on this, aren't you? It's another conspiracy to force me to do everything your way, right? Hardy starts giving me a lecture on using a computer and word processing crap, and in less than two hours I'm dragged here to have a computer shoved in my face."

Paranoid stepped in front of me. "Excuse me? Only idiots refuse to use computers these days, and if you'll remember, you asked us if we'd mind bringing you to your office so that you could see what you'd need to bring with you tomorrow so that you could work. He leaned down and put his ugly face within an inch of mine. "Do you remember that?"

I said nothing. He was right. I did ask them to bring me here. Now what do I do? "That still doesn't mean this isn't a conspiracy to get me to give up my typewriter. What's wrong with it? It's done a terrific job for me."

"Evan, you have to do your work on a computer." Ed moved himself between Paranoid and me. "Once you start using one, you're going to find that editing your work is a breeze and so much more efficient. If you're up to it, you can stay this afternoon and I'll take you home this evening. I can have one of our computer techs give you a couple of lessons. You're going to type your work up just as you always have, but you won't waste reams of paper getting your final product."

I must have had that "deer in the headlights" look. Hardy, Paranoid and Ed stood in front of me and, like a chorus of old women, they assured me I'd do just fine and that it wouldn't take any time at all for me to love computers and word processing programs. I could feel tears filling my eyes. I loved my typewriter. It was my friend.

"Tell you what…" Ed moved closer. "I've got an extra laptop that you can learn to work on at home. You can write whenever you want to. True. Most of the work needs to be done here, but the laptop will allow you to have some flexibility. You're going to need to do a lot of research for the book. You can go online here and just do writing at home."

I didn't understand a word he was saying. Laptop? Right!

"Evan, you have to do all the writing on a computer so that it can be carried from machine to machine." Ed was looking at me like I had some idea of what he was talking about.

Hardy took over. "I think Evan needs time to let all of this sink in. He's been very proud of his hatred of modern technology, Ed. It'll take a little getting used to for him to move from his beloved typewriter to a computer keyboard."

I nodded my head in agreement and asked if it was okay to take a better look at "my office." Everyone moved behind me. Paranoid seemed to understand that I wanted to try sitting at the desk I'd sat behind for the last five years. He helped me into the desk chair. I sat and looked at the desk and the computer keyboard. I hadn't realized there was a keyboard drawer below the middle of the desk. For that matter, I hadn't seen the top of the desk for five years either. I looked at the monitor.

"That's your paper, Evan."

Ed moved to stand beside me. "You're a very bright guy, Evan. You'll be computer savvy in a flash. The first time I sat down with a computer was scary as hell. But I couldn't live without one today. It's a key to a whole new professional world for you."

I stood and moved back into the wheelchair. I was ready to go. Hardy and Paranoid got me back to the car.

"I swear they've done that whole place over. It's brighter and cleaner than it used to be."

Hardy and Paranoid looked at each other. Both turned and threw "I'm sure it is" back to me in the back seat. I got quiet and wondered if they really meant it was brighter and cleaner or if they meant that I was brighter and cleaner. I decided to not figure it out and just watched the beautiful city go by.

That evening I sat in my dingy living room looking at my dingy Smith-Corona and mourned the loss of my old life. I touched the typewriter and said good-bye. I never typed another word on it. The conspirators left me no choice but to use a computer. But I promised myself I was never going to like it.

CHAPTER 4

I spent the next two weeks learning about computers and word processing. I can't say I'm friendly with the contraption, but I do see some clear advantages. Not having to white-out stuff makes for a much cleaner page. And editing on the computer screen makes a lot of sense. I haven't said that to anyone and doubt I ever will. I've got my pride, you know. Madge and Hardy helped me learn the laptop. Hardy gave me a full-size keyboard that I can use here at home and he and Paranoid rigged up a two-tiered typing table that allows me to roll the wheelchair right into it. I noticed that the softer chairs caused my broken bones and troubled back to hurt a lot. The wheelchair was designed to orthopedically support my body better than ordinary chairs do. I realized I'd do better physically if I used the wheelchair most of the time.

I mostly did research while I was in my new and improved office, where I was able to get on the Internet. I have to admit that the Internet is amazing. I downloaded a bunch of materials on addiction treatments and lists of books in the San Francisco Library System that might help me broaden my perspective of the work EG and her colleagues are doing. In fact, the library delivered a fairly large box of books to me just the other day.

My head is swimming with pro and con arguments about spiritual disconnection.

When I'd printed up several articles on-line, I took a few of the articles into Ed and asked if he wanted the book to be a tome, full of cites and quotations. He looked through the articles and said we might use some quotes, but it was his understanding that Martha Bullock wanted the book for the general public, not professionals in the field. He told me to use my gut instincts. If I came across something that helped people understand the idea better, use it. He also said that if I came across something that refuted EG's work, then I was to use that, too. But most of all, I was to write about the human aspects of this thing called spiritual recovery.

And then Ed said the damndest thing to me. "Be careful where you go on that computer, Evan. Our computers are checked regularly for illegitimate use." I nodded like I knew what he was talking about. Enough alcohol had drained from my brain that I could process a lot of information on an emotional level. My gut told me that what Ed just said was important, but my brain made it clear to me that I needed to find out exactly what he meant by that. In an unusual display of candor, I asked, "What do you mean, Ed?"

Ed looked at me with a questioning look and then, in an instant, he seemed to understand my question. "I forget that you've never used computers before, Evan. There are places you can go on the Internet that are destructive and can create new addictions in us. Those of us who are in recovery from any kind of addiction are particularly vulnerable."

I guess I looked at him like he was speaking Greek.

"Pornography sites, Evan. They're highly addictive and are destroying a lot of good people and their careers."

"Oh." That's all I could say.

"Just don't go to any of them, Evan. As a friend I'm telling you they're dangerous. As your boss, I'm telling you you'll be fired. That's what happened to Mike Johnson. His computer here at the magazine had a history of kiddie porn sites. A couple of other people lost their jobs because of adult porn sites."

Chapter 4

"Really?" I always wondered why Mike was let go. He's a crack journalist and we'd had some good times together after work at a bar down the street. Now that I think about it, Mike got fired a month before Ed laid down the ultimatum to me. I think Mike's firing played into my agreeing to do the article. Everything around that day was still a bit fuzzy, but I'm pretty sure I remembered that a really good journalist had been fired recently and the same could happen to me. And then I wondered if the pornography online was as good as some of the magazines I had tucked away in my closet. Just as quickly, I stopped the thought. I have to have this job. I knew that in every cell of my being.

I took the articles from Ed and went back to my office. It was late and the MediCab would be arriving soon to take me home. I packed all the printed materials into my wonderfully weather beaten briefcase. I straightened everything on my desk, grabbed a book from the library box, turned off the computer and headed for the elevator. As I approached the elevator door, the thought ran through my head that it was time for a drink. It was the first time that thought had crossed my mind, and it felt like I was reliving something that used to be important to me. That had been the last thought in my mind every single time I got on that elevator for the five years before the "do the article or else" day. It felt strange, but the pull was very strong. Fortunately, MediCab will only take you to the specified address on the orders. The driver will make no stops other than that. Soon I was delivered home.

As we drove through the city to Van Ness, my sister's face popped into my mind. "Good ol' Teri," I thought. "I wonder how she is." I hadn't had contact with my older sibling for several years. I had trouble with being in her presence for years and I never wondered why. She looked and sounded like our mother. She had been totally estranged from Angela Howard for years, but I couldn't ally with her in the way that the Monahan children had allied with each other. That turned my mind to the question of parental alienation. Did our father turn us against our mother as Matt Monahan seemed to have done with his children? Because Teri looks like our mother, did our father dislike her, too? Did I pick up on his dislike of both my mother and my sister? Hmmm. The van pulled up to my apartment complex and I was glad. I didn't really want answers to my questions. But something inside me said that I needed those answers. This was another part of what Paranoid called "recovery crap"—knowing we don't want to feel or understand certain things, and at the same time knowing we need to feel and understand those things. Hardy said that was just another one of life's little ironies. I've promised myself that if there is a God, I'm going to ask him or her what he or she was on when he or she created us.

CHAPTER 5

My apartment seemed more welcoming than usual this evening. I wheeled myself through the living room, tossed my briefcase down next to my typing table, and kept on rolling into the bedroom. I was beginning to enjoy wheeling myself around. My upper body was beginning to look pretty good from the constant exercise I got from operating the chair. By this time I'd cleaned up the mirror in the bathroom and the full length mirror in my bedroom so I was able to get a pretty fair look at the bod. My face still looked pretty haggard. Paranoid said I actually looked pretty good for all the drinking I'd done. Hardy and Madge were more tactful. When I asked what they thought of my face they replied in unison, "It's a good face."

That took me back to the old doctor who delivered Teri and me. Mom—uh, Angela—said that whenever anyone had a new baby, ol' Doc McKinley would look at the baby and then at the proud parents and he'd say "Now that's a baby!" Every parent thought he was commenting on how gorgeous the child was. Angela would say that was Doc's way of avoiding legal problems later on when the kids didn't win beauty contests. I chuckled to myself. I'd forgotten that there had been many humorous, gentle moments like that in my early childhood.

I stood beside my bed and pulled my tie and shirt off. I struggled to the closet, got out a hanger and hung them up. Madge gave me an old towel rack and I carefully draped my pants over it. I couldn't stand too long, so it was easier to fall back into the wheelchair and straighten the pants out sitting down.

I chuckled again as I thought about Doc McKinley. He was beloved in our town. And then I started feeling something else. Just thinking of Doc and the town I grew up in made me anxious. "Oh, God. Please don't let me get nostalgic. Please, please. Anything but that." I'd spent more than twenty years trying to forget everything about my childhood years. Especially people like Doc McKinley. And then I remembered why I grew out of liking him. He met with me and my parents when I was sixteen. "Son," he said, 'you've got grandparents on both sides of your family who are alcoholic. That means you're probably genetically predisposed to alcoholism. You're in serious trouble already because of drinking, so I'm advising your parents to get you into treatment." I was incredulous.

"I don't need to go into treatment. I can handle it. Why don't you tell my mother to get into treatment, Doc? Huh? Why don't you tell her that?" I was livid. From then on I made a point of avoiding Doc McKinley. As I looked back on that memory, I thought how brilliant I was even in my teenage years. I could see better than a medical professional what was really wrong in my family, but I wasn't ready for what happened after Doc left the house.

My father, James Evan Howard, stood up and slapped me across the face. "Don't you ever bring anything like that up again. Do you hear me, Evan? You don't take our problems out of this house!"

"Wait a minute. You let Doc McKinley come here to tell me about alcoholism and to tell me to go into treatment and that's not taking a problem out of this house?" I was screaming at the top of my lungs. My mother and sister sat like statues. "I'm getting out of this nut house as soon as I can."

Chapter 5

"You will finish high school and you will not get into any more trouble or you'll end up hospitalized, and it might not be in a treatment center," said my father. He'd been a Marine and I could see that he was ready for combat. I wasn't. So I settled down and finished high school and even got through two years of college before I left my parents' home. I left when they divorced. Teri was already married so there really wasn't anyone left at home to leave.

I sat in the wheelchair and looked at myself in the mirror. I saw tears coming up in my eyes and turned myself away as quickly as I could. I went to the living room, picked up my briefcase and started reading one of the articles I'd downloaded concerning mental health professionals promoting the spiritual aspects of clients' needs in the Twenty-First Century. That took me completely back into the intellectual, and I was grateful that all feelings stopped. I was back in my mind and truly happy to be there.

I read for a little while and then felt my stomach rumble. I pulled a supposedly healthy meal out of the freezer and stuck it in my brand new microwave. I punched in the recommended time and then sat there and watched the turntable turn. I wondered what I was coming to. I'm using a computer, and I even purchased a microwave and I'm using that, too. Two things I promised myself I would never do. I vowed years ago that I would never become dependent on electronics. I felt a feeling of betrayal. My own betrayal of my long and dearly held principles. And then the microwave beeped and I removed my dinner. I lifted the rest of the film that covered the meal and let the aroma swirl past my nose without a fight. Madge turned me on to a line of prepared dinners that were a little more expensive than most. I had to admit the meals were surprisingly good. And then I felt that dark feeling of betrayal again. I couldn't think of Madge in any way these days without feeling hurt and angry.

I ate and turned on the news. Nothing but the usual insanity for which the San Francisco Bay Area is known. The world news wasn't any better. People blowing people up. Religions fighting religions. Hmmm. Religions fighting religions. I picked

up EG's book and went to the chapter on spirituality versus religion. EG claims that no one can escape the spiritual, but that
one must agree to a set of dogmas or beliefs if one is to belong
to a religion. Ergo, the spiritual includes all. Religion excludes
anyone who doesn't agree with its dogma, rules and regulations.

I thought about what I just read. Madge had been trying to
get me to understand the difference between spirituality and religion for years. I remembered sitting in her kitchen one night
years ago while she tried to explain to me that there is a vast difference between the spiritual and the religious. I kept telling her
there was no difference. She kept telling me there was. "I hope
to God you get the difference before you die, Evan," she hollered. And then I think she told me to go home. I probably came
home and had more to drink, because I have a vague memory of
really hating her but not wanting to. I felt myself thinking about
how stupid I believed Madge was. And then I thought how odd
it was that I still kept bumming things off of her. It dawned on
me that Madge might think I'm nothing but a bum—a drunken
bum who uses people.

So what is Madge's problem, I wondered. Why would she
put up with my insolence, my rudeness? I was terrible to her for
years. I took advantage of her generosity and still she helps me.
All of a sudden I felt a wave of blackness come over me. I
reached for the phone and dialed Madge's number.

"Hello."

"It's me, Madge. Evan."

"Uh huh."

"I need a friend—I think I need to tell you some things."

"Can you wheel yourself over here? I'm just getting ready
for dessert."

"I can."

This was the night I began to actually be a grown up. I told
Madge that for the first time in my life I felt truly sorry for having hurt her and for taking advantage of her goodness for all
these years.

She cried. I cried. I ate her strawberry shortcake and choked
on it just about every other bite. But it was the best damned

strawberry shortcake I'd ever eaten. We talked about recovery for an hour or so after the dessert was gone. And then Madge helped me home and we were really friends. She helped me through my door and gave me the biggest hug I've ever gotten from anyone. Here I was, eating more of Madge's food, drinking more of her coffee, but this time it was okay for both of us. I slept like a log that night, and I was still feeling that hug when I got up in the morning.

Madge popped in while I was having breakfast and asked if I knew which Step I had worked the night before.

"I didn't know I was working a Step."

"You were. The Ninth Step. Made amends to those we had harmed except when to do so would injure them or others."

"I guess it didn't injure either of us."

"It didn't. In fact it was wonderful for me, Evan."

"It was pretty wonderful for me, too."

And then Madge left. And I wondered, how could an amend hurt anyone else. That lesson would come later in my recovery. I shrugged the question off and went about my day.

CHAPTER 6

My friendship with Madge changed dramatically after that night. The edge of anger I always felt when I was with Madge was gone. It took a while for me to realize that she never was angry with me. The feeling I had was anger at myself. I always knew that I was an ingrate and that Madge deserved so much more than I gave her. About a week after my big amends night with Madge, there was a gathering at the magazine offices and I was the center of attention. I was asked to be at the office on a Saturday afternoon. Strange.

EG was there. So was Denise Kinzler. Madge, Hardy, Paranoid, T.R. Atkins, Margarita Lopez-Sanchez and Ed sat around the big conference table. I sat at the end of the table in my wheelchair. Martha Bullock chaired the meeting. This was the first time I was aware of being in the presence of all the conspirators at the same time. Marshall Grayson was there, too. He sat quietly a little to the side of me and back a little.

I turned to him. "Did you know about the conspiracy?"

"Sort of. I've learned over the years that folks in recovery have a very different, very powerful sensitivity to people who struggle with addictions. I don't have that sensitivity but I don't question theirs. I've seen too many miracles to doubt it." Marshall Grayson was a quiet force in his own right. His presence said, "Listen to me." So I did. He touched my shoulder and squeezed it lightly as though to say he, too, cared. Tears came. I fought them. Everyone waited quietly for me to come back to them.

Martha Bullock spoke first. "I believe that each of us in our own way has spoken with you, Evan, about our part in what you like to call 'the conspiracy.' We're here to tell you how much you've given us. The article was excellent—very good work under the conditions you struggled through while writing it.

My mouth still wasn't as carefully connected to my brain as it should have been. "What all of you did was despicable. How can I trust any of you?"

No answer. Not a word.

"I have to admit that it took a lot to help me realize how out of control my life was." I thought that sounded very grown up.

No answer. Not a word.

"What is it with you people? Why aren't you explaining why each of you did what you did?"

Ed spoke. "Because you're the only one who has to figure out why we did what we did. You were on the fast track to death or to skid row at best. We don't owe an explanation for why we worked very hard to save a friend's life."

"But most of you aren't friends. You're bosses or strangers."

"That's where you're wrong, Evan. We share the same disease. We're comrades in arms with you." Elizabeth Grayson was the speaker. "We didn't do this conspiracy thing as well as we might have. Clearly, we didn't think things through as carefully as we should have. The article seemed to be a product of a mind that was clear and beginning to be quite rational. We thought we could relax because you seemed to be on a solid path of recovery. Alcoholism, addiction, is always more powerful than the human mind can grasp, no matter how many years of recovery we have behind us. You must have walked from your apartment to Pine Street drinking all the way. But all the police found was a pint bottle, empty, in a brown bag. We may never know how you got so drunk so far from home. We all carry regret because we didn't better anticipate what you might do."

"I have to admit that I breathed easier once the article was finished, Evan," said Ed.

"All of us did. We forget how people in early recovery can snow the people around them. You were really good, Evan." Hardy sat back from the table, his elbows on his knees, hands clasped between his knees. "I'm not carrying a shit-load of guilt about your accident. Part of recovery is accepting that I'm here to save my own life and no one else's. But I'm truly sorry for anything I did or didn't do that contributed to that accident."

I looked at Hardy and thought about the hours and hours of time he gave to me, not only in the two weeks prior to the article, but for all the months since. I didn't know what to say. I felt helpless to say anything.

It was Paranoid who lightened things up. "Listen, Bro. You took yourself out in a few minutes. It took me ten years to finally get low enough that I had no choice but to let people help me. I'm thinking you're a hell of a lot smarter than I am. Two weeks after starting the program you got yourself rendered powerless of everything. Put my ten years up against that and I lose every time. But that doesn't mean you've left the category of dumb shit."

We all laughed. I loved Paranoid's honesty and his earthy way of seeing reality.

"So why are we here today?" The minute I asked the question I got that sick feeling that told me I didn't really want to know why we were there.

"We're doing a reality check. We're checking to see if you're still on track about the book. We don't want any more secrets or surprises coming your way. We've done enough of that." Martha Bullock looked directly at me and I looked directly back at her. I didn't see a bitch of a boss. I saw kindness and concern.

"Boy, are these people changing," I thought.

"Thank you for that," I said. "But I don't know if I really feel trusting of any of you."

"We don't expect that you do, Evan." Again, Martha Bullock looked me straight in the eye. "Now, how we can we help you with the book?"

"I don't know."

"I like that you're keeping a journal of what you're learning and understanding each day, Evan. Maybe the book should come from your Tenth Step journal work." It was Hardy who was looking me straight in the eye now. My eyes were really getting tired of all this intense looking into. He had explained to me that the Tenth Step of 12-Step programs requires us to keep constant check on ourselves and to write every day about new things we're learning or things that bother us and need to be resolved, either within ourselves or through talking things out with others. I had to admit that some of my journal work felt like chapters in a book. I would feel so tired when bedtime came around, but I'd followed orders every night and was always amazed at the flow of thoughts, and yes, God forbid, feelings that poured out of me. And I have to admit, doing it on the computer made it a whole lot easier. I was actually feeling powerful when I sat down at that keyboard without my bottle of whiteout.

"I do have some questions, Mrs. Grayson." She nodded for me to go ahead.

"Why haven't you made some attempt somewhere to get your side of the story out—I mean other than through the article?"

"Because, Evan, this work is too important to be a sideshow on TV. What you're not understanding is this. There are millions of people in what, in the 60s, would have been called an underground movement. Millions of dysfunctional families have been torn apart like mine was, and there was a scapegoat in every single one of those families. I'm not a rarity. You've seen a thousand or more people in your short months in recovery here in the Bay Area. Many are estranged from their families. There are millions around the world who are beginning to understand the issues that force us to try to medicate our pain one way or another. I'm not going to go public and risk hurting myself or my children further." Elizabeth Grayson was as composed and seemingly sincere as it's possible to be. "I'm going to let the grass roots recovery movement do the work in God's time, not mine."

And then there was silence. Dead silence.

"That's it?" I asked.

"The book, your book, will do more than a talk show ever could, Evan." It was Margarita Sanchez-Lopez speaking. I turned to look at her. "More than anything, a simple explanation of what Elizabeth codified as a primary, underlying factor in addiction, will make sense to the many millions of people inside and outside the recovery movement around the world. We socialize children to *not* feel certain feelings according to their gender and to *not* use their imaginations and to *not* listen to their intuitive voices. We cut them off from their spirit centers and, as a result, children become anxious. When we're cut of from any of our fifteen senses, we become anxious because our abilities to navigate safely through the world are diminished. The anxiety sets in pre-memory, and anxiety grows as the child grows. And then we program the kids to drink beer with everything they do and we wonder why they get in trouble with alcohol or other drugs. And the society programs them to admire violence and to believe the solutions to all their problems can be found through guns and brutality. Males resort to violence and females resort to fairy tale beliefs that men who control their every move are the ideal. It's a deadly combination."

"Can I get you to say that on tape so that I can include it in the book? That makes more sense to me than anything I've heard so far."

"Be glad to go over it with you anytime, Evan."

"If you want input from folks who don't struggle with addictions per se, Evan, I'd be glad to be one of those and to connect you with others who have been codependent with alcoholics and addicts. Millions of people are addicted to addicted people, and the pain of that is excruciating." It was Marshall Grayson speaking.

Chapter 6

Ed Wainwright spoke next. "Most of us in this circle, Evan, are the scapegoats of our families. When we came into recovery and refused to continue the role of bad boy or bad girl, our families disowned us one way or another." Ed pushed the arm he was leaning his head on further onto the table. He looked me straight in the eye. "You may not have known that I was the family scapegoat when we were kids because you were too busy being your family's scapegoat."

Now that was news to me. I'd always believed that Ed was the perfect son, the kid I should have been.

"No way…"

"Oh yes. My family was very good at looking perfect to the outside world. But I was the pariah in my family. Why in the hell do you think we became such good friends and did so much drinking together through high school and college?"

"Okay, but you grew out of it."

"No I didn't. I just lucked out and realized that I needed help, and was ordered to go to AA after my first and only DUI. I was very lucky to not have to go further into the disease. But I had lost what it takes to live successfully in this world, Evan. I had lost myself by the time I was fifteen."

As a reporter, this was absolutely fascinating. I'd known this man for close to forty years and I had never once suspected that he was alcoholic or a problem to his family. I thought we didn't drink together anymore because he was my boss and above drinking with the "underlings."

Everybody seemed to read my mind.

"You're going to learn more than you ever imagined possible as you go through this thing called recovery, Evan. I hope we've accomplished our goal with you this afternoon. If you have any questions about anything, please don't hesitate to ask us." With that, Martha Bullock rose from her chair and the meeting adjourned. What I didn't understand was that I'd just been to an incredible 12-Step meeting with some very old-time recoverers. I'd learned that alcohol wasn't the problem. Relationships with people were. I was emotionally exhausted but I also knew that I'd just heard a lot of stuff that conflicted with just about everything I'd ever been taught about life.

On the way home, Hardy handed me a meditation book called <u>Daily Reflections</u>. He asked me to read the meditation for April 6th. Bill Wilson outlines the worthlessness he felt as an un-recovered drunk. And then he wrote:

> *Those words remind me that I have more problems than alcohol...that alcohol was only a symptom of a more pervasive disease...*

"As you learn more about Mrs. Grayson," said Hardy, "you'll find that she read everything she could about Bill Wilson and this statement. She realized that he was talking about the disease of spirit disconnect. And that's where she took off on this new understanding of alcoholism. Put any word you want where the word alcohol is—sex, food, work, cocaine, pot. It doesn't matter what you're addicted to—you're trying to medi-cate the loss of your spirit abilities.

CHAPTER 7

About a week after the Saturday meeting at the magazine, I got a powerful feeling that I needed to call my sister Teri. When Hardy and Paranoid picked me up for the day's AA meeting, I did something very unusual for me. I told them about the feeling. Hardy was driving, as usual. I was sitting in the back seat, as usual. Paranoid's head began nodding up and down. Hardy threw his voice back to me. "Follow your feeling, Evan," he said.

"I've got to say that I got the feeling to call and then started thinking about it. My thinking says not to call her. Why open that Pandora's box?"

"Your thinking is what's gotten you to where you are, Bro. Call your sister!" Paranoid hit the glove box to emphasize his message.

And that was the extent of their advice to me on that subject. So I thought I'd bring it up at the meeting. It was a fairly small group. All men. I was sure I'd get some validation for not calling Teri there. Wrong. I still hadn't learned that no matter what you bring up at a 12-Step meeting, someone's going to have experienced what you're currently struggling with and will tell you what happened to them. A man in his thirties proved that point to me that day.

His name was Mel. He looked me straight in the eye and said he'd had a very strong feeling that he should call his sister, but he decided against it because he didn't want to hear from her that his drinking was out of control. The very next day his sister was killed in an accident. "I never got the chance to talk to her again. But it was her death that made me realize that I'd put my drinking ahead of everything else in my life. And life taught me what was most valuable the very next day. I cry every day for her. She loved me when no one else could or would. Maybe if someone else calls his sister because of what I didn't do, I can rest easier and not miss her so much."

And then the meeting went on to other things. What more could be said? Nothing. Mel said it all. He came up to me after the meeting, reached down and hugged me. He looked me straight in the eye and asked, "How much do you have to lose before you wake up?" With that he walked away.

Hardy and Paranoid took me home after lunch and I called Teri.

"Hi, Sis."

"Evan?"

"Yeah."

"How are you? What's wrong? I haven't heard from you in years. I've sent cards and never heard anything back. I gave up on calling you. Please tell me you've gotten an answering machine."

The dam broke. Teri listened quietly as I went on for half an hour telling her all that had happened over the past several months. I started with the day when Ed ordered me to write the article, and brought her up to the present and the meeting earlier in the day. I took a breath and went silent. This was my first contact with anyone in my birth family in more than seven years. Tears were streaming down my face.

Apparently Teri wasn't sure I was finished. There was silence.

"Are you there, Teri?"

"I am. I don't know if you understand how long I've prayed for you to stop drinking."

"Was I really that bad?" I was hoping she'd say I wasn't bad at all.

"Your drinking was horrendous!"

This was why my intellect didn't want me to call Teri. She could be brutally honest. She was like our mother in that way.

But Teri didn't go any further in assessing my drinking.

"I have to be honest, Evan. I've been in touch occasionally with Ed Wainwright. I've kept track of your career. I knew you got fired from both newspapers and that Ed had hired you."

"Were you in on the conspiracy?"

"No. I knew nothing about it. But I can tell you honestly that I would have been had there been any reason for the group to invite me in." Teri's words felt angry to me. "I'm so sick of alcoholism. I'm sick of people who think that because they don't drink they're perfectly okay."

"Who are you talking about now?" I was beginning to get lost in the conversation.

"I'm talking about our father. I've watched my own husband try to turn my children against me because I come from a dysfunctional family—just like our father turned us against our mother."

We talked about parental alienation. I told Teri that I'd just learned about it. She said she's been studying it for years. She told me that she became aware that her husband was making subtle statements about her behaviors that were causing her children to be suspicious of her.

"So are you still married to Bert?"

"I am. There was no need to destroy what is otherwise a good marriage. We both went to counseling and realized that we'd both grown up in families where one parent pitted the kids against the other parent. It's all over the place, Evan."

"So were you in touch with Mom before she died?"

"Unfortunately, I wasn't. But it was her death that really brought me up short. Today I focus on the good things she did for me. The most important thing she gave to me was her example of quitting drinking and changing her life. Sadly, my awareness of what was really going on came after she died."

"Are you excusing Angela's drinking? I won't Teri. If that's the price of rebuilding a relationship with you, then I guess we're back to ground zero." The anger against the verbal abuse Angela heaped on our father came back into focus and I was ready for a fight.

"We're not going to do that dance, Evan. Mom's dead and Dad's still being Dad. He's unreachable emotionally and that was a big part of his fifty percent of that dynamic. He was just as much at fault as Mom was. She was just louder and looked more guilty."

"Wait a minute…wait a minute. Are you blaming Dad for her outrageous behaviors?"

"I am blaming him for fifty percent of every single problem that ever existed in our parents' marriage. After the divorce, Dad started to pull me into the role of surrogate spouse. He started giving me the cold shoulder and silent treatment that he always gave Mom if I displeased him in any way. Do you remember talks we had when we were just teenagers and we agreed that Dad had never loved Mom and why the hell didn't she give up trying to get him to love her?"

"Vaguely." That was a lie. I didn't remember much of anything from my teen years. I was already involved with checking out from the family and was already heavily involved with alcohol and pot.

"Don't give me 'vaguely,' Evan. You were the one who first realized that Dad didn't love Mom and never did. I remember the first time you said that to me. It was a big light bulb moment. I actually felt sorry for Mom. She loved him. But she became so frustrated with his coldness that she could spit. She didn't drink when we were little. Life was really good for us as long as she was operating under the illusion that she had a good and loving husband and that we were a normal family."

"Teri, I have to go. I'm getting overwhelmed and my sponsor says that I need to go quiet and do some praying or phone calling."

"I totally understand, Evan. Can we talk again? Soon?"

"I guess so."

Chapter 7

"No. I want a promise."

"I promise. I'll call you next weekend. Teri…"

"Yes…"

"Is Dad still alive?"

"Yes. He's living with a lady friend in the Chicago area. I see him occasionally. The girlfriend calls me once in a while, and she has the exact same complaints Mom had."

"Yeah. I'm getting overwhelmed."

"Call your sponsor as soon as you hang up, Evan."

"Okay." And with that I hung up. I went to the laptop and began writing out some of my feelings. Angry. Frustrated. Confused. And then I remembered my promise and called Hardy.

"Did you call your sister?"

"I did, Hardy, and I don't know what to do with most of what Teri said. She's gone over to the other side."

"She hasn't gone over to the other side, Evan." Hardy took a deep breath. "She's just looking at the big picture and what was really going on between your parents."

"How can you say that? You don't even know what she said."

"She told you that your father was just as responsible for what went on in your childhood home as your mother was. Right?"

"Okay. She said she wasn't in on the conspiracy. But she's lying, isn't she? You guys have been in contact."

"I've never spoken to your sister in my life. Don't you get it, Evan? Families are families and what happened in yours happens in millions of families. Those of us in recovery from addictions are unusually aware of the dynamic because many of us played the role of the bad guy. We wanted so badly to just be loved. Unfortunately, we didn't believe we were lovable and we made sure through our addictions that people couldn't love us— at least not for long. The underlying factor in all addictions and compulsive behaviors is self-loathing, Evan. And we find people whose attitudes and behaviors enable us to hate ourselves even more. Your parents weren't bad people. But they were a matched set when it came to poor self-esteem. Your mother wasn't able to bear the pain of her poor self-esteem without some liquid help. That played right into your Dad's need to feel superior to her in some way."

"Did that happen to you?"

"It did. I drank myself into oblivion and right out of a family. I have a family who feels about me as you feel about your mother."

"That sucks." I didn't realize that my reaction was an indictment of my own unwillingness to look at my feelings toward my mother. But as I lay in bed that night, I wondered how anyone could hate Hardy. He was a good heart and helped a lot of people to come back to the land of the living. I heard that quiet voice within say, "And so was your mother." If I thought or felt anything more on the subject, I'm not aware of it. I was glad for sleep to take me over.

CHAPTER 8

The week following my conversation with my sister, Teri, was uncomfortably emotional for me. I put on my nice face with my so-called recovery friends. I began to realize that time was slipping away, and as nice as everyone seemed to be at work, there was a deadline I was going to have to meet. I was loving the journal work because I could spin it however I wanted. But my conscience was coming back to life, and I actually did some reverse spinning on some of the things I wrote about. Hardy put a new rule in the mix. I had to go over what I'd written every day with Hardy or Paranoid. I was surprised to learn that I liked doing the work with Hardy better. He could be tactful and diplomatic. Paranoid was just plain brutal at times. I'd get this twist in my gut whenever Hardy said he couldn't listen to me. It began to dawn on me that Hardy actually had a life outside of taking care of me. "What a concept," I thought. One time I asked him if I'd sometime have a life of my own.

"All you've ever done is have a life of your own, Evan. When was the last time you ever thought about someone else's needs."

I didn't answer. Couldn't think of any time in recent history that I'd thought of someone else's needs, but I was sure I was quite altruistic in reality. "I'll get back to you on that," I said.

"You do that," replied Hardy.

That evening, as I was doing my journal writing, I thought about Hardy's question. As hard as I thought, I could not remember thinking about someone else's needs, much less putting another's needs ahead of my own." I wrote about the level of selfishness I seemed to have displayed to the world. It dawned on me that even as a kid I expected others to serve me. I made a note that I wanted to talk to Madge about this. Outside of Ed and my sister Teri, no one had known me longer than Madge. I knew that conversation might not happen for a couple of days because I had to go to Walnut Creek to meet with Elizabeth Grayson and Margarita Sanchez-Lopez. I maneuvered things so that Margarita extended an overnight invitation, so I planned to be gone the better part of two days. Hardy and Paranoid said they'd get me on a BART train to the East Bay and they'd pick me up when I came back. I'd been getting a pay check, and had some extra money in my pocket, so I planned to get Ms. Sanchez-Lopez to take me back to that fabulous Mexican restaurant—my treat. I'd actually been submitting articles that were usable besides doing the research for the book. That made me feel less like a freeloader. But, back to the Mexican dinner with Ms. Sanchez-Lopez.

So there! I was planning to do something nice for someone. The thought was comforting. Maybe I'm not such a selfish asshole after all.

***

Hardy and Paranoid were at the door at eight the next morning. I'd surprised myself by getting up, fixing a healthy breakfast and being ready when they arrived. I'd even thought to have a full pot of coffee on so each of them could fill their travel mugs and enjoy the fresh brew on the way to the BART station. As they filled their mugs and bantered back and forth, I thought again about what a nice guy I really was. I remembered to make extra coffee for them.

Denise Kinzler picked me up in Walnut Creek. She was as beautiful as ever, and just as professional, which translated in my mind to untouchable—a no-no. I kept hearing people talk about no relationships for at least the first year of recovery. It was the "at least" that troubled me. So I thought this would be a great way to ply the waters and see just how untouchable Denise Kinzler was. I watched as she drove the convertible down Mount Diablo Boulevard. "So when 12-Step people talk about not getting into a relationship for at least a year, what's that 'at least' mean?"

"Most people are in enough pain in early recovery that they can hear that the biggest reason for relapse comes from disappointment in relationships." We were stopped at a light and Denise looked me straight in the eye. God, I hated those straight-in-the-eye looks. "So everyone with any time and good sense tells newbies no relationships for a year. If a person really gets sober and works the program, by the end of the first year they know pretty well that they are not ready for a relationship and won't be for a while. If we don't have a good relationship with our Higher Power and our selves, we'll never have a good relationship with anyone else. Sexual relationships are extremely dangerous for people in early recovery."

This was not at all what I wanted to hear. I knew that I wouldn't like the answer, but part of me would always hope to get something that fit my agenda, not reality's agenda.

"If we've gotten into trouble with substances or obsessive-compulsive behaviors, Evan, we're trying to fill a hole within us. Believe me, there is nothing in the world that will fill that hole except the love of God and healthy self love."

This was really, really, not what I wanted to hear. "And you believe this with all your heart, huh?"

"No. I don't believe it, Evan. I know it. I've watched hundreds of people go back out because of failed relationships. The people who I've seen find healthy relationships have a love affair with God and themselves first. They find a healthy relationship later in recovery. I know what works and I know what doesn't work." Denise smiled at me and turned the car into the Grayson homestead. I said nothing more. As she parked the car, Denise gave me another straight-in-the-eye-and-don't-argue-with-me look that went straight through me. I literally felt like a lance, or a very large needle, had just been thrown through me.

"No relationships for at least a year, Evan. If you really want to have the best life possible, don't try to go around that piece of advice."

"Yes ma'am." She helped me get the wheelchair out of the car. I was able by this time to use the chair like a walker. I got into the house and sat myself in it and rolled down the hall to the bathroom. I felt at home, even though I hadn't been back since the day of my interview with Matthew Monahan. I went back to that day and felt sad to have brought such terrible information to EG. But the house was welcoming and familiar. I took care of business and washed my hands and looked at myself in the mirror. I felt the feeling of "being at home" more deeply. I opened the door and managed to get back into the chair where it waited for me in the hall. The chair felt good to my back. I was grateful to have it. I sat there for a minute and wondered what the hell was going on with me with all these gooey feelings. I decided that no one was ever going to know I was feeling what I was feeling. I didn't want anyone making fun of me.

"Evan? Do you need some help?"

Elizabeth Grayson was coming down the hall.

"Nope. Nope. I just needed to freshen up a little."

"Well I'm glad to see you. You look well." EG leaned down to hug me. I put my arms out to hug her back. It was a very motherly hug. Nothing sexual. But it touched something deep in me, and I felt more of that gooey stuff that scared me. She must have sensed my fear because she moved back and out of the way so I could move the chair into the family room. I rolled into the room and there it was—that piece of glass. The sun was beaming through the window and glistened through the glass. The refracted light danced on the couch and the wall behind it. I stopped and stared at it. I remembered looking at it this same way when I was very young. Angela always kept it polished. She'd let me hold it but always asked me to be careful not to drop it. I wondered why I hadn't dropped it and broken it. I broke a lot of Angela Howard's stuff. By the time I was ten or twelve, I knew how to get even with her for her nasty attitude.

I suddenly realized that EG was watching me as I stared at the glass.

"Would you like some coffee, tea or soda, Evan?"

Thank God she didn't ask me what I was thinking or feeling. "I could use some soda. Something like 7-Up or Sprite?"

With that she disappeared for a few minutes. I looked back at the piece of glass. It was made from volcanic ash. Different colors swirled through it, depending on the metals present in the ash. Had it been anyone else's pieces of glass I would have thought it was beautiful. I realized that the piece was beautiful even though it had belonged to my worst enemy. I wasn't having a gooey feeling. I was aware that I was experiencing very mixed feelings. Part of me still wanted to smash the piece, and another part of me realized how wasteful and foolish such an act would be. I'd had all I could stand of that piece of glass, so I turned my wheelchair away from it. I took out my recorder and note pad and laid them out on the couch. EG came in with the soda. She pulled a small table over for my soda and then sat on the end of the couch, leaving plenty of room for my things.

We talked about EG's struggles to accept the loss of her children and how she believed that any struggles we have are part of a bigger plan. She explained that her pain and her recovery program had led her to do life quite differently than she would have done it had she stayed in her first marriage.

"I'd spent the better part of my life trying to get people to love me, accept me, approve of me, and understand me. I wrote letters. I made phone calls. I sat and had heart-to-heart talks with my children when I was still in the marriage. What I didn't understand, Evan, was that my children heard those conversations as me indicting their father for all the wrongs in the marriage. I drove them crazy with my 'talks.' What I've come to understand since is that most of us spend the bulk of our life energy trying to get love, acceptance, approval, and understanding from other human beings. We'll never get it from others until we totally love, accept, approve of, and understand ourselves."

I made note of the subject at that point in the recording. I didn't understand a word that EG was saying, but I knew she was saying something that would be critical to the book. And then EG told me about her understanding of the 12-Step Process.

"You have to remember, Evan, that I and many of my friends thought I was pretty savvy when I was in my forties. I'd accomplished a lot. That said, I was in a black hole of despair and going deeper every day. I constantly looked outward for answers. I went to therapy several times. Each time, we went over what was wrong with my childhood. Each time, I came out in more pain that I had started with. Finally, I heard a voice say to me, 'Elizabeth, you're dying. Alcohol is killing you. Do something.' Mind you, I'd felt for some time that my drinking wasn't healthy. I was waking up with god-awful headaches. I dragged through mornings and promised myself I wouldn't drink that day. But I got to five o'clock, or five-thirty at best, and I had to fix myself a drink. I know I didn't stop and say to myself that I was enslaved to alcohol, but I knew something wasn't right."

EG took a sip of soda. We both sat and thought a while.

"I remember thinking that I shouldn't drink the way I was drinking." I froze in my chair. These were the kinds of statements that always came back and bit me with whomever I was talking to, sober or drunk. I braced for a lecture.

"Most alcoholics have those feelings. But the addiction is much more powerful than good sense. For me, I listened to that voice that asked me to do something about my drinking. A good friend who was head of a small company here in the Bay Area had gone to rehab. I asked him if he thought it might help me."

"Did he jump in and try to take over your life? Did he build a conspiracy to get you into AA?"

"No, Evan. I asked him for the name of the rehab, called up and asked for them to get me in as soon as they could. I was all by myself. Divorced. I had a good income from my own little business. But I knew that I was going down and that there was no one who'd catch me if I went over the cliff."

EG was very good at deflecting my anger. I made note of where her statement was on the recorder. That information would probably be important to the fleshing out of her story. And then we talked about some of her experiences in the rehab. That was where she met Margarita, her addiction therapist.

"The minute I made that phone call and asked the hospital to get me in, my whole being broke out into the light, Evan. I knew I was going in the right direction. For the first time in my life, I knew I was doing the right thing."

"That's a pretty powerful statement, Mrs. G. Like you say, you were pretty savvy even before recovery."

"I was savvy in the business sense and in making myself look good to the outer world. Internally I was just a black hole. When I went to the hospital, I was greeted by a staff of people who told me I'd be okay and that I'd be amazed at how much better life would get for me."

"Did they promise you that you and your children would heal?"

"They did not. They promised me I would heal if I worked the Steps and built a healthy spiritual life. They were brutally honest with me. They told me that many scapegoat families continue to see the scapegoat as the problem, no matter how changed and healthy the scapegoat becomes. They literally freeze the scapegoat in time and will never accept that the person has changed. And this history repeats itself over and over and over in our society. I see it every day in my practice."

"Do you feel angry when you see it in your clients?"

"Some. But not much anymore. My heart goes out to the entire family. I just work with the client to help them accept that others have the right to reject us but that doesn't mean we're unlovable. It just means that certain people blame us for their problems and there's nothing we can do to change that. Acceptance of reality for good or ill is a critical factor in recovery from any dysfunction, Evan. I am angry that this society encourages contentious relationships and that we, as a society, are so disconnected from our own intelligence and common sense that we can't see what we're doing to children and to each other. I'm very angry about that."

A thought passed through my brain about my mother. I felt compelled to say something and immediately thought better of it. "Don't go there, idiot," my nasty voice said.

"Were you going to ask me something, Evan?"

"Ummm. I was but it's slipped my mind. Senior moment or wet brain, I guess."

EG nodded. "How about a break? I feel the need for some sunshine." She rose. I nodded agreement, then turned to stop my recorder and put my notepad and pen on the table. She was on her way out to her garden. "Join us if you wish." I saw Marshall wave to her as she headed toward him.

I had to stop and think what I wanted to do. In the past, I would have considered EG's statement an order and would have felt trapped and angry. But this wasn't an order. She said I could join them if I wished. I decided I didn't wish to. I wanted to rest and think. What she just said troubled me, but I didn't have a clue as to why it troubled me. I got out of the wheelchair and stretched out on the sofa—the same sofa I crashed on during my first visit to EG's home. It felt good to lie down, and before I knew it, I was asleep again.

CHAPTER 9

No one woke me up. I slept about an hour and woke up naturally. EG was still in the garden. My body felt refreshed but my mind felt distressed. I looked at my notes and listened back to the last things EG had said.

I felt as though a bomb had been dropped and that EG was blaming me for my mother's unwillingness to make amends to her children—the amends she should have made before she died. It felt like a bomb because I couldn't stand the thought that any of the estrangement with my mother was not Angela Howard's fault. I was totally taken off guard by EG's anger at the outer society. It wasn't difficult to figure out that EG's anger felt exactly like my mother's anger. Once I understood that, it was easy to move into dislike for Elizabeth Grayson. I thought about returning immediately to the city and to hell with lunch. But my mind was clear enough to remember that my entire financial well being rested in doing what Martha Bullock considered a good book on Elizabeth Grayson and her work.

I didn't feel the anxiety as I listened again. Hardy and Paranoid would listen to this tape and they'd tell me to hear what was really said, not what I wanted EG to say. What I didn't understand while at EG's house was how Teri and I were responsible for any of our problems with our mother. I played the part of a grown up and had lunch with the Graysons and Denise. Both Denise and EG worked with me during the afternoon hours to better understand the broader application of the 12-Step process.

"The 12 Steps are simply a therapeutic process for healing wounds from childhood, or even adult experiences that contain a spiritual component." EG sat near me and let that sink in. I noted the number on the recorder and nodded that I was ready to hear more.

"Many people find out what caused their problems while in therapy, but they're not given the mechanism to permanently remove the erroneous beliefs, attitudes, and behaviors that came out of those experiences. Most human beings develop strategies that allow them to survive their childhoods, but those strategies almost never work in adult relationships—unless one is in a relationship with someone who developed matching coping mechanisms. The relationships are unhappy, but the couple is stuck together like they've been super-glued. The Seventh Step is the silver bullet in this process, Evan. We have to become aware of what needs to be healed or what we want to change in ourselves and then we take it to our Higher Power and ask that Power to change us. And it always gets healed or changed. All of the great religions teach us that all things are possible with the Divinity, whatever one calls their particular divinity." EG took a breath. "The wonder of the 12-Step process comes from the fact that we take ourselves to God like children taking broken toys to a loving parent. Our Higher Power does the heavy lifting."

This sounded familiar and I said so. "It's in my book," said EG.

"Oh."

Denise told me how she struggled with addiction to legally prescribed tranquilizers and how the 12-Step process in therapy helped her get off the downward slide. Before I knew it, the afternoon was gone and it was time for Denise to take me over to Margarita's house. I said goodbye to EG and to Marshall Grayson. I used the wheelchair as a walker again. I couldn't stand the thought of having Denise Kinzler help me into and out of the car. I was even able to put the wheelchair into the trunk of the car. We rode silently across Walnut Creek.

"You have so much to learn, Evan. You were fifty percent of your problems with your mother, and no matter how much you want to argue with that, you'll never change that fact."

"I have no idea how you have reached that conclusion. Angela Howard was the mother. She didn't do her job well at all."

"I can't disagree with that, because you're just about the most immature person I've ever met." We were at a light again and Denise gave me another one of those straight-in-the-eye looks. That look caused me to feel hurt, and the tears were right on the rims of my eyes. I turned my head and looked away. I didn't want to brush my hand near my eyes for fear that she'd know she hit something very painful. I was grateful to have the wind dry my eyes as we neared Margarita's house. Denise parked in front and pulled the trunk lever. She didn't get out of the car. I did, and went to the back of the car and got the wheelchair onto the sidewalk.

I waved as Denise drove off. She didn't look back. "Heartless bitch," I thought. And then I felt real loathing for myself. I knew she was a good, caring person. Tactless, maybe. But basically a good person. She didn't deserve to be called names. Again I wondered what was becoming of me. In the past I'd felt all women were heartless bitches.

Margarita came through her front door.

"Hey."

"Hey to you," I said. I used the chair to get to the front door.

"Want to go to dinner first?"

"Sure."

The Mexican food was good, but my stomach was a bit upset that evening. I paid the bill and left what I thought was a good tip. I got the wheelchair back to the car and into the trunk and then out of the trunk and into Margarita's living room. This being crippled thing was exhausting. I sat heavily in the wheelchair as Margarita did some fussing in the kitchen. She brought in some coffee and Mexican cookies. Fortunately, my appetite was still hearty. She'd told me not to order dessert at the restaurant because she'd made some cookies she wanted me to try. They were delicious. But then I hadn't eaten anything in my months of recovery that wasn't delicious. Drinking had starved my body of nutrients for years, and it was still trying to make up for what had been lost.

"So—how's it going, Evan?"

"It's been a rough day."

"Oh?"

I told her about the morning's interview with EG. I played back the tape so she could hear exactly what had been said."

"And?"

"Where does she get that Teri and I were just as responsible as our mother for the way our relationship with her was once we became adults? I never set a boundary with her, and I'm damned if I'm going to be blamed for Angela Howard not making amends to my sister and me."

"Amend means to change, Evan. Your mother changed in so many ways. When I first met her she was willing to throw herself under any bus just to talk with you kids."

"So?"

"So, the professionals who were working with her struggled for a long time to get her to understand that she was making matters worse with all her phone calls, letters, gifts and cards trying to make you kids understand why she was who she was and why she did just about everything she ever did. Every attempt to get you to see her side just made you angrier."

"And?"

"And finally, she got a letter from you and Teri. She brought it to me. I told your mother that you kids were well over twenty-one years of age and that if she wanted to stay sober and get truly healthy, she would not dishonor the boundary the two of you were setting with her."

I said nothing.

"Do you want to see the letter? She gave it to me on her deathbed in case either of you ever asked why you weren't contacted when she was dying."

Chapter 9

Margarita went into her bedroom and came back with a book—a journal. "This is for you and for Teri if she wants it. Read the letter you two put together and sent her."

I unfolded the yellowed piece of paper. It was cheap paper. The letter was typed. Our signatures were at the bottom of the very short paragraph:

> *Angela -- This is to inform you that we are disowning you. Do not attempt to contact us in any way. You are not to send anything to us or to your grandchildren. If you do, it will be sent back by return mail.*
> *Evan   Teri*

It was dated June of 1993. It was definitely my signature and Teri's.

"I swear to you, I don't remember doing this."

"Oh, you did it all right. To the very last minute she struggled to accept your decision."

Margarita's eyes filled with tears. I began to sob. She let me sit with my own pain. No one could take away the reality of what Teri and I had done.

"If either of you had given Angela just one smidgeon of forgiveness, she'd have died the happiest woman on the earth." Margarita looked me straight in the eye, and this time I heard her and I felt the weight of my own hatred for my mother. I felt my thoughts swirling in the old effort to justify what I had done. Margarita handed me a box of tissues. "Go to bed, Evan. Read a little of your mother's journal if you can. If you can't, take the journal to Teri and let her read it."

With that Margarita left me. I knew where the bedroom was. I felt at home in this house, too. What I didn't feel comfortable with was what I was learning about life and myself. At that moment I hated me. I would have loved to have had a drink. Fortunately, I was in Margarita's house and that wasn't going to happen. I tried to begin reading my mother's final journal that night. I reread the letter Teri and I had sent her. Some of what

Teri had told me was now making sense. I was beginning to realize that I always saw my mother through my father's eyes.
Now, life was demanding that I do what Hardy had been telling
me to do for months. I needed to see what was and what is
through my own eyes. I washed my face and pulled my own pajamas out of my battered old case. I hung up my clothes and
crawled under the covers. I read the first page of the last chapter
of my mother's life and ended up in a very deep sleep. I
dreamed about my mother that night, maybe for the first time
ever. She opened her arms and held me just as EG had done earlier in the day, and I swear I could smell the lotion my mother
used to wear.

CHAPTER 10

I woke up the next morning feeling as confused as I've ever felt in my life. I could smell bacon cooking. I grabbed the wheelchair and walked myself into the bathroom. I took a shower, holding onto doors, handles and lavatory tops to make sure I didn't fall. My legs were getting a little stronger. Margarita had several towels laid out. I put one on the seat of the wheelchair and sat my wet butt on it. I used another towel to dry the rest of my body. The warm water felt wonderful. The lather and a clean shave felt good, too. I was beginning to appreciate little things. But none of the good feelings countered the heaviness I felt in my chest. I brushed my teeth and stood up to comb my damp hair. I looked myself straight in the eyes and then had to look away.

I dressed and straightened the bed to the best of my ability. I was never good at housework. Nothing I ever did was good enough for Angela Howard. I decided I didn't want to go into more thoughts about my childhood, so I focused on getting the quilt straight, the pillows in their proper place, and myself on the way to the kitchen.

"Good morning, Sunshine." Margarita was in her happy-happy-happy mode.

"Good morning," I replied. I pulled myself up to one of the tall stools behind the breakfast bar.

"We don't have to sit at the bar, Evan. We can sit at the table."

"All I want to do is be a grown up, Margarita. Let me get myself up on this stool."

She turned back to the stove. "Want your eggs over easy?"

"Yes, please."

Thank God for all the weeks of muscle building I'd had with the wheelchair, because it took all I had to get up on the stool. But I made it up and put both arms on the counter top.

"So—how'd you sleep?"

I tried to figure out if I should tell Margarita about the dream. In the end, my mouth started pouring out the dream and descriptions of all the feelings I was going through. I'd lost control of my own mouth. Margarita put the filled plates on the counter and came around and sat beside me. She put my napkin on my lap and a fork in my hand.

"Eat. You need lots of good food."

So I ate. And so did she. We said nothing more until the food was gone. Margarita served cinnamon-raisin toast and I absolutely loved it. My mother used to try to get me to eat cinnamon-raisin toast and I refused to try it. My father hated cinnamon-raisin toast and he grumbled every time she served it.

"So did you know that my mother and I used to have a war about cinnamon-raisin toast?"

"No, Evan, I didn't know that. I just happen to love cinnamon-raisin toast and that's what I had on hand. I knew a lot of things about your mother, but we didn't have the time to talk about toast, for God's sake."

"Can I have some more toast?"

"Sure. So tell me about the war over the toast."

"I'm beginning to understand this stuff about role models. I never questioned anything my father said or did."

"Most kids don't, unless their role model is the scapegoat. Teri's the one who got an extra load of confusion, because the most powerful person in your family saw her role model as a problem. At least as a male you got to think you had the upper hand."

Again, I had no idea why she was saying what she was saying. But I wolfed down the cinnamon-raisin toast and asked if we could just get to work on the book.

Margarita and I worked most of the rest of the day as professionals. A good lunch, some more work and a hug at the BART station summed up my time with her that particular day.

CHAPTER 11

Hardy and Paranoid were waiting at the station in the city. I came out of the elevator to see the two of them laughing. They were telling each other lawyer jokes and wanted to know if I wanted to hear some of them. I made it clear, without saying a word, that I wasn't in the mood.

"What happened, Bro? Did EG and Margarita beat you up?" Another of Paranoid's attempts at humor.

"No. I beat myself up." I was aware that they were giving each other that "he just got another insight" look that 12-Steppers give each other all the time. When we got to the car I told them that I was now able to get the chair into the trunk by myself. Both men stepped back and let me do it. When I turned around to guide myself into the back seat, both of them looked me in the eyes. The looks said they were proud of me and happy for me. I sat down heavily and closed the door behind me. We pulled away from the curb.

Hardy spoke first. "Do you want to talk about what happened?"

"I don't think I can without breaking down. Give me some time to process all this new stuff, okay. I guess I could use some lawyer jokes."

Chapter 11

They were off and running and didn't stop with the jokes until we were in front of my apartment. I was able to get with them and laugh by about the third or fourth joke. It was a good ride home and just what I needed. I got my chair out of the trunk. I still needed Paranoid to get it up the steps, but I knew it wouldn't be long and I'd be able to get it up and down the stairs myself. It was important for me to do as much for myself as possible. That's what the accident was teaching me. I was beginning to realize that all the walls I'd built around me to keep people out never really made me an independent person. I was just a frightened kid with walls around me.

Paranoid and the chair went first. Hardy followed me. By the time I got to my front door, I realized that something different was happening. I used the chair as a walker, unlocked the door and went in. The two of them followed me right in. They weren't going to let me off the hook.

"What?"

"So what happened? Come on, man. Process it with us." Paranoid was giving me a gentle order. I wanted to look anywhere but in his deep dark brown eyes, but he held my gaze."

"I think I told you at the BART station that I need to process all that went on first."

"Uh-huh," said Hardy. "If you need to cry, you're going to goddamned learn how to cry in front of us. Hell—we'll probably cry with you. You're not any different than we are, and we had to learn to feel all of our feelings with other men, healthy men who are no longer afraid to show the soft side of their selves."

"It's the divine side," said Paranoid.

"The divine side?"

"Never mind," said Hardy. "You'll understand soon enough. Just tell us what happened in the East Bay."

So I went through the meetings with Elizabeth and dinner with Margarita. And then I told them about Margarita giving me the letter Teri and I had sent to our mother so many years ago. I took the letter out and showed it to them.

"I've been trying to remember signing this, and I have a vague recollection of Teri sitting at her computer typing out the note. I think we were both drinking and we were talking about getting even with Mom."

Both men shook their heads.

"What I don't understand is this boundary crap. Angela was the mother. She was supposed to contact us and get things straightened out."

"Were you children under the age of eighteen when you wrote this note?" It was Hardy asking the question.

"No." The truth was we were both well over thirty if I remember rightly.

"And who taught you that you had the right to tell someone to never contact you again and that you then had the right to expect that person to ignore what you said and humiliate themselves by begging you to allow them back into your life?" Hardy was in my face by this time. I pushed backwards and moved away from him. He stepped forward.

"When you put it that way…"

"Oh yeah…when it's put that way it sure looks different, doesn't it?" This time Paranoid was moving into my space.

"Come on, guys. I'm beginning to understand. Give me that, will you? I'm thinking of flying down to L.A. and seeing Teri either this weekend or next."

Both men said that was a good idea. They hugged me and left. And there I was. Alone with knowledge that I couldn't deny or escape from. I truly was a piece of shit. I didn't feel love for my mother, but I was beginning to feel compassion for her. I was just beginning to realize that I had been truly unfair to her. I looked over and saw that there was a message for me on my answering machine. I rolled over to it and punched the playback button.

"Evan, this is Teri. I hope this doesn't upset you, but I've been thinking about you in recovery and things you're learning about Mom and Dad. I made reservations to fly up there this weekend. We need to talk. Don't worry about accommodations. I'll stay at a hotel. I think there's a Marriott on Van Ness— pretty close to your place. I'll be in Friday afternoon. See you."

CHAPTER 12

I called Teri back and told her that I'd thought about flying to L.A. but was glad to hear she was coming to San Francisco for a visit. On Friday I took a cab to the airport to meet her when she arrived. I insisted she stay at my place. Madge and I had cleaned things up and bought some new sheets and towels so that Teri would have comfortable surroundings during her visit.

We picked up a rental car and drove home from the south peninsula, stopping on Polk Street for a bite of dinner before coming back to my place. We talked all evening. My memory of Teri typing out the short paragraph to Mom was correct. She said we were both pretty well loaded. Ever since I came into recovery I'd been hearing all about the meanness of the disease of alcoholism. Now I was beginning to see up close and personal just how mean I could be under the influence. We both acknowledged that Mom could be mean under the influence, but we also acknowledged that Mom's respect for the boundary we'd set wasn't the intended outcome of that note.

Teri cried when I gave her the note. I told her about my rather one-sided conversation with Hardy and Paranoid. I'd never thought that Angela Howard might need to respect the boundary we had set with her.

"I didn't see it that way either, Evan. Mom fought to get through to Dad for more than twenty years. I think I assumed that she'd do the same for me—for us. I've been going to AA, Al Anon and Codependents Anonymous, and I'm learning that Mom had to escape our family if she was ever going to survive mentally, much less physically. Both Mom and Dad came from abusive families. I think Dad shut down as a very young child. His father was a junk yard dog drunk from what I remember."

"What was Mom's problem? I think we always knew he didn't love her. I thought she was insane to keep trying to get him to love her. Why couldn't she be satisfied with the fact that he brought home his paycheck and supported her?"

Teri reared her head back. "You're a Neanderthal, Evan. I can put myself in Mom's place. Dad took vows to love and cherish her. There were witnesses to that. She had a right to be loved by her husband."

Teri began to cry, and all I could do was turn my wheelchair away from her.

"Don't you turn away from me. Look at the tears, Evan. Face human emotions for once in your life."

I turned back to her and there it was again. She was looking me straight in the eyes. I threw my arms up in the air in a fit of frustration and aggravation. I clenched my fists and didn't know what to do with myself.

"Just like Dad—that's what he'd do every time he didn't know what to do with Mom. And then he'd walk away and that would end the fight. And Mom would go crazy. She couldn't stand cold shoulders and the silent treatment. Oh, she'd come back days later and try again to engage him, but he'd always close her off. I remember so many of those fights. And I always thought he was right and she was wrong."

"Oh, that reminds me. Do you remember Dad saying anything that set us up to think Mom was the only problem in the family?" I wasn't changing the subject. There seemed to be a connection to what Teri was saying and what happened to EG's kids.

"Like what?"

"Well, Elizabeth Grayson's first husband told her children from the time they were little that if they had problems when they grew up it would be their mother's fault because she was the active one—she was the doer. Do you remember anything like that coming from Dad?"

"I remember both of us watching him shrug his shoulders at Mom and we'd shrug our shoulders right behind him. I don't know about you, but because she was the one who fought and screamed and kicked and cried, I always thought she was the problem. I never thought there was anything wrong with Dad. It was only when I noticed that my husband was doing the same thing, and the children were being triangulated against me, that I began to understand Mom's side of the story. I had begun using alcohol to medicate my feelings, and I worried about becoming alcoholic because we're genetically predisposed to alcoholism on both sides of the family. So, I went to a therapist and she sent me to AA and Al Anon and it was the best thing that ever happened to me."

"Why haven't you had contact with me, Teri?"

"Evan, I called and called and invited you for visits. You never called back and you never came to visit. I was getting messages from my friends in recovery and from my therapist to just let you go and pray that someday you'd want to rebuild our relationship. I had to let you go just like Mom had to let us go. But I did have some contact with Ed Wainwright and I knew your drinking was progressing. There was no point in calling you."

We talked a little more but I soon began nodding off. I used the bathroom while Teri did some readings and yoga meditation. And then we went to bed. I slept on the couch with my old sheets.

We both slept deeply that night. I got up first, sneaked past Teri's sleeping body and used the bathroom, then went out to the kitchen to make fresh coffee and a good breakfast. I had a wonderful sense of belonging that morning. I felt a warmth that I may never have felt before in my life. I had a member of my family in my home. My sister had come to visit me. We were talking about emotional things and we were sharing recovery. It was like we had a shorthand language between us. Not just recovery language, but family language, shared experiences. I loved cooking in my kitchen that day. I made bacon, eggs, pancakes with real maple syrup, fresh orange juice and fresh brewed coffee. The smells were wonderful.

"I've got to get a picture of this!" Teri stood in the doorway watching me move pretty easily around the kitchen. I pushed the back of the wheelchair against the stove and locked the wheels in place. I knelt on the seat and put the meal together like a pro. I'd thought to get everything I needed out on the counter next to the stove top. I even had the table set with new place mats and napkins. I was so grown up I could hardly stand myself.

"How do you want your eggs?"

"Over easy, thanks."

Teri poured the juice and waited until I had the plates dished up. She put them on the table while I unlocked the wheels and scooted to my place at the table. Teri poured the coffee and got cream out of the refrigerator and sat down in her place. We ate in silence. I enjoyed every bite.

"This was delicious, Evan. I'm impressed. Really impressed."

"Thank you. I was thinking—I'd like you to meet some of my recovery friends. Madge lives just down the porch, and I'd like to invite her to ride with us to the Saturday morning meeting."

"Great. Will I get to meet Hardy and Paranoid?"

"Count on it. I called them after I got your message to say you were coming and that you planned to get a rental car. They offered to pick all of us up, but I really prefer to drive with just you and Madge."

"Whatever works for you, brother."

I called Madge. She said she'd meet us out front about twenty minutes before the hour. I got myself ready. Teri cleaned up the kitchen. I showered and shaved and looked myself straight in the eyes in the mirror. Feelings, all of them good, were running through me. I actually smiled at myself. The itty bitty shitty committee, as Hardy called the voices in my head, didn't have a bad word to say to me that morning. I realized I was having another first-in-a-lifetime experience.

Teri and I left the apartment at the appointed time. Madge was waiting for us. Teri walked straight into Madge's arms.

"You look just like your Momma," Madge said. She started to cry. So did Teri.

The two women held each other for a moment. They turned around and grabbed my wheelchair in concert. I got down the stairs and held onto the handrail as they brought the chair to the bottom of the stairs. Madge signaled that she'd drive her car. Teri and I obeyed. I got the chair into Madge's trunk, slid into the back seat and listened as the two of them chattered back and forth as though they'd known each other all their lives. Teri cried. Madge cried. I rolled my eyes a lot. We were soon at the meeting. I rolled myself to the table holding the food and got myself a sweet roll. Madge and Teri took seats in the front row, right at the end where I could roll my chair up next to Teri. I certainly felt like the third wheel. I felt that way because I was. But I was able to sit back and watch something very magical happen between my sister and my old friend. I still hadn't been able to talk to Madge about her knowledge of the note that Teri and I had sent our mother. If she knew anything about it, she certainly wasn't holding any anger toward Teri because of it. Maybe some of Madge's anger at me over the years came from knowing about that note. Right now it didn't matter. The meeting started. I looked around and saw Hardy and Paranoid sitting a few rows back.

I didn't get a lot out of that meeting. I felt a new energy swirling about me. I wasn't terribly comfortable with it, but I didn't dislike it either. I would get an even bigger dose of that energy after the meeting. Madge, Hardy and Paranoid said they wanted to take Teri down to the restaurant behind Union Square for a corned beef sandwich. They told her that it was our mother's favorite food in the whole world, and could they treat her to one of those sandwiches. Teri agreed and glowed in the light of all the attention she was getting. I felt left out and started to pout. I realized what I was doing and told myself to grow up, or to at least get the pouty look off my face. I think I succeeded.

So we had corned beef sandwiches and everyone freely talked about their experiences with Angela Howard. Teri listened and cried a lot. I had mixed feelings. I was still struggling to accept that I might have been wrong in some instances about my mother. Paranoid sat next to me. Teri sat between Hardy and Madge. When she laughed or cried, she'd lean against one or the other's shoulder and they'd hug her.

I ate and thought. Paranoid punched my shoulder a couple of times. All of a sudden, Hardy turned his attention to me.

"What's happening in you, Evan? This has to be churning things up for you."

All of a sudden all four sets of eyes were looking at me. Except for Paranoid, it was straight in the eyes.

"To be honest, I don't know what's going on in me. I'm really, really happy to have Teri here. But I have to admit, I think I feel some jealousy to have to be sharing her with all of you."

Silence. I looked at Teri. "What's with this sudden love affair with Madge? You've just met her."

"She knew Mom, Evan. She's a connection to the parent I disowned. That hug on the porch this morning felt like it came from Mom. I'm two years older than you. I remember being loved by our mother. Maybe you don't."

The problem was that I was remembering some loving moments with our mother. I'd successfully buried them for years, but I hadn't been able to kill them completely. I waved my hand because I couldn't say anything. Paranoid put his arm around me and squeezed. I wanted to cry but was damned if I was going to let that happen. Everyone seemed to understand because no one pushed me in any way.

"I was hoping to take you and Teri to Muir Woods either today or tomorrow," said Madge. "Your Momma and I went there together often. Would you be up for that? They have electric chairs built to work in the woods, so you'd be able to go right along with us, Evan."

Chapter 12

I looked at Teri.

"I'd love to go there. It's redwoods, right?" said Teri.

"It is. And you're as close to God as you'll ever get," said Hardy. "I brought my big car in the hope that we could all go there. Would that be okay, Evan?"

I looked at Teri. She nodded her head.

"I guess so." Damned. They're going to take me to be close to God of all people. And so we left Union Square. We took Madge's car home and then headed to Muir Woods with Hardy in the driver's seat.

CHAPTER 13

The five of us traveled north into Marin County. Teri had tons of questions. Madge and Hardy had lots of answers. Hardy and Paranoid were up front. Madge, Teri and I sat in the back. While they talked about Angela Howard, I thought about the car we were riding in. It just didn't fit my picture of Hardy. It was a luxury SUV—a Cadillac Escalade. I realized I actually knew next to nothing about my sponsor except for excruciatingly minute details of his drinking history and recovery. I didn't know if he was married, worked, was retired—nothing. He probably would have told me if I'd asked. But I never thought to ask about anyone. I was busy trying to get the article written so that I had an income. Now, I was too busy trying to get the book together.

"You're awfully quiet back there, Evan."

"I was just thinking about your car, Hardy. It's really nice. Do you have two cars?"

"I do. This is one of my splurges. I bought it after my wife died two years ago." And then he explained to Teri that he'd only been married a few years. He'd met his wife in the program. Both of them had more than twenty years of recovery under their belts when Marilyn moved to San Francisco. She was retiring from teaching and wanted to be closer to her kids. They

282

fell in love and got married, and not long after they married, Marilyn was diagnosed with brain cancer. It didn't take long for it to kill her.

"I'd worked through the pain and loss by the time you landed on my doorstep, Evan. My friends in the program got me through it."

Teri launched into a rather long winded description of how her recovery program had helped her weather her kids' growing up years, and that her greatest comfort is getting to meet the people who helped our mother through her recovery and death. My stomach turned. And then it got quiet. My sister is in recovery, too. And she's happy. So why did her statement upset me, I wondered. Maybe I was still mad about the conspiracy and feeling like they were all laughing at me. Ah, yes. That was it. I felt like the whole car was laughing at me. But they weren't, and I'd had enough recovery to know that. So I did something that was new behavior for me. I kept my mouth shut.

When we arrived at Muir Woods, Hardy got me as close to the visitor's center as he could. He gave me my chair, and I got myself to the center while he parked the car in the regular parking area. The other three came with me and helped arrange for an electric wheelchair with big fat, cushy wheels. Hardy caught up with us and off we went into the woods. It was a very warm day outside of the woods. It was a constant fifty-two degrees inside the redwood forest. Madge had thought to bring extra sweaters and jackets. I pulled a big old plaid, woolen jacket around me. We read the information panels as we went along. It was so quiet. The birds were so high you could hardly hear them. The smell of rotting vegetation was clearly present but not objectionable. The chair moved quietly and easily over lumps and bumps on the natural walkway. In about an hour we reached the top of the walk-through loop.

"This is where your Momma came and sat at least once a month for years." Madge pointed to the bench in front of us.

"I want to sit here for a while, too," said Teri.

Madge sat down next to Teri. Both women closed their eyes. A terrible feeling ran through me. I was actually feeling physical pain. Hardy and Paranoid walked to the next nearest bench and sat down. They closed their eyes. It looked like they were in church. I looked at Madge and my sister and felt my pain and asked myself what the matter was. That still, small voice said, "You're jealous. Madge is your friend, you're neighbor. Don't be jealous. There's plenty of love for you and for Teri."

"Can I sit on the bench, too?"

Madge and Teri both stood up. Without a word they helped me out of the chair and onto the bench. I plopped down between them. Madge had an extra throw with her and she put it over all three of our laps. I don't know how long we sat there, but it was magic. Hundreds of people could have passed by for all I know. I sat there cooled by the air and warmed by the two women's bodies. I nestled down between my sister and my friend. Madge pulled me to her and held me. Teri rubbed my back. I let go of a lot of shit that afternoon.

Madge kept going "shhh, shhh, shhh. Your Momma loved you no matter what, Evan Howard."

I couldn't see Teri's face but I could hear her sniffling and blowing her nose. I don't know if our mother was present that afternoon, but I have a strong suspicion she was. Madge insists she was. The three non-Howard people waited for us. After a very long period of quiet, maybe the longest period of quiet I'd ever experienced in my life, Teri took my hand.

"Are you okay?" I looked my sister in the eyes.

"I actually am okay, Teri. I feel okay. I have feelings of sadness and loss."

"They're about what might have been, Evan. We could have had a relationship with our mother if we weren't so damn self-righteous. Dad never meant to alienate us from her. She didn't get up each morning and ask herself what she could do to make us hate her that day. Mom and Dad were a bad combination. Unfortunately, we were kids and we went with the power person in the family. Dad was so quiet. He looked like the 'sane' one. But honestly, if things were as bad as he indicated to us they were, why didn't he get Mom help? Or why didn't he get himself and

Chapter 13

us out of the marriage? No. He chose to do nothing. Finally it was Mom who ended the misery."

"That's really interesting, because EG asked pretty much the same questions. If things were so bad, why didn't Matt Monahan get his kids out of the misery? And here we sit asking the same questions about our father."

Hardy, Paranoid and Madge were listening to every word. All three heads were nodding up and down with every word that Teri and I said. I looked over at the two men. They were looking at the ground, but their heads were still going up and down even though Teri and I had stopped talking.

"So what are you three thinking?" They knew who I was talking to.

Madge spoke. "We've been waiting for years for you two to 'get it.' It's nice to be here with you in this blessed place, this sacred place."

And that's all that was said. Madge and Teri helped me back into the chair. I went ahead of the column. I stopped after a few feet and dug out some tissues from my pack. I needed to wipe the wetness from my face. The cool temperature seemed to almost freeze the tears on my face. I started up again. Part of me wanted to speed my way out of the forest. Fortunately, the chair was built to go slowly, probably a couple miles an hour. So I pushed the throttle to full tilt and the other four kept up with me quite easily. I may have been ahead of them physically, but I was eons behind them spiritually, and I knew it just as surely as the sun comes up in the east and goes down in the west.

CHAPTER 14

Teri stayed two more days and we talked until both of us were talked out. She insisted that I go to an Al Anon meeting and a Codependents Anonymous meeting with her. I began to understand that I was codependent with alcohol. I depended on it to help me deaden feelings and to cope with everything that ever wandered through my life. I began to understand that Mom was codependent with Dad and vice versa. She did become codependent with alcohol, but more than anything, she needed to get Dad to love her and pay attention to her. He unconsciously needed to fix her alcoholism, or to punish another alcoholic for the love his alcoholic father couldn't give him. Maybe he was really trying to fix his father's alcoholism, but his father died when Teri and I were very young. That didn't change his need to fix the problems of his childhood. Dad did tell us that his father was a raging drunk. It took Mom years to become that, but his behaviors, his emotional deadness drove her to scream at him in her efforts to get some kind of a reaction out of him. All of this made intellectual sense, but I really struggled to put any responsibility on my father for any of our mother's screaming. Teri had no trouble doing that at all.

"You seem so unemotional about all of this, Teri."

"I'm in total acceptance of both of our parents. I'm in total acceptance that I am fifty percent of any relationship."

"So how does that affect us as individuals?"

"If someone hits me, then shame on him or her. If they hit me again and I do nothing, then it's shame, shame on me. I've allowed the bad behavior to continue. Mom worked hard to be a good wife. Dad felt his only responsibility was to bring home the money and everything else was Mom's to do. Neither of them understood how unbalanced their relationship was. I had the same kind of marriage for the first ten years, and then I began yelling and screaming. Just like Mom. That's when I went to counseling and that's when I was directed to go to Al Anon *and* Codependents Anonymous. I was contributing my fifty percent to replicating my childhood home by doing nothing that would actually change the dynamic. Bert was just like Dad. Just a quiet, pleasant, non-entity except for his paycheck. And I was beginning to use alcohol in the evenings, just like Mom. So I went to meetings and I stopped using alcohol and told Bert I wasn't going to spend twenty more years trying to reach him. I was ready to walk, and I guess he knew it because he started going to counseling and to men's support groups. He actually began to bond with the kids and me. I took a hundred percent credit for everything that happened, and I hated Mom more because she could have done it too, or so I thought.

"What caused you to forgive, or let go of the belief that Mom could have or should have fixed our family?"

"Dad's girlfriends. They all have the same complaint. They all leave for the very same reasons. And to be honest, I've spent a lot of energy trying to get Dad to love me and approve of me and he's nothing but a stranger to me. I love him with all my heart, but I don't expect to have any more emotional exchanges with him than Mom had with him. That's just how it is. I remember Mom saying that she didn't know any more about our father than she did three days before she met him. I had no idea what she was talking about then. I know exactly what she was saying now."

We sat in silence for quite a while.

"Evan?"

"Yeah?"

"You've always been just as remote and unreachable as Dad. I understand that some of that is probably genetic. It was also modeled to you, so you've worked very hard all your life not to get close to anyone. I can't tell you what it means to me to see you actually expressing emotions. I'll hold our time on that bench in Muir Woods yesterday dear to my heart forever. I truly feel at peace with so much right now. I wish this weekend could go on forever."

My heart warmed to those words. I got out of the wheelchair and sat on the old beat-up couch next to my sister. We held hands and cried. We fixed a light supper and went to bed early. We were both exhausted. The next morning, Teri drove to the airport. I rolled the chair out onto the porch of the apartment building and watched her put her suitcase into the trunk of the car. She turned and looked up at me and threw me a kiss. I promised to get down to Los Angeles as soon as possible to meet my nieces and nephews and to honestly get to know my brother-in-law.

Madge came up behind me and waved to Teri as she got in the car. Teri threw Madge a kiss, too.

"Want some coffee?"

"Uh-huh," I answered. I rolled into Madge's apartment. She handed me a box of tissues. I just sat and cried for a few minutes. I felt like something wonderful had just been ripped from me. For the first time in my life, someone I was actually related to by blood had been in my life. I needed family. I needed my mother, father and sister. Madge stood behind the chair and held my shoulders as I spit out those thoughts. She pushed me up to the table and poured a cup of coffee, then sat down across from me and looked me straight in the eyes—again.

"You have your family, Evan, if you'll just open your mind and heart. They may not love you exactly the way you want or think they should love you. But they love you the very best they can."

"Ya think my Mom's loving me right now?"

Chapter 14

"I know she's loving you with all her being, Evan?

"What about my father?"

"He's loving you the best he can. You know there are some spiritual laws that are in effect at all times, Evan. You can fight those laws all you want but you'll never change them."

"I guess you'll tell me what those laws are."

"We can only feel love to the extent we love ourselves. We can only love others to the extent we love ourselves. If we don't think well of ourselves, we'll set up every relationship to reflect that poor self image."

"Would you write that down for me? I think my brain just locked up."

"I'll bet it locked up." Madge walked over to a cupboard and pulled out a notebook. She pulled out a printed sheet that was in a folder in the notebook. And there it was:

> ### The Spiritual Laws That Govern Relationships
> *You can fight these laws as long as you wish to but they will never change no matter how long and hard you fight with them.*
> - *You can only love others to the extent you love yourself.*
> - *Others can only love you to the extent that you love yourself.*
> - *You can only feel the love of others to the extent you're able to feel your own love of self.*
> - *Health draws health, sickness draws sickness. If you're convinced that the person you're in relationship with is sick then you have to honestly admit that parts of you are equally sick or you would never have been attracted to that person.*
> - *The only sure source of love, the only relationship we can truly depend on, is our relationship with our Higher Power and our selves. The only feelings of true security we can experience come through this relation-*

289

> *ship and no other. People change, people die.*
> *They're no more dependable than we are.*
> • *When we no longer "need" others to love,*
>   *accept, approve of, and understand us, we*
>   *then get these things from human beings. Our*
>   *first source of these things must be our*
>   *Higher Power and our selves.*

I read the so-called laws.

"Absolutely everyone is governed by those laws, Evan. Your parents could only give you what they were given. I knew your Mom when she first came into the program. She was about as beaten down as anyone I've ever known. She came in believing that she'd failed as a wife and mother. The treatment you, Teri and your father gave her—cutting her out of your lives completely—almost killed her. But she stayed with the program and she let us love her until she could love herself. She died in grace. She loved her new life, and the only dark spots in that life were the holes you and Teri used to fill.

"Madge, I've been wanting to talk with you about the conspiracy."

"Yes?"

"Of all the people involved, I was most hurt by you. We've been neighbors for years and I know I spent hours griping and complaining to you about my rotten mother and all the while you were having a friendship with her. Somehow that doesn't seem right."

"Well, Evan, it's possible for healthy people to love two people who are in conflict with each other. I loved your mother and I loved you. I never carried a single word that you said back to your mother. Never."

"Why not? You had a lot of good gossip to take back to her."

"Why would I carry things you said back to her that would hurt her? We try to live all of the 12 Steps, Evan. We don't gossip and we don't repeat things that would be harmful or hurtful to others. Or do you not get that yet?"

"I guess I don't. Did Mom know we were neighbors?"

"Yes she did. And she never asked me to try to get a message to you. She did ask me often to give you a hug for her if you'd let me. Unfortunately, you were not very open to hugs until recently."

We drank our coffee in silence.

"Going to a meeting today?" Madge asked.

"I guess. Can I go with you?"

"Sure."

"And then I've got to get busy and get the book written."

"Yes. You need to get that book written."

EPILOGUE

August, 2007

Dear Reader:

The book did get finished and it continues to enjoy good sales. It turned out to be a very different book from the one I thought I was assigned to write. "The Committee," i.e., the conspirators, informed me as I was pulling things together that they simply wanted me to use my journal work to explain my pathway out of addiction and hatred for my mother. Naturally, my story explained beautifully what had happened in the Monahan Family and why Elizabeth Grayson was so hated by her children. It hit a chord in the American psyche. Apparently there are all sorts of families torn apart by parental alienation. The magazine and I split royalties and we're doing pretty well to this day. Every week letters come in from people who were harmed by parental alienation, and a substantial percentage of that alienation happened inside the marriage, not during divorce.

I'm now three years sober. The relapse on Pine Street was the last one so far. Hardy is still my sponsor and Paranoid is still my bro. I'm still working at the magazine, but as I got further into recovery I realized that I needed to finish my undergraduate degree and maybe get an advanced degree and do something more with my life. So I'm now in graduate school pursuing a Master's Degree in Psychology. I may continue writing for the magazine or I could go into a therapeutic setting myself. I take meetings into the county jail twice a month. Paranoid is my partner and I feel a whole lot safer being with him. I'm learning that there are a lot of alcoholics and otherwise mentally ill people housed in jails all over the country. I thank God every day that I didn't end up in that situation.

Paranoid is working at a youth center. He's gotten several large grants to support sports programs and after-school programs. He can talk to troubled kids like no one else can. I help him out once a month with reports he has to turn in to the agencies from which he got the grants. It's one of the best friendships a guy could have.

I've tried out lots of meetings. I was amazed to learn there are almost 550 different AA meetings in the city and county of San Francisco every week. There are hundreds of other 12-Step meetings every week, too. There are Al Anon meetings, Al Ateen and Al Atot meetings, Codependents Anonymous meetings, Emotions Anonymous meetings, Families Anonymous meetings, and others too numerous to list. Churches and synagogues are implementing 12-Step groups within their belief systems. Mental health professionals are losing a lot of their anti-12-Step biases and employee assistance programs are insisting on long term, consistent participation in 12-Step recovery groups as a condition of continued employment for employees who have gotten into trouble with substances or troubling behaviors. It's amazing how deep the 12-Step movement has gone through society today. It truly is a grass roots movement that's finally getting some attention from the power structures of the Twenty-First Century.

I'm still living in the same apartment. You wouldn't recognize it if you saw it today. I celebrated my first anniversary of sobriety by getting the entire place cleaned and freshly painted. Got some new carpeting and drapes. Real adult stuff. I threw out all the old furniture. None of the charities would take it. You know stuff has to be really bad when even the charities turn you down.

Madge is still my neighbor and I notice she and Hardy getting awfully chummy lately. I wonder where that friendship is going. I don't know if I like them getting closer or hate them getting closer. Paranoid says it's none of my damned business.

Ed Wainwright and I have mended our friendship. He's still my boss, so it's not quite as loose as it was when we were in high school and college. But then we're not drinking anymore and we're not that young anymore either.

I still have to use the wheelchair quite a bit, but I get around well. I've had a couple of lady friends over the past three years. I really want to have a good, loving relationship someday, but I know in every cell of being that I have a lot more work to do on learning to love and accept myself before I'll be able to fully love another person and be truly fair to her. Right now I'm putting all my energy into my recovery, work and school. I love all the new things I'm learning. I've gotten really good with the computer, too. I buy quite a bit of what I have to buy online and it gets delivered to me. Me and the chair are a real pain in narrow store aisles.

I never got to have a date with Denise Kinzler. But I did dance with her at her wedding. She was very patient as I used a walker and she held onto my shoulders. I went home really sad that night because the immature part of me really hoped she'd wait for me to grow up. She married a nice guy, and we all socialize when the Graysons have a picnic or a party. She still works for EG and seems to be very happy in every respect.

Margarita Sanchez-Lopez and I have had a professional relationship. I go out to the East Bay twice a month for sessions. She gives me lots of homework to do. Most of it is Sixth and Seventh Step assignments, or new books to read. If I do become a counselor, I want to work the way Margarita does. I've met some of her other patients in groups and they all have positive feelings about themselves and the new knowledge they're gaining about how the Higher Power intended life to work.

Teri and I are close today. We talk every week and we see each other several times a year. I actually spent Christmas and New Year's with her and her family last year. She does it just like Mom did. I can say Mom today and feel tenderness for my mother. I've seen my Dad, too. He's had some more mild strokes, and his current girlfriend says that's why he's so emotionally distant. I won't argue with her, but he seems exactly like the Dad I grew up with.

You're probably wondering about that piece of glass that used to be our Mom's. Teri did ask EG for it and EG was happy to give it to her. Teri had a very special place in her living room for it. The sun hit it just like it did in our childhood home. The first time I visited Teri's, I couldn't resist picking the piece up several times. I just held it and had a lot of feelings. Teri caught me holding it once and she decided we should share it. So I brought it to San Francisco and put it on the nightstand beside my bed. Since I've been keeping the windows clean, the morning sun got caught in the prism every day, and I awoke to flashing lights and colors falling all over the room. When Teri came to visit again, she took it home with her. So Mom's beautiful piece of glass wanders between San Francisco and Los Angeles. It's been good for both Teri and me. For me personally, I believe that we're reconnecting with Angela Howard through color, light, and love.

EG's children still are estranged from her. I tried to speak with them shortly after the book was published to explain how far off base I had been about my own mother. They refused to talk to me. Mr. Monahan told me that the article was a complete betrayal of him and his children. He said I clearly hadn't heard a word that any of them said. And that's just how it is.

I did call EG's former sister-in-law. She was married to one of Matt Monahan's brothers. She confirmed that the oldest brother got three shares of his father's estate and yes, he drank it up in a few months. So EG and her fetus went hungry when more money could have been available. I called Mr. Monahan to ask why he allowed that to happen when his wife was pregnant and he hung up on me.

Epilogue

And so ends this chapter of my life. I'm happy and as healthy as it's possible to be after years of hard drinking, a crippling accident, and feelings of pure hatred for the woman who gave birth to me. The years of self-hatred have taken their toll on me, too.

Friends are asking if I'll write more books. Maybe. Maybe not. I'm still basically a lazy person who wants to get by with as little effort as possible. The article was difficult. The book was an absolute bear. Hardy, Paranoid and Madge all say I'll be writing more. You know how far I've gotten arguing with those three. So I plan to stay in recovery, go with the flow of life, and if there's another book in me, I'm sure the conspirators will browbeat me into doing it somewhere down the line.

I hope you've learned some about human nature, and perhaps about your own family, by reading this book. I've gotten the equivalent of a Ph.D. by writing it.

Peace, love, and joy,
Evan Howard

Lightning Source UK Ltd.
Milton Keynes UK
15 December 2009

147528UK00001BA/4/P